THE RHINO'S HORN

BRYAN HOPE

authorHOUSE®

AuthorHouse™
1663 Liberty Drive
Bloomington, IN 47403
www.authorhouse.com
Phone: 1 (800) 839-8640

Published by AuthorHouse 02/02/2017

ISBN: 978-1-5246-6074-1 (sc)
ISBN: 978-1-5246-6075-8 (hc)
ISBN: 978-1-5246-6073-4 (e)

Library of Congress Control Number: 2017900936

Print information available on the last page.

Any people depicted in stock imagery provided by Thinkstock are models, and such images are being used for illustrative purposes only.
Certain stock imagery © Thinkstock.

This book is printed on acid-free paper.

FOR SARAH

PART 1

1

A MAN WITH A PONYTAIL AND a week's worth of beard, reeking of cologne and stale sweat, approached Kenneth without an introduction. A weak handshake followed by a weaker hug granted him the proximity to whisper into Kenneth's ear.

"Four thousand views." His breath was warm and strangely sinister. "The funeral has four thousand views right now. And it just started." Like the number was some score for how well she did in life. Like internet popularity could be offered as some kind of condolence. Like any of it had the slightest importance. The man videotaping the funeral or the thousands watching it from their homes within walking distance; Kenneth didn't know which was more condemnable.

It all seemed wrong, but not just how all death seems wrong, unfair, and tragic. Everything was superficial and backward. Women donned short skirts and blouses bedazzled with sequins that spelled out the names of websites. All of the sobbing seemed so rehearsed. Beyond sympathy, beyond grief, beyond any natural emotion, those in attendance seemed more concerned with putting themselves in the limelight, like they were there only because they saw an open stage.

Two young men he had never met approached his wife's casket to pay their respects. The red-haired man, looking unmoved, advanced toward the coffin, turned one hundred eighty degrees, and frowned insincerely. The other took his picture in front of the casket, then showed it to him to see if he approved. Kenneth, not confrontational enough to cause a scene yet not meek enough to let it go, grumbled the word, "Assholes," just within earshot. The red-haired man twisted to face Kenneth, but was pulled away by his accomplice. Before retreating to the back of the crowd to post the picture online, Kenneth heard him say to his friend, "Did you hear that old man?" At thirty-six, he didn't feel *physically* old, but in the presence of others, Kenneth felt as archaic and useless as an abacus.

He looked to his son for his reaction. It seemed strange for a father to admit, but Paul was now at an age where he could stand up for his old man, even physically defend him. Paul's eyes were wet, but his face was vacant. Oblivious to the situation, he was using his index finger to trace the curve of his bicep back and forth. His arms were crossed just below his chest to accentuate his pectoral muscles, presumably. Kenneth looked back to the box that contained his deceased wife, trying to mute the disgust that pressed in from all sides.

The contempt he felt wasn't entirely external. He never told anybody, but as her casket descended beneath the horizon of Astroturf, as the sobs were piercingly audible over the howling autumn wind, as they began to pour shovelfuls of dirt atop his wife's coffin, Kenneth's tears that were streaming down his face came from two entirely separate places; one of mourning and one of relief.

Kenneth believed that all marriages were doomed from the start. All of the arguments and uncertainties had no possibility of a positive outcome. There were options – counseling, experimentation, long vacations to wipe the slate clean – but he viewed them all as a water buffalo struggling to stand and run away while being gnawed upon by a pride of hungry lions. It was futile. There was no *fixing* a marriage. All you could do was accept uncertainty and dissatisfaction into your heart and keep moving. Keep dying.

As the monotony of the hugs and handshakes petered out, the endless condolences blurred together, and the faceless and nameless people summing up their parts in the senseless tragedy into his ear as everyone behind them shifted closer and rehearsed their own weeping eulogy in their heads, his wife's casket was swallowed into the earth and all of those problems and uncertainties were finally resolved.

And now, only two hundred days later, he was dying.

Doctor visits made him feel like a kid. While in years previous, doctors would spew out medical jargon like it was common knowledge, making Kenneth feel infinitely inferior, now they were more often than not silent, running their tests with few questions and no eye contact, making him feel more like a child lost in a department store, kneecaps and pelvises staring at him, but never giving him any attention, everyone oblivious to the fear and hysteria he was going through.

His diagnosis came in the form of an e-mail to his phone, a message that he was refusing to open. Although he had no symptoms, since leaving the doctor's office he had been surrounded by an eeriness so thick and palpable that he could taste it on the back of his tongue. The doctor never hinted toward anything – at least, not verbally – but after every test, he had the perplexed expression of a child opening up his favorite book to find that it had been written in Braille.

"I haven't felt this sort of anxiety since asking out my prom date." Kenneth was making confessions to a man he had never met before, a man in a suit who waved his arms around animatedly in front of a map of south Texas. When Kenneth was distressed, he would turn on the weather channel – the only station that hadn't changed over the past decade – and put it on mute, confessing to the meteorologist who always wore a smile and seemed to be the only one who was happy to listen to Kenneth's sorrows. "I know I've got nothing to worry about. It just feels so shitty, hearing these sorts of things from a phone, you know?" The meteorologist laughed with a wide smile revealing his large, horse-like teeth, nodding in confirmation.

Staring at his phone, he once again felt like a child. As a boy, he would sit cross-legged on the living room floor, bare calves warmed by the carpet, Sunday evening programming that had coincided with – and eventually, catalyzed – the gloom of another weekend coming to an end, and would look closer and closer into the television, the world receding as his forehead would gently touch the glass screen, the flickering lights illuminating and dimming almost imperceptibly, until all he would see were thousands of tiny rectangles divided equally into three vertical strips – one red, one blue, and one green – like flags from some unknown country. He would be mesmerized, perplexed at how three colors could brighten and darken at the exact levels to create one larger and impeccably illustrated moving picture. Perhaps it was that childish intrigue that pushed Kenneth toward his career as an electrician. Maybe the memory was some omen of things to come, some sign that merely needed to be decoded to sway him toward an intended path. Maybe it was nothing. As the memory floated to the surface of his thoughts, emerging like a stone beneath a receding tide, then descending once more, back into the abyss, forgotten, Kenneth felt that old Sunday melancholy and a distant wave of nostalgia.

An oversized beam of white light enclosed by the blue perimeter of the phone's plastic casing lit up Kenneth's face. Red letters ominously stretched across the top spelling out the name of the hospital he had left just twenty hours ago. In the center of the screen, in plain blue lettering, read his results.

Diagnosis: Pancreatic Cancer

Beneath the words were five tabs: Prognosis, Probability of Survival, Treatment Centers, Support Groups, and Contact Us, each title driving the shocking pains of imminent doom deeper than the previous. No solace could be found beneath the first three tabs, and no further crushing reality could be sustained at that point, so Kenneth skipped straight to the fourth. After touching the Support Groups tab, the screen listed links to social media circles and online forums for others with the same disease, to his dismay.

Contact Us. Kenneth chuckled disdainfully through a thick, building mucus and repeated the words to the meteorologist incredulously. No face-to-face consultation. No sympathetic physical contact. Not even a lollipop. Just a phone message with a list of e-mail addresses to direct his concerns, his questions, and his problems with receiving a death sentence on a touch-screen device.

How long had everything felt this way? So impersonal, so vacuous. For as long as he could remember, everything in Kenneth's life bore the breath-stealing cold of emptiness. Every errand ran, every workday completed, every movement was characterized by futility. With every breath, something inside him was leaving, hollowing him from within, and now that feeling had manifested itself in a cancerous tumor.

He denied himself the comfort of doubt. Although it seemed nearly impossible for someone of his age and health to be dying, Kenneth didn't allow hope to enter the equation. Illusions as such were distracting, calming, uplifting, but mostly, fruitless.

And all of this mere months after the death of his wife. Her body might not even be fully decomposed by the time his would be lying beside it. It was cruel and unfair. But more than feeling like a man being beaten on the ground, Kenneth felt like a caged animal living in captivity for years only to be released unto a den of hungry predators.

He tried to distance himself, to detach from the severity of it all, but it seemed he couldn't back away any further than he already was. For so long, everything seemed like fiction, like he was only watching a movie of his life, like if he focused hard enough on any one point, it would all fade into ambiguity, into tiny boxes of blue, red, and green, and the meaning and emotion of it all would be lost.

Kenneth summoned the little remaining strength in his body in a deep, shuddering breath and touched the little blue words that read *Chance of Survival.* He looked to the meteorologist for a smile suggesting he wasn't alone, but the program had gone to commercial.

10 percent.

Just like the child of his memory, the space between his eyes and the screen of his phone diminished slowly, the bulb of his nose touching the screen until the colors were no longer discernable, until the light burned his retinas and life gently faded to the background. His eyes shut tight as green lights that had burned into his vision danced over the curtain of black, and Kenneth wept.

2

Election Day.

THE YELLOW SUMMER SUN WAS still high in the sky and making the sidewalks burn like stovetops. All of the stores in Corpus Christi, Texas were set to close in half an hour so employees were free to vote. The few who were still on the streets were hustling to purchase a last minute item, their faces concealed behind dark sunglasses and headset microphones. Still, it was good to see people.

Kenneth was summoning all of his strength to remain optimistic today. In his current state, optimism felt more like being *delusional*. He had just finished setting up new bank accounts and moving money around, an errand much easier done from home, but Kenneth enjoyed getting out. He hadn't spoken to his son in weeks, but today, that was going to change. *Everything* was going to change.

Kenneth's thin lips snarled in a half-smile as he ran a red light. The streets were vacated anyway, and being that Kenneth was one of the 2% of drivers who didn't own a self-driving car, the flow and timing of traffic was quite predictable. It felt good not to care about the inevitable ticket that was to come in the mail. It seemed that there were some perks to terminal illness.

His beachside city had become the proverbial ghost town, not to say that it was normally bustling. It was strange, he thought, to shut down businesses for a voting process that took seconds. The part of the process that Kenneth didn't participate in was the time-consuming portion, and that was posting about the outcomes afterward. The election was a normal occurrence that happened every other week, but the shops closing was more unusual. As the sun beamed through the windshield and sizzled the leather seats, Kenneth put on his sunglasses, listened to the engine grumble, and enjoyed the road that seemingly belonged to him only.

His yard was freshly mowed, and the white siding that ran like latitudinal lines was clean and gleaming. He threw open the cherry red door and grabbed his globe from the living room. He held it like a football as he raced up the stairs.

Paul was in his room posting about the election that was now set to begin in twenty-two minutes. Kenneth entered without knocking as the door was left slightly ajar, a rule in the house; a rule that was arbitrary as Kenneth never went upstairs for *fear* of seeing what his son was up to in his bedroom.

Paul was shirtless, his skin shiny with sweat, and his torso lined like a map with muscles and tattoos. His vanity was well-known to his father, but whether he was showing off to those who could see him through his webcam or to himself was arguable.

He was visibly shocked by his father's entrance, but didn't know how to verbally react to the situation. Kenneth plopped the globe down on the desk between Paul and his computer monitor. Paul instinctually switched his webcam off.

"Anywhere you want to go." Kenneth looked hopefully into his son, digging beneath his eyes for some likeness of himself. They offered back nothing but confusion. "I want us to take a trip. And I want *you* to decide where we go."

"Why do we need to leave? I don't understand."

Kenneth's thoughts screamed. *Because I'm dying, you little shit! Because you've barely ever made it out of your room! Because I want to find some reason to like you before I die!* He collected himself and replied calmly, "I think it'll do us good to get out of our routine. I'd like for us to do something fun and different together. And wouldn't you like to see somewhere different, with different people and different cultures? Try some new foods? Do something exciting?" The word 'exciting' was a strategically placed landmine, camouflaged in innocuousness, but was meant to imply that there was nothing exciting about Paul's way of life. Kenneth and Paul alike knew this.

Paul looked at the globe, scanning the surface with curious fingertips, crawling like spiders around the world until his index finger arrived at a destination, pressed firmly, then offered itself in Kenneth's direction to reveal that it was placed on that spot where the green met the blue at the Gulf of Mexico, right where they were sitting.

The two of them stared at one another in a silence that was thick with abhorrent confusion. Kenneth's eyes darted around as he searched for some argument that would show his son why he was most definitely wrong, but no such argument presented itself. It seemed no amount of persuasion could make them like each other.

Kenneth scratched the balding crown of his head and retreated, all formalities spared.

Unfazed, Paul went back to his computer. The forums were blowing up. The issue to be voted on in thirteen minutes was one that had been predominant in the social media threads for the past two weeks, and one that involved Paul's most prized possession, The Suit, which hung from his back wall and looked like scuba gear, but felt like a medieval knight, an ominous presence that just witnessed the awkward father-son interaction.

The Suit was a relatively new product and was just as its name suggested - a full-body enclosure. It had a USB connection that would sync with dating sites and programs that would pay an annual fee to be Suit-compatible. After uploading self-images from all angles into The Suit's database, it could detect every slight movement and project it onto the other party's headset, only that in the projected image there was no Suit, just naked flesh. It was fitted with hundreds of thousands of tiny appendages like the fingers of an anemone that would imitate a person's touch, mimicking the movements and exerted pressure of the person on the other end of the conversation, whether she was in Boston, Prague, or the Moon. Larger appendages existed in the areas surrounding the genitals of The Suit. There were obviously different versions, depending on gender. After The Suit underwent several transformations and revamps, it could simulate intercourse nearly identically.

Upon its initial introduction to the marketplace, The Suit had a negative public reaction, being that it was making sexual intercourse – albeit *touchless* sexual intercourse – readily accessible to any and all, but as sales escalated rapidly, new trends emerged. Sexually transmitted diseases plummeted. Teenage pregnancy, which had become nearly inevitable to most of America's youth, dropped back below 5%. Bars were suddenly vacated and closed down, thus drastically cutting down on alcohol-related fatalities. And while immorality was a great argument, no one could fight against the statistics that The Suit produced.

Today was to be the day that the public decided whether or not it was morally permissible for the manufacturers of The Suit to create and distribute a version made for physically underdeveloped clients – specifically, for children.

As most controversies go, statistics battled ethics, numbers battled ideas. While the idea of eleven-year-olds being enabled to freely fornicate in the virtual world was an idea that was easy to see as morally despicable, millions were posting images, videos, and stories of their pregnant or diseased adolescent family members. Selling The Suit to children, it was argued, would mollify these issues, just as they did for the adult population upon The Suit's introduction to the marketplace.

The election opened, and Paul voted with the touch of a button. Chrysanthemum messaged directly after:

Let's Suit up.

The outside of it was a viridian green. It was the thickness, texture, and softness of an aerobic floor mat, yet it fit tight like a wet suit. Paul first slid his left foot into the leg, his heel sliding along the thousands of rubber appendages so densely packed throughout the inside of The Suit that they bore a resemblance to transparent kernels of corn, but beneath the heads of each appendage was a long, unseen stem allowing it maximum flexibility and movement. The right leg was open as the seal ran along the outside of the leg, up around the pelvis, cutting across the chest and ending finally just underneath the chin. It was a watertight seal like that of a sandwich bag, only thicker and with more layers. Both of Paul's legs were in, and now came the more delicate task. The Suit had what essentially was an entirely separate compartment for the genitalia that attached to The Suit and acted almost freely from the rest of the apparatus. While The Suit ran off battery power from the headset, the genitalia compartment had its own separate battery so it could perform other tasks before the rest of The Suit was connected to power. Paul carefully slid his flaccid penis into the compartment, a job that would be much easier with an erection, but it was always difficult maintaining stiffness while performing the intricate and monotonous duties of getting suited up. At the press of an external button, about eighty appendages at the base of the genitalia compartment constricted gently around Paul's shrunken member, a thousand or so more stationed behind them awaiting Paul's manhood to grow as the others did their job. Next to the startup button on the genitalia compartment existed a small opening resembling a microphone jack. Paul slid his arms into place, the outside of the hands looking like large, puffy mittens while on the inside they fit snugly around each finger, and retrieved a bottle of Suit-issued lubricant, the bottle with a large nipple on the lid like that of an old restaurant-style ketchup bottle. He inserted the nipple of the lubrication into the jack on the genitalia compartment and filled the reservoir. The lubrication would be intermittently pumped to the heads of the appendages once Chrysanthemum – or Chrissy, as he called her – made genital contact and sensors inside the genital compartment would regulate the necessary amount to apply. Paul then grabbed the headset and fastidiously pulled it down over his eyes, fit the earpieces into each ear, connected the power cord to the female end on the neck of The Suit, and adjusted all four headset fasteners, one in the back of the head, one on top of the head, and two underneath each eye. He fixed four adhesive sensors to his face. Each was a black line like a leech, three inches long and a quarter inch wide, paper-thin. One topped the upper lip like a mustache, another mirroring it beneath the lower lip. The two others went vertically down each cheek. The sensors would detect facial movement so the image projected on the other party's headset was accurate. The screen inside the headset doubled as a camera and detected eye movements. There also existed a mouthpiece that helped simulate tongue kissing and oral sex, but most found the apparatus and its stimulation as obtrusive and that it obstructed breathing. Paul angled the microphone down over his mouth and did a quick sound test. Now, every task was to be handled digitally.

In the screen of the headset were sixteen white squares around the perimeter of his vision, each with a different label that he could reach out and touch to take him to some different part of the virtual world. After passing through a few different virtual doorways, he could type in the code to access the e-room that he and Chrissy had allotted.

Paul waited alone in the e-room for Chrissy, who was probably busy suiting up her own genitalia compartment, something that was entirely enigmatic to Paul. One drawback of The Suit was that it mimicked every exact movement you made in perfect relation to the rest of your body, and that prevented one from masturbation, seeing as the genitals were underneath three solid inches of rubber appendages, lubrication, and lithium batteries. Had that not been the case, Paul would have been touching himself as he anxiously anticipated Chrissy's arrival. Instead, he occupied his time playing with different lighting schemes, choosing different settings, then holding his hand in front of his face to see how it translated visually.

Chrissy entered confidently, gracefully, and slightly perturbed, yet still wearing that melting smile of hers.

"ISTG [I swear to God]," she said, standing naked on one foot, the other bent and crossed above her knee, her fingers tapping methodically in the air a few inches from her toes as she was presumably fixing a crease in her Suit in the RW [Real World]. "These promos we have to suffer through before we get to fuck are getting longer and longer. What was yours about?"

"Mine was urging me to vote for a program that identifies all immigrants in the VW [virtual world] so you know who you're dealing with. And yours?"

"Mine was wanting us to allow them to document all of our sex so they can see trends and, I guess, like, know what kind of positions we like so they can make a better Suit."

"Are you gonna vote for that?"

"I don't think so. I don't want anyone to see the terrible things I'm about to do to you." She smiled seductively and advanced.

The two had created a ground rule based on a mutual agreement that stated that every other month they were not to see one another. This rule was meant to act as a preventative measure to ensure that neither would get too attached, although Chrissy knew men, and she knew that it would have the reverse effect on Paul.

It was their first time to have sex since their last hiatus, and it was so much better than Paul remembered. Everything that could have gone wrong, did go wrong. Paul accidentally tapped a button and transported him out of the room suddenly, the quick absence of sensation feeling ghoulishly strange on Chrissy's end. When he came back, Chrissy's father was talking to her from outside her bedroom door, leaving Paul waiting awkwardly naked and erect. At one point, Paul was taking her from behind and he noticed Chrissy's back gradually contorting with every thrust, the back of her head directly above her ass, her spine curved concavely, her knees bent in a strange position, until she had to stop him as he realized she was up against her dresser in the RW. But what made all of these mishaps so rewarding for Paul was her smile. Each time something would go wrong, Chrissy would crane her neck and grin playfully and tenderly as her eyes looked sideways to meet his. It was this meeting of the two worlds, of the playful kinship and the animalistic sex, that bored into the core of Paul. Laughing while groping one another. Smiling while massaging one another's nether regions. Constant eye contact. These were the things that he didn't get from his various sexual outings with girls from other 7-codes. These were the things that made him belong to Chrissy.

Aside from all that, one thing that he and Chrissy exclusively shared was post-coital pillow talk. The only problem was that this couldn't directly follow intercourse as the two had to separately clean their respective Suits. Every version of The Suit had a detachable hose with a female nozzle affixed to the top of the right shoulder that could be attached to an ordinary sink faucet. An intricate series of valves and infinitesimal tubing directed the water flow to every nook of The Suit's interior. From there, a drain plug on the end of each foot could be removed to allow all the liquid to drain presumably into a bathtub after being hung from the shower curtain rod. This was primarily just for perspiration. The genital compartment detached and had a similar system, but you had to be a little more thorough with this part of the contraption, for obvious reasons. After all of that was completed, Paul and Chrissy would usually Suit back up and return to their e-motel room to talk and gently trace each other's bodies with their fingertips. If time was pressing, they would spare each other the ordeal of Suiting back up and merely video message one another, but today was not one of those days.

Chrissy's body had tightened up since he had last seen her. Subtle and sexy variances in her body shape presented themselves now that he got to pay closer attention. Her top three ribs were made visible in gentle dips and rises in her skin as she lay on her side. Her collarbone was slightly more accentuated and glided seamlessly to her long and slender neck. This meant two things. One, she had worked on herself during their little hiatus, and two, she had uploaded new self-images to her Suit database. Otherwise, despite her newly sculpted body, the same, slightly chubbier Chrissy would have been tracing Paul's deltoid with her index finger.

"So what all has happened since we last talked?"

Paul's cheeks tightened and his forehead crinkled as he thought about the question, all of the facial expressions identified by the sensors and shining back at Chrissy through her headset monitor. "Not much. The old man's still crazy. He just tried to invite me on a trip."

"A trip?"

"Yeah, like, to another country or something. I think he's losing it – for real, this time." Paul did notice something different in his father during this last confrontation, aside from the invitation. He always had a certain sense of superiority that never failed to belittle Paul, although he never let it show, but today there was a shame in him. It was slight and ambiguous, but something was most certainly askew. It was like he wanted to be *friendly* with Paul, as opposed to judgmental, aloof, and hateful.

"He just wants to be your *dad* again, now that you've become a man and all."

"Trust me, that's *not* it."

Her fingers crept their way up to his neck, yearning to trace his jawline, to tickle his lips, to slide down the bridge of his nose, but The Suit's effects didn't enable these sorts of sensations as the touch simulators only went up to the neck. Whatever slight variance Paul had detected in his father's face seemed to be surfacing in Chrissy's, only softer, sexier, as she whispered two words, words as plain as the kitchen knife that cuts to your heart, as simple as the boulder that smashes your head before you ever notice it falling.

"Marry me."

Paul withdrew, obviously shocked, unsure of how he was supposed to feel. To his fortune, election results came in at that exact moment and flashed across both of their respective monitors, granting him a moment of reprieve.

Allotting $1.2 million to revamp education websites
  DENIED

Both proposals, his father's and Chrissy's, were invitations to the RW, and it was the RW that terrified Paul. The virtual world had walls, walls that shielded him from pain, from fear, from shame, but the real world was so unforgiving. Events couldn't be deleted with the touch of a button. The touch sensors of his Suit couldn't replicate the pain of a punch or a stab wound, and although most of his presence in the virtual world was with little, if any, clothing, the idea of stepping outside and into the sunlight with real people and real interactions made Paul feel infinitely *naked*.

Publication of all citizens' medical, legal, and financial history
    APPROVED

The human psyche was a twisted and manipulative engine. It would take an emotion and mold it, reshape it, and present it as something different. Negative emotions would be projected onto external factors.

It's astonishing, really, how quickly the mind can work, can identify and transform, can manipulate. Those two words were instantly processed in Paul's brain, conjuring imageless emotions, fears, and uncertainties, of the vast enigma of the RW and all the caustic mystery that it possessed, then recycled into indignity and self-deprecation, then transformed into wrath, all in the course of nanoseconds. *How could she put me in this position? How could she back me into this corner? How could she present it as an order rather than a question?*

Legalization of production and distribution of Youth-Suits
    APPROVED

Both Paul and Chrissy's votes had been heard and their views, apparently, were the views of the majority of the general public, but they delayed rejoicing as the question still hung in the air like a toxic fog that didn't allow them to breathe. Paul's eyes locked onto hers, but were presented slightly averted in her headset, as he made his reply.

"No."

3

AFTER THE INITIAL IMPACT OF the cool blast of air conditioning contrasting from the scorching summer heat, the first thing about the grocery store that Kenneth noticed was the silence.

Motorized shopping carts quietly hummed, cans tapped gently against metal shelving, and the soles of shoes squeaked as they skidded on the linoleum flooring. And silence.

Like most Americans, it had been years since Kenneth went to the grocery store. It reminded him of childhood, of pushing the cart into his mother's Achilles heels, her reprimanding him, all to the gentle soundtrack of pop music from some other decade, from some other plane of existence, echoing softly throughout the store. Kenneth usually wouldn't even notice the music until a good half hour of shopping, but once he stopped racing the basket through the aisles, when the candy section was long passed over, he would stop and listen to the music, its smooth, repetitive melody as soothing as it was annoying.

But now there was no music. How long had it been since they turned it off? The few shoppers who, too, had abandoned the amenities of at-home online shopping were tuned in to their earbuds and tuned out to the world. Whether they were listening to their own music, tuned in to another snippet (displayed behind one lens of a pair of sunglasses), or – as most were – speaking to their social media as it transcribed onto their personal web pages, narrating their adventurous journey to do their grocery shopping like barbarians, they were all not really there.

On the one-inch barrier that ran horizontally between shelves shined a scrolling news marquee that read:

MILLIONS GATHER NATIONWIDE IN TWO SEPARATE PROTESTS, ONE AIMED AT OVERTURNING THE LEGALIZATION OF YOUTH-SUITS AND THE OTHER IN RESPONSE TO THE TERRORIST ATTACKS IN SOUTH DAKOTA.

Kenneth wasn't sure what the word 'protest' meant anymore, but it conjured the image of millions gathered in the VW in some digitally-enhanced setting, a powerful image to most, a laughable image to Kenneth. He imagined all of those individual people shouting angrily in their own living rooms wearing scuba gear and marching in place while they heated up their microwave dinners.

A middle-aged woman with purple hair and too many gold necklaces, a beak for a nose, and kind yet piercing eyes was perusing the shampoo aisle and glanced up to meet eyes with Kenneth. She smiled. Kenneth smiled back. It felt immediately wrong. It wasn't wrong in the sense of betrayal, but because he couldn't even separate his lips to show teeth. He couldn't maintain eye contact. The smile looked more like a child pursing his lips trying to hold back laughter. For once in his life, Kenneth was free to pursue a flirtatious smile, and with his recent death sentence, there were literally no consequences.

She looked derailed by Kenneth's reaction, and her eyes went back to the endless shampoos, the ivories, the seafoam greens, lavenders, that made a thirty-foot rainbow that drew a straight line from her shopping cart to where Kenneth's was turning around and retreating. With one last glance, Kenneth noticed the freckles that speckled her cheeks and neck, just like his dead wife.

Meredith was cute. It was such an easy and clichéd adjective used to describe a person, and the only one that could describe Meredith. She was intentionally, spuriously, vacuously cute. When Kenneth first met her, she was giggling childishly, yet with confident, grazing eyes, after their high school English teacher corrected her pronunciation of 'libary.' He took notice of her colorful bracelets, her frizzy, unkempt hair, her skin-tight jeans with a hole strategically ripped across the front of her upper thigh. At the time, it was an ensemble that elicited intrigue, infatuation, a glimpse of a personality that he had to uncover. Retrospectively, he saw the outfit as the uniform of someone masking insecurity, fear, and a *lack* of personality.

They conceived a child twelve minutes into their second date, three weeks before graduation.

Kenneth told her they weren't ready, that he wasn't ready, but an abortion wasn't something he was willing to force on anyone. By the time little Paul had extended Meredith's belly beyond her belt, the future was solidified. They would be a family.

No matter how solid his place in the world was, no matter how concrete was his will to be a faithful husband and father, the life he was leading felt like cross-threading a screw. It would turn with building resistance until slipping to the next thread with ease, then again, would grind back, impossible to turn. His marriage suffered hardships and ecstasies, but just as we define everything by its defining characteristic, by its brightest color, Kenneth's marriage was *wrong*. Just thinking about that first year, turning that screw that would never bottom out, left an acidic taste on the roof of his mouth.

But Kenneth wasn't thinking about that.

For the first time since Meredith died, he actually *missed* her. It wasn't her personality that lingered on. It wasn't memories that would resurface. Kenneth was just *alone*. More alone than he had ever felt. He felt out of place, like a circus animal that had spent its entire life in captivity to be released into the wild, yearning to return to its cage.

Kenneth glanced down the cereal aisle and, for some reason, expected to see his mother, the fringe lining the bottom of her sundress dancing an inch above the floor, her chocolate hair resting delicately on her shoulders, fingers grazing the cereal boxes, eyes scanning the nutrition facts. Instead, he found two teenage boys fixed with a series of colorful rods and fittings secured to their shoulders and supporting a small camera in the shape of an eyeball dangling twenty inches in front of their faces. One boy was holding up a box of Marshmallow Yellows and giving a one-sided dialogue to his camera like some space-age news reporter posting his trivial findings on the web, probably watched and followed by tens of thousands. The other boy looked lost and awe-stricken, marveling at the high ceilings and endless supplies of sugary treats. Kenneth wanted to hit them. He wanted his mother, his childhood back. More than anything, he wanted to pretend that these two hollow boys didn't remind him of his own son.

How had Paul grown so far beyond reach? He came from Kenneth, his DNA making Paul the person that he was, yet neither of them knew how to communicate with the other. They could have spoken different languages and still been no further apart than they were now.

Paul was definitely his mother's son. She saw Paul's need to fit in with his peers, with his generation, but it was only Kenneth who questioned the morality involved. Meredith was the one who took Paul to get his tattoos, that hideous barcode written below his neck like a necklace. *3612016.* Their area code and the year of his birth, probably his two most defining qualities. How many people had this exact tattoo? How did becoming a clone make anyone feel special? Paul's lifestyle was so foreign, so *repulsive* to Kenneth. His entire life existed online. Destroy the web, and Paul had created no mark, no evidence that he ever existed. Kenneth knew about The Suit, but Paul had followed a path paved by his generation and provided by his mother for so long that there was little Kenneth could do to deter him.

Paul was an adult now, as much as Kenneth hated to admit it. It was a petrifying idea. Kenneth felt like he had done so little, had failed so completely in making his son a man, in preparing him for the world. Then again, the world was something that Kenneth didn't know anymore, and Paul apparently did.

His feet slid languidly across the floor, his toes dragging underneath his ankles. He slowly sulked over at the waist, putting more and more weight on the shopping cart in front of him. He strolled aimlessly through the aisles.

He had been putting all of his weight on Meredith for so long as she dragged him to wherever she pleased. He resented her for it, but he was beginning to realize how directionless he was, how much he needed her support. Without ever vocalizing such concerns, he always believed she wasn't smart enough for him and worried that her lack of intelligence would surface in little Paul, possibly making him resent that part of his own son. But it was Meredith who did their taxes. It was Meredith who organized Paul's homeschooling and acted as his teacher with help from online schooling programs. It was Meredith who formulated their daily routines, packing the lunches and marking the dentist appointments on calendars. More pertinently, it was Meredith who got them covered with life insurance. It surely couldn't be called 'suddenly' given that it was eight months delayed, but Kenneth felt like her absence was the ground beneath his feet giving way with the quickness of a magician pulling the tablecloth out from under a vase and place settings.

When little Paul was first enrolled in school, it was only Kenneth who found it odd to homeschool a child from the computer. Meredith would create a curriculum downstairs and Paul would complete said curriculum from his room. Meredith would then grade his completed assignments (something that she always claimed to be doing despite the fact that the programs did the grading themselves) and sent feedback in the form of compliments and criticism posted to the education section of his social media page.

The entire process seemed absurd to Kenneth and counterproductive to all of the potential benefits of homeschooling. It completely eliminated the advantage of keeping Paul at home to create firmer family bonds, but as the rest of the country was undergoing the same process, Paul formed an online class and began learning socializing skills for the twenty-first century. In other words, this form of schooling proved ideal to everyone except for Kenneth. As much as he disdained the way things were heading, he had to concede to the fact that it was probably the most directly aimed tactic in preparing his son for the world into which he was born.

He had been in the store for an hour. He looked into his basket, which held only a box of crackers and a stick of deodorant. He didn't even know what he needed. He didn't know where to go next. A pain of uncertain origins clenched his insides and sucked air from the outside in, pulling everything into his core like a black hole. He doubled over as every breath was icy and weighted.

He reached for a loaf of bread and caught another line of scrolling news.

PITTSBURGH, RW: THOUSANDS OF SUITS ARE PILED IN CITY CENTER AND BURNED IN RESPONSE TO TODAY'S ELECTION RESULTS

Kenneth read the words aloud. It wasn't until moments like this that the reasoning for coining the term 'RW' was made apparent. It wasn't easier as it had more syllables than reading the words out, but the acronym disarmed the feeling of the words, the implication that the *real* world was somehow more significant than the virtual.

The purple-haired woman turned the corner in front of him and brought the two face to face. Kenneth issued a wide and rehearsed smile. She smiled back and said unabashedly, "Wanna GAM?" The acronym stood for 'Get a Motel,' but Kenneth was obviously confused.

"Huh?"

"You want to get an e-motel?" Kenneth wasn't sure if he was more repelled by the idea that meeting in the real world only elicited desire to meet in the virtual or that their introduction was an invitation for sex.

"How about we go get a cup of coffee?"

"Like, in the RW?" Kenneth nodded quickly like a child being asked if he wanted dessert. Her eyes squinted in distaste. "I don't think so." She exited the supermarket, leaving Kenneth somehow exponentially more alone than he was a few minutes before.

As the woman left, a horrible epiphany bloomed in the pit of his stomach, somewhere near his cancerous tumor. It was envy, not blame, that was the source of his discontent for Meredith. She was the one bold enough to do the things that he could not. He used her chains as a symbol for why he couldn't achieve more in life, but she also gave him the key. While he couldn't even smile at another woman, Meredith was more than likely on her way to another man's house to venture out of their marriage when her car skidded on a stretch of wet road and careened into a palm tree.

4

A DRONE SCANNED THE BARCODE OF a tube-shaped package in Hive #6. Hive #6 was one of seventeen warehouses that existed within the city limits and resembled an actual hive as drones swarmed the interior, hovering over the ocean of tan, cardboard packages, racing in and out to make their deliveries. The drone had two fingerlike appendages that existed beneath the main structure, long and metallic with three knuckles. They were exactly eighteen inches apart, as were the red O-rings that emerged from every parcel. The fingers hooked inside the O-rings of the tubed package, bent at each knuckle to lock the package in place, then sped swiftly out the bay door. After reaching an altitude of one hundred sixty feet, it headed southeast.

A man at the delivery headquarters located on the north side of town tracked the drone's flight path on a computer. All flights were computer-programmed and didn't require manual control, but every delivery was to be monitored, mostly for the residential arrivals. If any activity was detected in front of the house where the delivery was to be made, the person monitoring the drone's flight could manually drop it down to ensure that no one would catch a propeller to the head and no drones would be run over by a car backing out of the driveway.

The drone arrived at Kenneth and Paul's house and dropped the tube in front of the red front door. By the time the package touched the ground, an alert was sent to Paul's FlashConnect page notifying him of the delivery. Although he saw the alert, he didn't come downstairs to retrieve it.

Fifty minutes later, Kenneth returned home from the supermarket to find the long tube resting on his front porch, the two red O-rings not allowing it to roll away with the wind. Kenneth took it inside and inspected the label. The sender was unknown to Kenneth, and it was addressed only to 'Burke Residence,' so Kenneth popped the round plastic insert at one end and pulled the rolled poster from its container.

Paul watched from the bottom of the staircase, spying on his father as he inspected the poster.

The face of a teenage girl with caramel skin and heavy eyeliner sat atop the body of an enlarged raven. The wings were made of computer keyboards and stretched the width of the poster menacingly. A trail of crimson bled behind her. Across the top were the words "Meet Me in the RW," and on the bottom, "Time To Get The Boys." The initials of the latter phrase were made much more prominent, so at first glance Kenneth only saw "T T G T B." Unbeknownst to him, this was an acronym that usually stood for "Time To Go To Bed," a phrase that was posted every night by most normal individuals and was done as routinely as brushing one's teeth.

Also unbeknownst to Kenneth, "Meet Me in the RW" was the title of a snippet, a short movie that lasted an average of four to six minutes, about a group of girls who lured their male nemeses to a rendezvous at a warehouse in the RW, only to lock them inside and set the building aflame. But Kenneth only saw the letters 'RW.' As common as they were, they never lost their disgusting impact on Kenneth, and seeing them printed on the poster, he audibly scoffed.

Paul, still watching from the staircase, snarled as his father mocked his artwork.

Simply as a hobby, Paul enjoyed designing images expressing the theme of his favorite snippets. He would post them on his FlashConnect page for all to see. As Paul honed his skills and his friend list climbed quickly toward seven digits, he began getting contacted by producers of snippets aiming to escalate their sales. In exchange for designing a promotional image for their snippets, Paul was offered compensation in the form of memberships to e-motels, discounts on technology products, and minimal financial compensation.

Meet Me in the RW was Paul's latest project and his proudest accomplishment to date. Seeing his father puff cynically at the picture had him seething.

Paul emerged from his hiding place and took the poster from his father's hands.

"That's mine."

Kenneth let the glossy paper slide from his fingers as Paul took it from him and turned away. He wanted to reprimand him for the crude way in which he talked to his father, but he knew it would only send him back further into seclusion.

"Is that for one of those snippets?"

Paul stopped his stride just before reaching the stairs.

"Yeah. I made it. I get paid to make these, remember?"

Kenneth suppressed the urge to scoff at the word 'paid' as Paul could never make any sort of living off his so-called *salary*. He struggled for words to engage his son, constantly battling between his need to connect and his need to scold.

"Do you make any for *real* movies?"

Paul grumbled as he stormed up the stairs. Kenneth felt his son, like his life, slipping through his fingers, and panicked as he felt all of his tribulations being sealed in permanence.

"It..." he stuttered, "it looks really good." His words were drowned out by Paul's feet wrathfully slamming into each stair as he retreated to his room.

In the sanctuary of his bedroom, Paul scrutinized the poster. He ran his fingers over the smooth, glossy surface. He held it close to his face and inhaled deeply, taking in the hypnotizing scents of the inks and adhesives. While it was more common to buy a digital poster that would flash through hundreds of images, Paul enjoyed the texture and scent of traditional posters. He used four thumbtacks to fix the poster to the wall beside his four previous works. He tried to appreciate it, to allow the image to inflate his self-esteem, but the recent events in his life kept anchoring him to an anxious depression.

Although the scene downstairs was thoroughly aggravating, it was superficial in comparison to the things that were really bothering Paul. He was eighteen. He was developing an actual career. His girlfriend had just proposed to him. Pivotal decisions were on the horizon, and he couldn't even feign enthusiasm about any of them.

While it may not have seemed admirable, Paul enjoyed a more static existence. He was perfectly fine with the present, and he had no need to alter his course. The fact that he was being forced to change made him loathe Chrissy.

Paul's life was small. Most of his days were spent in the same room, lifting the same weights, talking on the same computer. He even had the same teacher for every class of his entire life – his mother – although her classes were mostly offered electronically via various schooling sites and posted through his FlashConnect page. Paul's life offered few variances, and

Paul was content with that, but when his mother passed away, something in him hollowed. It came in waves. When her death was fresh, it was almost unreal. It seemed like a tragic event in a story that didn't concern him. Before her funeral, Paul had to rub shampoo into his eyes to ensure that he would cry. His lack of emotion was more troubling than grief. Grief was explainable, logical even. Not mourning for your own mother was a heartlessness some circles of Hell didn't even know, and as the weeks passed, Paul only felt the strange hole in his schedule. He constantly felt like he was supposed to be doing something, but he didn't know what. He felt like she was waiting around the corner, but the hallways were always vacant. He began turning in assignments, then logging in to his mother's FlashConnect page (hacking into it was a simple chore) and messaging himself with a 'Job Well Done' or a 'Wow! I'm impressed!' Initially, it did nothing. But when he went back to his life and navigated the web, returning to his home page and seeing the comments posted to the main screen, they became just a background symbolizing that nothing was askew. Her profile picture would pop up two or three times at the bottom of his page next to some encouraging words, rather than her absence, which was much more noticeable. As colossal of a presence she had in his life, her persona was surprisingly easy to replicate.

There was a freedom that came with his mother's passing. Being the chief organizer of daily agendas for the family, her absence left the men of the house with ample amounts of free time. The first couple of weeks felt like a rite of passage for Paul. He had to take over some of the household duties and discarded his sense of responsibility and inferiority. He washed the dishes every morning, a chore that went unnoticed by a grieving Kenneth and chilled the already frigid waters between the two. The rest of the day he spent perusing the internet and using his Suit to fornicate with various women. And as it always does, this time spent in idleness led to a directionless, tailspin type of boredom. The monotony and anxiousness finally made way for some form of grief.

It wasn't the lack of updates on his class schedules or the takeout dinners that set him off, but the merriment lost. Meredith was essential to the aura of the household, and that absence went seemingly unnoticed for quite some time due to how little time Paul, Meredith, and Kenneth spent together when it wasn't obligatory. Paul and Kenneth, not to mention their tumultuous relationship, lacked the jocundity that Meredith provided. As the pizza boxes stacked up in the kitchen, as Paul's already uneventful agenda thinned out, and as every day lacked the blithe smiles that Mom would bestow, Paul found himself one night weeping incessantly. It was right around that time that Chrissy came into the picture and filled the void that was hollowing out Paul from the inside.

Chrissy was perfect as far as Paul was concerned. They met just under a year ago when the 7-code groups were formed. They were both in 3612016 and also were placed in the same subgroups based on similar interests in music, movies, and internet celebrities, so dating came naturally. As per routine, both parties exchanged spin-vids, which were short video clips of the person in his or her best and most revealing outfit (sometimes being no clothes at all) doing a slow three-hundred-sixty degree turn in front of the camera so the other party could decide to reject or give it a go. If both parties issued a GIAG, they would experience each other sexually by means of The Suit. If they complemented each other sexually, dating, in its most recognizable form, would commence. As distasteful and backward as the process seemed, the normal first date stuff, as well as second, third, and fourth date stuff, was previously taken care of thanks to webpages displaying all likes/dislikes, age, family members, most defining sexual orientation, hometown, tastes in music and movies, and, if any existed, hobbies.

Paul and Chrissy went through all of this a year ago. They would meet in an e-motel (Suit-compatible web program) on a daily basis. Weekly, they would invite a random third party from a different 7-code into their e-motel to keep things adventurous, but Paul didn't care much for these encounters, although he sensed that Chrissy did. Paul (without consent from Chrissy) met with several other girls from different 7-codes on a regular basis for sex. But it was Chrissy who kept fuel in his tank. She was the one he connected with. She was the one who consistently stroked his ego during their romantic encounters, who told him how gorgeous he was, who took the time to run her fingers down his muscles, to gaze at all parts of his body intently, to make him feel *sexy*. That was important. All of the other girls were more like practice for Paul. He had only been sexually active for two years (ever since his advertising earned him the money to pay for The Suit) and would still think of new things to try. When he did, he would try them out on girls from different 7-codes and gauge their reactions before bringing those ideas to Chrissy.

Although the prevalent theme of love in art had long been replaced with *compatible*, Paul still believed in love, and he believed that he loved Chrissy. It was an idea that he didn't know how to address, an idea that he wanted to ask his father about, but every time the feeling got strong enough to actually act on it, his father would come into his room and gawk awkwardly at The Suit in the corner, ask him to accompany him to the store, or invite him on a strange trip to a strange locale. As per usual, love was always so quickly replaced with dissatisfaction and anger.

Although his relationship with his father was the opposite of ideal, his relationship with Chrissy seemed perfect, aside from two obvious problems. First, although Paul's life was small and stagnant, he always believed that he would do something much larger. Locking himself down in marriage was the perfect deterrent to any plans to achieve greatness. And second, deep within the labyrinth of Paul's mind, he knew that Chrissy was somewhat of a replacement for his own mother, and it felt backward and wrong.

To distract himself, Paul was scrolling through news memes. After countless police brutality scandals, all police officers were legally required to wear cameras on their uniforms. As a byproduct, high definition pictures of arrests were made public. Within minutes of an arrest, the video was made publicly available online and hundreds of "reporters" would create a witty quip or provocative headline, attach it to a still-frame of the video, and let it go viral. Different news agencies had dozens of these reporters working for them and would create a page of entertaining news compiled of memes, mostly presented comically. This was how most would receive their knowledge of current events.

Burglar Breaks in to House, Crawls into Bed with Sleeping Couple

The picture showed an Anglo-American couple, mid-forties, obviously wealthy, lying in bed in silk pajamas with startled and confused looks on their faces, as a raggedly dressed dark skinned man with sunken eyes grinned obliviously, arm extended across his body in an attempt to spoon with the female.

It's Getting Easier to Get Away with Robbing Fast Food Restaurants

Three police officers were shown trying to handcuff a morbidly obese man outside of a McDonald's, apparently struggling as his arms could not reach each other around his massive belly, and were having to cuff him up around his chest.

Curry-Terrorism on the Rise

Three different pictures were displayed, each one divided vertically down the middle. On the left side of each box showed a detonated building, some with burnt bodies strewn about the grounds outside of the explosion. On the right, three different Indian men were shown being cuffed and put inside squad cars.

Between news memes, a message appeared on the screen.

Care for a pay raise?

Paul glanced down at the address of the sender and knew immediately the implications of the message.

Five years prior, politics had been altered drastically and irrevocably. Voters had all grown tired of electing crooked politicians who campaigned on policies forgotten their first week in office, yet all citizens were complacent with the fact that the entire country was run by lawyers and judges, all of whom were in the pockets of billionaires, an entire corrupt system to which the public was completely aware of. The problem was that there was no alternative solution. Sure, the leaders were all despicable human beings in a violent circle of bribery and injustice. But everything was still afloat. Things were running smoothly. And most important, the enemies were just too large and powerful to be confronted. And then came Fair e-Lect.

Once registered on the Fair e-Lect site – something that required minimal time and therefore, was done by 98% of the public – a citizen could vote on his or her tablet or other device. The initial phenomenon that this new tool incited was the high voter turnout. Voting was now done with not only the ease, but with the minimal thought that was commonly put into a common text message. Once again, morality was beat out by statistics.

But that was merely the beginning. Once Fair e-Lect caught on and all arguments made against the system were refuted, Fair e-Lect elections broadened. No longer were elections held biannually and only for elected officials and major policies, but every issue the government faced was brought to public attention, and then public opinion. To promote transparency in local government, all policies and budget expenditures were to be brought to the public eye, then voted on. If the citizens didn't like it, it didn't pass. And these elections would happen biweekly.

The initial problem with this system was that not only were people as a whole stupid and arrogant, but the public didn't see the entire picture. You couldn't expect John Doe to say things he likes and doesn't like and that will be how his government spends their money when Mr. Doe doesn't know exactly how deep the government's pockets run. The government couldn't be entirely transparent because the average Joe simply couldn't comprehend it all and make an educated decision. New positions were made within the local governments and old positions were deemed antiquated and unnecessary. Entire committees were formed just to present information to the public in ways where their votes couldn't capsize the economy. Whereas high-ranking government officials and leaders used to be commonly referred to as 'puppets,' puppets were becoming their actual job descriptions. Their responsibilities became fewer and fewer, and began merely acting as ambassadors, working only to create the connections necessary to execute the wishes of the public.

After the first couple of years, all of the kinks were worked out and the system ran smoothly. Then Fair e-Lect made it all the way to the federal government. For once, the people's voice was going to be heard. Anything from foreign policies to gun laws to declaring war was to be decided entirely by the people. It was a cataclysmically horrifying time.

Luckily, the people didn't e-Lect to blow any innocent and unsuspecting country off the globe, and those giving the information to Fair e-Lect still hid enough and presented the issues in such a way that all the collective missiles in the world didn't aim at the U.S. in unison, or vice versa. The president was nothing but a mascot, presenting the people's opinions to other leaders around the world in the most diplomatic way possible. And the country seemed to be run by the people. In all actuality, the country was run by the marketing strategists.

It was vividly apparent how inattentive the modern American had become, not to mention how addicted to a virtual state of constant interaction. As the modern American achieved new heights of power, the government put all of their proverbial eggs in the marketing basket. No longer could they fight the public's ability to *choose*, so now they simply had to persuade that choice. Before Fair e-Lect took total control, the federal government made one last large expenditure in buying up all social media and video-sharing websites, including all dating sites and Suit-compatible e-motels. Every online interaction was preceded by an advertisement swaying the public to vote for or against a certain proposition posed during the following week's election. Given that all ads were to remain under thirty seconds, the most brilliant of marketing strategists ran the world.

And Paul had just joined the ranks of dictators.

He sprung out of his seat and didn't quite shout, but unleashed a quick exhalation that came out in a kind of elated squeak.

After issuing his obvious acceptance of the position being offered, he was immediately assigned a task. He was to design a twenty-second advertisement persuading the public to put another $3.5 million into local road construction. Anything goes. If anything submitted was not in compliance with the laws regarding Fair e-Lect marketing (namely presenting false information), their team would identify it and either modify or terminate the ad. The rest was up to Paul.

In a state of jovial excitement, Paul went straight to work. He first searched the web for all arguments for and against road construction. He had to use some arguments to support his own and had to figure out how to disprove the others. He searched for images that would look appealing in his advertisement. Both of these searches came up with a minimal amount of useable material. He searched other similar advertisements used in bordering states and counties. None offered more than the basic message; more money = better roads. He knew that something of that caliber wouldn't allow his career to go any further than this one assignment. He had to create something bold and unique, but it just wasn't coming to him. Disillusion hit him like a sledgehammer to the forehead. Advertisements for snippets had been easy. They were something he was passionate about. They were something beautiful and artsy. How could he turn an idea as bland as road construction into something beautiful?

Paul looked hopelessly down at his keyboard. His fingers only felt comfortable when perched readily across the middle row of keys, yet they had nowhere to go, like two long estranged friends meeting again to find they had nothing left to say to one another. Just like his father downstairs, he felt a despair that ached to get out, but he didn't know whom he could confide in or how to do so.

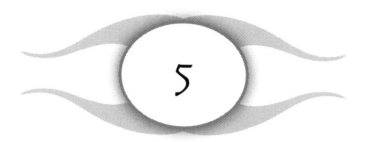

5

THERE WAS SOMETHING ABOUT THE sound of the ocean; not the crashing of waves on a sandy beach, but far out in the ocean where it was nearly silent, save for the gentle pops when two small waves would collide, subliminally separating water in minute droplets milliseconds before reforming. Something about that sound, the subtlety of the infinite, would make loneliness so much more profound and on such a grander scale that it became almost sublime, as opposed to debilitating and horrendous. Sitting on the edge of the drilling rig, sipping coffee and watching the ocean stretch out to the horizon, then beyond perception, eventually reaching some distant and unknown land, and listening to the waves whisper as they danced was one of the few perks of Kenneth's job. It was almost humorous, seeing as Kenneth initially took the job for the companionship.

When Meredith became pregnant, Kenneth went through jobs on a nearly weekly basis. The only jobs that he could see himself doing for an indeterminate period of time didn't offer the financial compensation to support such a fantasy. As his struggle for finding a career became apparent to a wider audience, a family friend of Meredith's who happened to own a small construction company offered Kenneth a job framing houses. The idea of being outside all day and sweating through the summers was actually quite enticing to Kenneth, but the real allure of the job presented itself immediately. Blue-collar workers had a way about themselves. Perhaps it stemmed from discontent for their careers, but they found appealingly grotesque ways to pass the time. Crude dialogue was in constant abundance, as were hilarious practical jokes and inane banter. Despite their vulgar behavior, it exhibited a sense of camaraderie. Hammering nails and dirty jokes were a great way to spend the day, Kenneth thought. However, the tedium of swinging a hammer eight hours a day grew increasingly intolerable. Kenneth realized that while the rudimentary antics were quite gratifying, it did not challenge his mind. A more professional skill that would present new challenges would keep the job interesting when throwing a co-worker's gloves into a porta-potty wouldn't suffice. After three months of framing houses, Kenneth enrolled in an electrical apprenticeship. With his innate mathematical abilities and iron work ethic, Kenneth excelled rapidly. His mind was already bent toward over-analysis, which made him great at troubleshooting.

But as the years passed by so quickly, things began to change. Break time became much quieter as raucous repartee took a back seat to silently perusing internet memes on one's phone or other device. The more everyone was attached to his phone, the more difficult it became to incite any sort of traditional socializing. While everyone else was still having a good time, chuckling to themselves at random images posted on social media websites, Kenneth felt completely isolated, like he was drifting out into the ocean.

And that was exactly where he was sent. The company that Kenneth worked for had a long-standing contract with a drilling company that mostly dealt in oil. Kenneth worked a few jobs at sites all over south Texas, mostly desolate ranch locations, troubleshooting motors that had failed in one way or another. He was quick at isolating problems and even quicker at fixing them and immediately earned a sterling reputation with the customers. With that, he was sent to offshore drilling sites for weeks at a time. His pay increased dramatically, as did his sense of isolation. Where his first year in the construction industry provided Kenneth with some of the most cherished friendships of his life, the deepest connection he felt over the past couple of years was with the ocean itself. The job itself offered excessive amounts of idle time – another catalyst of Kenneth's loneliness. Before he was sent offshore, Kenneth usually would travel with a mobile drilling rig. This, in essence, was an eighteen-wheeler truck with a giant drilling auger mounted to the bed. It was used mostly to run tests when an area was thought to be rich in oil or a certain rare earth mineral. They would do spot tests where the rig would punch holes into the ground in various locations and samples would be tested to collect data and look for percentages of said mineral to find the most suitable place to set up a permanent drilling rig or pumperjack. Kenneth would follow these trucks around south Texas and basically just be on standby in case something went wrong with the motor. It was a superfluous expenditure on the customer's account, but that particular customer frankly had too much money and was doing all but burning it and throwing it off a cliff.

Once Kenneth was sent offshore, his leisure time multiplied exponentially as, once again, he was on standby, but denied the task of driving a service van around following a drilling rig. Most days he tried to spend changing light bulbs, taking amp readings, anything to stay busy. Every now and then he would come across a motor that had gone down. He was always quick at troubleshooting, but tried his best to stretch out the task of fixing the problem as long as possible.

It was his first day back since being diagnosed with pancreatic cancer – something that no one, not even Paul, knew about. He left the rig the previous Wednesday, had his appointment on Thursday, his diagnosis on Friday, and a full weekend of self-pity and gut-wrenching disillusionment before returning to work on Monday morning. Kenneth usually had to catch a helicopter ride at dawn out to the drilling site – something that had him begging for the job years ago, and something that, although it was no longer new and exciting, still brought him to work in a glowing anticipation. Once on the site, he was stuck for at least three days, usually five, before being choppered back to dry land. Whereas most contractors were only called out when needed and were paid around the clock, an agreement was made once Kenneth earned a reputation on site and it became known how much Kenneth enjoyed the work, and he could basically come and go when an available spot on a helicopter presented itself and take home a forty hour paycheck every week regardless of whether he worked eighty or zero. While the isolation was jarring, it was much easier to feel lonely in the middle of the ocean rather than surrounded by people, Kenneth thought.

After the helicopter ride, the sign-ins, the hellos and good mornings, Kenneth fell into the dull routine of sipping coffee and watching the waves skip across the horizon in front of the pink light of the sunrise. While he thought that coming to work would get his mind off things, it had the opposite effect. It wiped everything clean and pushed his cancer to the forefront of his thoughts, and the tedium that his job entailed amplified the fact that he was leaving no legacy behind, that the week following his death, his entire existence would be completely erased. The crushing weight of mortality was finally lowering down on him, and he wasn't sure he could bear it.

Kenneth had always felt he was bigger than his particular life, that something about him was destined for more grandiose conclusions than the one he was reaching, but the circumstances of his life thwarted his destiny. Even around his co-workers, Kenneth maintained an air of superiority, a feeling that while their present state of being was all that they would become, it was merely a steppingstone for Kenneth, but that illusion was quickly dissolved. He felt like a life-altering change was on the horizon, but he was being pulled away from it by the black hole of his death. He wanted to reach out and fight, to usher in a legacy of his own, to make one final charge for immortality before being dragged away, but it was too late. He was nothing. And maybe that was what was so frightening about death. More than the pain, the uncertainty, and the afterlife was the idea of being erased. Kenneth knew that that was exactly what was in store for him. No stories would live on telling of his greatness. No anecdotes of his quirky personality would be shared among colleagues. No, he would just be gone.

He spit out a sip of coffee with a sob that hit him like an uppercut to the solar plexus. He coughed out a few more sobs, the scalding coffee spewing from his Styrofoam cup and burning his hand, briefly bringing him out of his fit. He struggled to keep himself together, swallowing that lump of despair, but choking on it, trying to keep it down, but every breath felt like a forceful Heimlich. Luckily, before this episode could be brought to a point of no return, the intercom crackled before Les, the supervisor, called out for Kenneth to report to MCC3.

A motor had gone down, a small consolation from a cruel god that was relentlessly kicking Kenneth in the teeth. Kenneth gathered himself before collecting his tools and hauling them to MCC3 to set them up beside the motor. He traced the conduit runs and shut off the circuit, testing power thrice before even cracking open the peckerhead. He was being as meticulous as possible to delay the inevitable downtime and potential emotional breakdown that awaited him upon completion. After removing the ten hex-head bolts, the problem was immediately apparent. The motor was running on a forty-amp circuit, but the contractor that had installed the wiring had downsized the neutral to a ten gauge, and it had consequently burnt up. Kenneth had plenty of wire onsite and took his time mounting the wire on a rack, inspecting the other wires, making terminations. Other crewmembers gathered around. Some were ordered to do so to restart the motor and ensure that operations were running normally after it fired back up. Some were there to offer assistance or just watch Kenneth work and hopefully gain some electrical knowledge. Most, however, were there just out of boredom. Kenneth didn't mind the audience. He was confident enough in his skills and could hopefully gain some much-needed social interaction, but alas, most of the men surrounding him were scrolling through memes on their phones, occasionally glancing up to note the progress that Kenneth was making.

The job was completed and the men retreated to their corners, about half a dozen pulling up fold-out chairs to the area that Kenneth was previously occupying. Five of them he knew to some degree, but there was a new guy on the job. His skin was dark and he had large bags underneath his eyes. His thinning black hair stood a couple of inches off his scalp in a constant fluff before laying over to one side. He wore a white button down and khakis. His arms didn't seem to disconnect as they were constantly folded across his chest. His unusual appearance was intriguing to Kenneth, mostly because it was anything different, anything to deter his snowballing depression.

"I'm Kenneth," he said as he approached the dark-skinned man, right hand outstretched firmly yet with a quivering voice. The man shook his hand, but offered nothing back verbally. "And you are…?"

"Narayan." Having never heard the name nor the sounds of a thick Indian accent, Kenneth heard something like 'Nah-dine.'

"Cool. Where're you from?"

"India." His remarks were as stern as they were short.

"Oh yeah? What part?"

Narayan finally turned his head toward Kenneth to engage him.

"Have you ever been to India?"

Kenneth shook his head slightly.

"Do you know anything about my country?"

"Not...well....no, not really."

"Then why do you care?"

6

"**W**HY DON'T YOU GET A self-drive car, Ken?"

Paul was coerced into another outing with his father. He squirmed and twitched irritably in the passenger seat. The sun burned his eyes. The seat of the archaic pickup truck was as uncomfortable as it was embarrassing. He blamed all of his inconveniences on his father, and he always knew that calling his father by his first name was a small yet sharp prick in his side.

"You know, Paul," Kenneth said pensively, "there is something about driving a car – or truck, I guess. A feeling about controlling a machine this large and getting comfortable with it. And without controlling the machine, you can't truly appreciate the open road." Paul allowed the corniness. "You should let me teach you. What d'you say, huh? You want to drive the way back?"

"Nah." Paul's gaze retreated down to his phone. "No need, really." Truthfully, Paul was terrified. And he knew that stating his generation's ability to do everything from the slothful comforts of home and their lack of interest in doing otherwise would ignite a small candle of wrath within his father, and therefore, mask his own fears.

Kenneth stayed focused on the road. His lower eyelids tightened minutely as a small film of tears coated his green irises. Left hand still draped languidly over the twelve o'clock position of the steering wheel, his right hand hovered out toward his son. Paul flinched reflexively, but Kenneth, thankfully, didn't seem to notice. His hand made its way to Paul's shoulder and gave a firm squeeze. Paul's eyelids peeled back revealing white on all sides, uncomfortably. He knew that something had changed, that some connection was attempting to be made, like a flickering light bulb sparking futilely, but he just couldn't get past the awkwardness of it all. Kenneth sensed this, slightly deflated that the attempt fell flat, and withdrew.

"This guy whose house we're going to," Kenneth continued, trying to assuage the palpable tension, "he's a real interesting dude. I met him on Monday, and we *hated* each other. It's funny how that works. It always seems that the people I dislike the most initially turn out to be my best friends." Kenneth chuckled, "But it usually takes more than a few days to go from hate to love."

"I don't get that," Paul replied.

"Don't get what?"

"How do you become friends with someone you hate? I mean, I've never talked to anyone I hated. Once I hate them, that's it. They're gone."

"It doesn't always work like that in the real world." Kenneth noticed the pun after he said it and immediately regretted using the term 'real world.' "You have to be in close confines with people. You get to know them. You learn the way they work and the way they talk and such. You learn that what turned you off to begin with is just the way that they operate, and it might be something that isn't too far off from the way *you* operate."

Paul seemed unaffected by this line of reasoning and went back to glaring out the window.

The city flashed by, to Paul, a city of incredible buildings, of mammoth and menacing machines, terrifyingly endless roadways, everything so different from viewing it in pictures, so incredibly infinite and perplexing, everything so haunting. To Kenneth, it was the walls of his cell, the flat terrain, the stretches of shopping districts, the dry yet humid climate. He often fantasized about taking trips to faraway lands, to overwhelming geographical formations and inimitably fascinating cultures, vacations that he always presumed would follow Paul's graduation and passage into manhood, the latter something that he feared would never happen, the vacations something that he *knew* would never happen. Glaring into the distance, the heat distorting the horizon in blurred waves, he saw Corpus Christi, Texas as the absence of geography, the absence of culture, the cruel punchline to the joke of his existence. His entire life was an allegory of confinement, the town the concrete manifestation of that confinement.

Cranes and orange barricades lined the freeway on either side. "Fucking road work."

Paul's ears went up. "What's wrong with the road work?"

Kenneth turned to his son, momentarily perplexed. "Nothing, I guess. It's just damn annoying."

"But don't you want the roads to get fixed? And get them widened? It could make things a lot more convenient – and safer."

"Let me ask you something. You see how many streets are being repaired? Just about every road we've passed today has some huge project going on. That's millions of our tax dollars going into repaving this whole city. And all you see everywhere you go are orange barrels and steamrollers, giant dump trucks and asphalt stampers."

"Yeah…so?"

"So why are all their trucks empty?"

Walking into Narayan's house was like entering a museum, and just like a museum, the father found everything to be fascinating while the son found the setting boring, impersonal, and painfully uncomfortable, already counting the minutes until they could leave. Artifacts and keepsakes from vastly different countries lined the shelves, the various shapes and clashing colors making everything seem asymmetrical. Twiglike sticks of incense burned at every corner, and the smell enveloped the father and son even before crossing the threshold, the scent an alluring fragrance to Kenneth, a pungent stench to Paul, coating his stomach with a caustic bile and giving him greater regret for agreeing to accompany his father on this outing and further reason to remain incorrigible in his reclusive lifestyle.

"Welcome! Welcome!" Narayan exclaimed jubilantly, ushering the two into his domicile. He seemed drunk and gregarious, the antithesis of the somber and silent Narayan that Kenneth knew from work.

Narayan was born in a small village outside of Agra, India. His family owned a small gas station and saved every penny to send their only son to college. He excelled in school as he was burdened with the relentless weight of being the family's only investment. He went to school for two years in New Delhi studying chemical engineering and English before transferring to Dallas. There, he completed several degrees, he won enough trophies from various experiments and competitions to fill a thirty-five gallon trash can, he finished at the very top of his class, and he lost much of his personality. Narayan was warned of the culture shock he would face upon emigrating to the states, but mostly just of xenophobia-related issues, and with news memes bouncing repetitively between comedic small-time misdemeanors and large-scale terrorist threats, xenophobia seemed to be bubbling beneath the surface of the entire country. However, no one warned him of the lack of communication and social interaction. In India, there was no such thing as 'personal space.' Social circles peppered with playful banter and constant physical contact were daily rituals, and while some topics were off-limits in India, those taboos were all people wanted to talk about in America – via social media, of course. Everyone at his Texas university was attached to a device, impotent and useless without one. Narayan did not have the money to purchase any sort of smart phone or tablet and would have to borrow them from the school to complete some of his assignments, leaving him virtually friendless and left to studying and introspection in his lonesome dorm room. With silence being his sole companion, silent and detached were what he became.

Upon graduation, Narayan got a job with a drilling company called Echo. Echo was a large corporation that operated globally, usually hiring local craftsmen at each jobsite, namely electricians. Narayan did a few overseas jobs enjoying the company of the locals from each location, learning their cultures and customs, which were usually far more similar to his own than those of the Western World. But after the dramatic decline in oil prices of the late-2010's compounded with the boom of electric automobiles, Echo's stock price plummeted and their international work went on hiatus, sentencing Narayan to lockdown in south Texas.

And then came the emergence of what was known as 'Curry Terrorism.' It was a crude and abrasive term, deemed politically incorrect upon creation and thus dubbed 'Hindu Extremism,' but the latter term was only used by network news. To the rest of the world that got its news from entertainment-based news meme sites, it remained Curry Terrorism. To most people of the Hindu faith, the notion that someone would claim that their religious doctrines and codes of morality would guide anyone to committing mass murder was completely absurd and insulting. To Narayan, however, the scare was almost expected. Terrorist activities occurred among all faiths, even the faithless. The only common trend, Narayan thought, was that they only occurred among the imprudent and arrogant. What was expected was the Americans' need to target a specific culprit and give a face to all of their fears to make them more digestible. As long as the enemy had a name, they could destroy him. And when the name shifted from Islam to India, Narayan further withdrew into his shell of isolation, becoming more and more detached. With his cold and aloof disposition and the recent spike in Curry Terrorism, Narayan's co-workers at his offshore job in the Gulf Coast were not very quick to approach him. And so dictated his position at the jobsite; vastly intelligent and horribly unapproachable, a tool for gaining quick answers, then easily discarded, like an old calculator on the corner of a desk.

But not today. Today was Holi, one of the most important Hindu holidays, the beginning of Spring, the day that everyone would let loose, socialize playfully, and drink heavily.

"Come, come. This way. Have some drinks." He began pouring three shots of some unknown golden liquor, not bothering to ask for Kenneth's permission to feed alcohol to his teenage son. Kenneth looked at Paul and tightened the corners of his lips as if to say he didn't approve, but he wasn't going to stop it from happening. Narayan toasted boisterously to new friendships, and the three poured the mysterious poison down their gullets, Kenneth eyeing Paul for his reaction. To his surprise, Paul actually did have the grimace, the heavy breathing, and the shocking disgust of a first-timer. Kenneth's contentment was short-lived as he remembered that it wasn't Paul living dangerously that worried him; it was Paul not living at all.

A man wearing a pastel-striped button up and flip-flops emerged from the hallway, presumably the restroom. He had the same skin tone and disposition of Narayan, although his face was gaunter, more linear, and his hair hung down just above his shoulders, shining like one organ rather than millions of strands, wavy like a solid black flag, yet stiff and motionless despite his galloping strides.

"This is my greatest friend, Chalem," Narayan announced. Handshakes and forced smiles ensued. "He is the owner of the finest Pakistani restaurant in town." Chalem and Narayan bellowed laughter at this notion, Narayan guffawing from the pit of his belly in seemingly fake and sardonic chortles, Chalem chuckling in quick breaths like a rat.

"Pakistani, huh?" Kenneth questioned, ignoring the inside joke. "I don't think I've ever had Pakistani food."

"Neither has he!" Narayan exclaimed in another outburst of laughter. Chalem's eyes squinted shut as he shared Narayan's amusement.

"I… I don't get it."

"It's an Indian restaurant. I am from India, not Pakistan," Chalem replied, somewhat condescendingly. "But it is too dangerous right now to have the word 'Indian' posted on your business, so it is now simply called Little Pakistan. The food is still Indian, but no one seems to notice."

"No one seems to notice because no one goes into your restaurant!" Narayan shouted. Kenneth was still getting used to seeing Narayan in this state of raucous joviality. Although they had only known each other for less than a week, every moment was shattering Kenneth's image of Narayan. But as the evening progressed, other issues came to Kenneth's attention that seemed more congruent with the reserved and sullen Narayan whom he knew. As drinks multiplied and stories were shared, Kenneth realized the importance of the holiday he was now being accustomed to. This was their Christmas, their big celebration of the year, and it was only the four of them – two of them being a man Narayan had just met that week and his son whom Narayan hadn't ever met at all. The realities of Narayan's existence and the hardships facing his minority group suddenly funneled down Kenneth's throat, filling him with an icy hollowness. Given his own circumstances, it was difficult for Kenneth to really empathize with anyone else's problems, but when his own impending mortality relinquished some of its weight, it allowed an opening for new heartaches. But despite this realization of his new friend's loneliness and despair, Kenneth was feeling the first interruptions of the pain caused by his diagnosis. He was finally somewhere outside the house with his son, he was making a new friend for the first time in years, and he had a nice buzz going.

"So where did you score all this shit?" Paul asked Narayan. Kenneth motioned to reprimand his son's foul language, but his reaction time was slower than Narayan's.

"The company that I work for – it's Paul, right? – it is the same company that basically employs your father, and they used to send me to many places to do my job."

"And what is your job?"

"It is difficult to explain. In a nutshell – this is the expression, no? – well anyway, I test extractions and decide the best way to obtain the greatest amount of a desired element."

Kenneth was elated, seeing his son actually exchanging dialogue in the real world with a man three times his age. This outing was Kenneth throwing a marble at the concrete wall between himself and his son, but somehow the marble shot through, providing a peephole into Paul's world. Kenneth had been making these attempts for years with Paul, but now they were to multiply and bear a certain despair to them. Kenneth was dying. It wasn't enough that he still didn't truly know his own son. What was worse was that Kenneth was petrified, literally and figuratively being eaten from the inside, the parasitic fears of what was to come as physically detrimental and as lethal as the cancerous tumor inside him, and he had no one to confide in. He *yearned* to tell Paul, to let him know the upcoming events that would shape his entire future, but lately, shamefully, not as much for Paul's concern as for his own. The terrors that Kenneth was experiencing were too much for him to bear, but he didn't have the right to put that on his son; not so much because Paul was to have his own ordeals and fears that would continue to arise from Kenneth's death for decades to come, but because Kenneth didn't *know* Paul, and he hadn't quite earned the right to unleash his problems unto Paul's ears.

Narayan checked the thermometer that was suction-cupped to the sliding glass door to his back yard and announced that he now deemed it cool enough to relocate the festivities to the patio.

The moment they were outside, the need for relocation was immediately apparent. Four plastic bottles filled with water and brightly colored dyes lined the edge of the concrete. Narayan picked up the bottle containing the orange liquid and began pouring it over Chalem's head, the colors running down his chest and back, permanently dying his dress shirt. It wasn't until this moment that Kenneth realized he knew of this holiday in old pictures of crowded streets in foreign lands, everyone and everything colored vibrantly. Chalem then returned the favor for Narayan. His face was a picture of reserved enthusiasm as Chalem rubbed the green dye vigorously into Narayan's thinning hair. Paul slowly retreated to the corner in fright. His eyes wide and his lips pursed, he inched toward the back of the patio, terrified at the prospect of getting dirty, but too amused and proud to go inside.

Kenneth was next. He was not as good at masking his excitement as Narayan. With the open smile and the slight confusion of a child walking downstairs on Christmas morning, Kenneth slowly approached Narayan and awaited being 'Holied.' His color was a dark blue, almost black. Chalem and Narayan both rubbed the liquid in their palms and coated it firmly over the entirety of Kenneth's body. They were much more thorough with Kenneth as he was a guest to their tradition. With the focus of parents bathing a newborn, the two of them rubbed the coloring around Kenneth's eyes, down the bridge of his nose, traced his jawline, and scrubbed it into his scalp. Almost instinctually, the three of them crouched to the ground, Kenneth curving his back and bowing his head, almost touching his forehead to the grass, as they poured the coloring straight from the bottle down his spine, the blue soaking into his shirt and spreading out toward his ribs on both sides. Four hands massaged the color across his kidneys and shoulder blades. Trying a little too hard to embrace the tradition, Kenneth wanted to believe in gods he was never introduced to. He wanted to feel the cancer leaving his body through their hands and the blue dye, evaporating out his pores like a gentle cloud of smoke trailing off into the breeze and becoming invisible and, therefore, nonexistent. By the time they were finished, Kenneth felt cleansed. He didn't know whether it was some ancient healing power associated with the coloring of the body, if it was a mysterious potion in the liquid concoction, or just the idea of getting as irrevocably filthy without any concern that was so rejuvenating, but he didn't care. Above all, he enjoyed partaking in someone else's custom, a different take on life, anything apart from the ordinary, anything to distract. Paul, obviously, felt otherwise.

Chalem was approaching Paul, and his fear was smeared across his face. "No, no, no," said Narayan. "You can leave him alone. He doesn't look like he wants to have any fun."

Chalem looked content with this explanation and withdrew briefly before pulling a concealed squirt gun from his belt and opened fire with the quickness and cunning of a gunslinger. A bright purple speckled wildly across Paul's chest.

"What the fuck?!" Paul exclaimed.

"Calm down!" Kenneth was disheartened to be brought down from his Holi high by the ostentatiousness of his son.

"Didn't you hear your friend, asshole? He said to leave me alone!"

"Paul!" cried Kenneth wrathfully.

"Relax," said Narayan placidly. "It is just a shirt."

"Wrong, dickhead. This is a Mark Griffin, and it cost $250."

"Like I said, it's a shirt."

Paul's eyes whipped around from face to face, scanning for any signs of sympathy, but only seeing contempt, and so he turned and fumed his way indoors to wash the stains out.

Narayan glared at Chalem sternly.

"What? The boy isn't right. I just squirted him with a little food coloring. I mean, it's just a damn shirt! Did you see his —"

"Enough," Narayan said calmly, yet with all the power to silence an angry mob.

"No, he's right." Kenneth hung his head in shame, not so much at his son's actions, but more at the fact that these men knew about as much as he did about his own son, and they, too, didn't like it.

In the bathroom, Paul cursed Chalem. He cursed Narayan. He cursed his father, the holiday, and all of the real world. He wondered why he ever left the sanctuary of his room. He scrubbed vehemently as their taunts echoed in his brain.

But as he dried his now polka-dotted shirt and swore vengeance upon the entire assemblage, vengeance appeared to him. The bathroom door open and the bedroom door across the hallway left slightly ajar revealed a small ivory object underneath the bed, barely peeking out from the dangling corner of the comforter, at first a curiosity, then a sort of infatuation. He pushed the bedroom door open, oblivious and careless to the personal injustice he was committing. As he approached, the object seemed to have grown in size. He pulled it out from under the bed and stood it upright on the headboard. At first sight, he thought it was pocket-sized, but now it towered powerfully, reaching up a good eighteen inches. It was conical and slightly curved, sleek and flawless. Initially, Paul mistook it for a colonial style gunpowder horn, but no, this was something biotic, something that came from a beast of an animal. Of all the artifacts that decorated Narayan's house, none had any effect on Paul, no artistic quality nor intrigue. But this, this was *beckoning* Paul to touch it, to hold it, to *take* it. He couldn't identify the overwhelming power that it produced, but it had a hold of him.

Paul ran to the truck and retrieved a jacket to cover his stained shirt. He rejoined the party outside, losing the anger, but still unapologetic, as they all collectively had to pretend the last five minutes didn't really happen. Outside in the truck, underneath the back seat where his jacket was previously stashed, an ivory rhinoceros horn now resided.

7

PAUL STRAINED HIS EYES, FIXATED on the horizon, trying to see an end or an obstruction, but neither presented itself. Two straight and endless roads stretched out in front of him in the shape of a V, shrinking, shrinking, and finally disappearing where the land met the yellow sky. The wind gently jostled the reed grass that covered the ground everywhere the asphalt didn't exist. The white sun sent ripples through his vision, blurring the clouds with the sky. Paul squinted as he stared at the sun, then raised his right hand toward it, threatening it, then squeezed his hand into a fist and dragged the sun down toward the horizon between the forked roads, the color of it dulling to a tangerine orange as it dropped in the sky. His left hand pointed to the top-left corner of his vision and touched the small white square with his index finger. The square enlarged and divided itself into a four by four grid. Paul found the square that contained the word 'WIND' and gently raised the levels. The grass bent and vibrated as thousands of appendages tickled Paul's skin. With his right hand, Paul pointed to the clouds and squeezed the cylindrical metal and plastic Mouse Tail in the RW, then dragged the clouds behind him and out of view, and therefore, they disappeared. Paul felt like God.

The Mouse Tail acted as a computer mouse, but because the fingers were encapsulated by the mitten-like hands of The Suit, one couldn't press a button with a single finger. Paul aimed it at the sky after selecting a new color scheme and waved his hand out in front of him, painting the skies blue and purple. He then pointed in different spots throughout the now-night sky and squeezed and released, squeezed and released, over and over again, like he was shooting a gun, small holes of light shining through all the bullet holes in the form of twinkling stars.

It was a program to which he got a membership in exchange for one of his old snippet promotions. It was a place where he would go to think. It was a difficult program to navigate and manipulate, and therefore, an unpopular program, but Paul was quite good at it.

He retrieved a two-dimensional image of Chrissy that he had previously saved and placed her at the end of one road. The other road remained vacant. He peered out at the image of his girlfriend in the distance, enjoying the control he had over her. He looked down at the rocks held together by tar, searching for an answer, trying to find beauty in the job at hand.

Once again, he looked into the distance, this time down the road that Chrissy didn't stand on, and felt the urge to run and run and run, chasing the horizon, but he knew he would only make it six feet before crashing into his bedroom wall. He wished that he could live in the VW, that he would never have to leave, never have to feel the restraints of physical boundaries. If only he had been born a couple of decades later, maybe he would never have to feel the pains and shames of the RW. Maybe he could live here, constantly constructing and painting his own personal Utopia.

A message from Chrissy appeared onscreen, an invitation to an e-motel. They had reconciled their relationship after Paul rejected Chrissy's proposal. He explained to her in the most roundabout and superficial of words that he wasn't ready, but she was still the one for him. He employed various scapegoats; their young age, his still blossoming career, and, of course, his mother's death. By the end of the brief conversation, both were content to go back to their old relationship status with the ambiguous promise that the issue would be readdressed in time.

The two of them went about their sexual routine as if nothing had happened. It was nice for Paul to not feel the awkward tension of the past hanging over the moment. He attributed it to the fact that Chrissy was that cool, that she wouldn't allow misfortunes to spoil her outlook on life, but in actuality, Chrissy wore the face of the unfazed to elicit that exact reaction from Paul.

Paul told her about the ordeal at Narayan's house. He told her mostly of his anger. He omitted his fear. He said nothing of his embarrassment nor his overwhelming need for approval, and he also didn't tell her about the stolen artifact in his closet that he had now identified as a rhinoceros horn.

"What do you expect?" she replied softly. "They're fucking *Indians*."

"I know, I know. It was just fucking weird. And my damn shirt will never be the same."

"I've been seeing more and more news about those people. It's getting pretty scary."

"Aw, c'mon." Paul stretched an accusatory grin across his face. "Chrysanthemum? Scared? I didn't think you were afraid of anything."

"I'm not!" she playfully mocked outraged. "But I mean, it's like every *day* now. Someone or something else is getting blown up."

Paul's eyes lit up. His mouth draped open and his cheek muscles relaxed. He went blank for about two seconds before exclaiming, "Holy shit! Holy shit!"

"What is it?" Chrissy asked perplexedly.

"Holy-- Huh? Nothing. I mean, I gotta go. I'll tell you later. I promise."

With that, he logged out and ripped off his Suit as quickly as possible. He began scanning the internet for video clips. Within fifteen minutes, he had copied eight videos into a folder entitled 'First Ad.' Still, the primary video he needed was missing. He spent the next twenty minutes perusing the web searching for the perfect video, but came up empty. Just as his hopes started to subside, he remembered the car-cam.

Before self-driving cars made their way to the streets in astonishing numbers, traffic fatalities related to drivers distracted by their devices were rising exponentially. The government made all new cars be mandatorily issued a car-cam, or a camera filming the driver and passenger any time the vehicle was running. If an accident occurred, all vehicles involved were to have their car-cam videos reviewed, and if it were revealed that a driver was using any type of device, the result would usually be mandatory jail time.

This drastic move by the government, however, was quickly deemed null by the unexpectedly quick emergence of the self-driving car. When the first models were being tested, all predictions showed them to be at least a decade away from mass production. That estimate was disproved within eighteen months. So, two years worth of automobiles with car-cams installed were issued, then never manufactured again. Kenneth was one of the few who bought one of these vehicles, and one of the fewer who still owned one. To make Kenneth look even more the buffoon, during that two-year time span he also bought another vehicle for Meredith, a vehicle that she totaled nineteen months later, a vehicle that killed her.

Despite the fact that the videos taken by the car-cam were never watched, the camera in Kenneth's truck was an evil and taunting eye, watching them always with a wicked smile, a constant reminder of their lives gone wrong. Only one video of theirs had ever been watched. Truth be told, Kenneth didn't even know how to access the video footage taken in his truck.

"I've got something you need to see," Paul muttered. He had approached his father sullenly yet confidently, a laptop held out in front of him like an offering. Just as all videos of arrests were made public, as were car-cams at crime scenes – you just had to know where to look. Paul found the video of his mother's final moments on one of these sites and bequeathed the horrors of witnessing it to his father. "I wanted you to see it from me before anyone else."

Faded by years of marriage and motherhood – not to mention being a full-time teacher/housewife – Meredith's fashionable appearance that she constantly scrutinized had been wiped down to bare essentials. She rid herself of most of her makeup kits. Her hair took whatever form it held after her shower. To Kenneth, this was how she honed her beauty. Although it was her wardrobe and audaciously loud jewelry that first intrigued Kenneth, it was her natural beauty that appealed to him after the initial infatuation wore off.

And so she existed without the cosmetics to which she attributed her confidence. For years, the painted up beauty queen that Kenneth met in high school was replaced by a gorgeous housewife.

But in their dimly lit living room on the glowing screen of Paul's laptop, the Meredith of old shined back, as if from a window to the past; her blonde hair purposefully unkempt, her eyeshadow thick and green, applying lipstick in the rearview mirror as she drove, then finally adjusting her breasts, pulling them out the top of her blouse barely shy of exposing the nipple, then a sudden jerk as she was propelled forward, just to the right of the frame and, within a millisecond, out of view.

Although the video was never mentioned between the two, Paul always knew that it broke his father apart inside. Kenneth retained his hard exterior, but a definite crack emerged after seeing that video that did not go undetected by Paul. It was the most profound of Kenneth's reactions to his wife's death. It murdered him inside. Paul knew this, but he never mentioned it. He took the knowledge and placed it in his pocket, hoping for it to be useful one day.

Grief is a horribly difficult emotion. Grief commixed with apathy is even worse. Throw spite for the deceased into the cauldron and the concoction is beyond lethal. While there always existed a boundary between Kenneth and Paul, a barrier comprised of incongruent personalities and confusion, that was the first time that the confusion had transformed into contempt. *I wanted you to see it from me before anyone else.* Kenneth knew exactly what this statement meant. It was a strategic move by his son to feign concerned and to appear proactive in a selfless attempt to prevent unnecessary suffering, but in actuality was a selfish declaration of Paul merely wanting to be the first. He wanted to win, just like the guy in the office that spreads gossip like gunfire, playing the role of the messenger because it is the closest that he will ever get to fame, or even popularity. Paul had to know the implications of the video. He had to know that they would be the emotional equivalent to a searing hot blade burning its way into his father's abdomen. Meredith posthumously cuckolding him elicited so many unmanageable emotions. Where could he direct his anger? In whom could he confide his hurt and betrayal? How could he gain any closure when the culprit of his hurt was now a corpse? The questions bored into him like knife wounds.

Paul, on the other hand, had a much different reaction to the video. The implications were obvious, yet not conclusive. Still, they both knew. Paul lived in an era where infidelity wasn't the issue that it was during his parents' time. In fact, the term held an entirely different meaning, but Paul understood the betrayal and the hurt that his mother inflicted. Rather than feeling any sort of shame or anger toward his mother, Paul felt admiration and envy. Meredith was doing something real, something unexpected, and something in the real world. These were things that Paul strived for, and things that constantly eluded him. That video, almost as much as his mother's death, filled him with a void needing to be filled and a nameless ambition. Paul knew that he wasn't quite enough.

But now when he felt those same feelings of inadequacy, he peered up into his closet at the rhino horn and felt vindicated. Paul felt accomplished. He felt capable, capable of surprising himself, capable of doing what hadn't been done, capable of inflicting pain on those he felt deserved it. It felt good.

Paul took the memory card from the car-cam and ran it upstairs to his computer. It took hours to go through the footage and get what he needed. He was looking for seemingly heartfelt and normal family dialogue. It was supposed to be one continuous piece, but that was impossible. He was going to have to chop and edit the shit out of the video to obtain what looked like a normal father-son conversation filled with love and heavy with sentiment. The main problem was that they would be wearing different clothes, thus making it impossible to look like one continuous clip, but Paul knew enough to change the color of the clothing in the video enough to make its flaws virtually imperceptible. After a few hours, Paul had his advertisement.

A father (Kenneth) and his son (Paul) are enjoying a nice drive through a suburban neighborhood. Kenneth asks his son how he is doing. Paul replies simply, "Getting better." A voice narrates over the video footage and says, "Our road construction project won't just make your drive a little safer." The video shifts to show the back tires of the SUV (not the one that Kenneth is actually driving) slide in loose gravel. The video goes back to the interior of the car. Kenneth reaches out and grabs Paul's shoulder. "I love you," he says. Back to the exterior of the SUV, we see the front tire hit a pothole and go flat. The narrator says, "It won't just keep your vehicle in good shape." Kenneth glances in the rearview mirror with a look of concern as he presumably pulls over to the side of the road. We now see the tire come to a slow stop over a shoddily repaired part of the road, and suddenly, unexpectedly, almost comically, the vehicle explodes. "It will help stop Hindu Extremism." The screen goes black. "Potholes are one of the easiest places for terrorists to hide explosives. Let's not give them the option. Vote yes for the Save Our Streets Project."

Dramatically, just as Paul put the finishing touches on his advertisement, all of the lights in the house went out, his computer went blank and lifeless, and Paul felt terrified.

8

DEATH. EVERYTHING THE WORD STOOD for was the epitome of fear, uncertainty, despair, and tragedy. Death doesn't need a picture or a sad story to convey the weight of it all. It is the darkest of conclusions that awaits us all, the last page of every book scribbled in tears and sorrow. But just like everything else in life, the real horror was etched in the details.

Every minor ache in Kenneth's body was now questioned. Every mundane crack in his joints, every sore muscle, every sneeze was now interrogated for its reason for existence. He could draw a line from a hunger pang to a bleeding organ.

He had always had the habit of scratching and gnawing at loose skin around his cuticles. If the skin broke away more easily than usual, he believed it to be his approaching death, already decaying the flesh. When he would pull away too much skin and the blood would pool at the corner of his fingernail in a small droplet, it was toxic. He feared his own flesh, his own blood, and treated his own body like biohazardous waste. He began washing his hands compulsively. He showered three times a day.

Urinating and bowel movements were dreaded interruptions throughout the day. Despite Kenneth's research that didn't support his fears, he was always expecting an unexpected discharge, blood, discolored urine, dark fecal matter, grotesque variations in consistency, anything to show in plain light the horrors that existed within.

At night, he would lie awake for hours. Insomnia had never plagued him in the past, but now when the lights would go out, the darkness would heighten his senses, would make him aware of the ongoings beneath his skin. He would hear his stomach grumble. He would feel his digestive system operating. He would see the complex machine that resided in his abdomen, and like staring under the hood of a broken down automobile, his body was enigmatically damaged, smoking and hissing, but offering no implication on how to fix itself.

So he would twitch in his bed, his brow furrowed, body shifting in spasms growing in frequency until they resembled a seizure.

The psychological torture of the disease was pounding Kenneth into the ground without any physical symptoms. Kenneth had only gone to the doctor six months ago to address a potential herniated disc in his back from lifting a heavy spool of wire at work. As all patients at that particular clinic, he was to undergo a sonogram along with blood work and the usual checking of vital signs. Four different nurses asked the same questions without making eye contact – reason for visiting the doctor, family histories, surgical history, allergies, other known ailments, drinking habits, smoking habits, other medication currently taking, pain level. By the fourth round of the monotonous questionnaire, Kenneth's enthusiasm had sunk to the level of the nurses interviewing him. Then they would proceed to poke, prod, measure, and inspect.

His back was fine. His pancreas was not.

He never returned to a doctor. It was an oafish decision, he knew, to approach death with the macho man mentality, to face everything alone with nothing but tidbits of information and a pair of balls. He knew he was doomed, and any advice given, any treatment administered would be counteractive. The knowledge of the progressing cancer, just the words uttered by a doctor, would damage Kenneth's psyche far worse than any medicine could sway his health.

With Paul confined to his room light years away from Kenneth's recliner in the living room, Kenneth fought the illness alone.

The previous night's power outage sent Kenneth peering around the outside of the house with a flashlight, inspecting his main service panel. Everything appeared in order until he looked to the left of the breaker box. He didn't know how it took him so long to find it. The meter can was now just a large hole where the meter should have existed, exposing electrically charged lugs and the service wires coming down from the riser. The meter lay in the grass a few feet in front of the service, bashed with a blunt object.

Paul was livid. Kenneth knew that the boy was helpless without the luxury of electricity, but that confusion and fear turned Paul into an animal. He stormed down the stairs screaming at Kenneth to fix the problem, that he was an electrician and this situation should not exist in their household. Kenneth wanted to explain to him that this was out of his hands, that the city was responsible for the meters to which he had no access, to possibly teach his son about the intricacies of his trade, but really, more than anything, he wanted to belittle Paul for not being able to exist in the natural world without a computer.

"Is my little baby afraid of the dark?!" Kenneth roared back.

The argument escalated as the two took turns stabbing at one another's pride. Shamefully, something in Kenneth was exhilarated and satisfied by the squabble. It was the longest conversation that they had shared in a while, albeit a wrathful and petty one, and although the dialogue was comprised of insults, they were all fueled by raw emotion, not just sentence fragments aimed at ending the conversation and getting Kenneth out of Paul's room. It was something real, one of the few real things the two had shared in years.

The next morning, a city worker came out, repaired the meter can, and replaced the meter, a quick fix that restored their electricity. Paul, surely, spent the night in terror, perplexed at how anyone could live without modern technology to comfort them even as they slept.

Once order and normality had been restored to the house, Kenneth suddenly felt blank. He missed the excitement, the feeling of need, of anything on the horizon. Once the status quo was intact, the horrors beneath the surface reemerged.

Kenneth's life had always been lacking, but he also always found ways to occupy his time. While he refused to turn on a television or log on to an entertainment site because he knew enough about the atrocities that existed in both, he would entertain himself by working in the yard, modifying his house, changing out his electrical panel, installing a ceiling fan, remodeling a bathroom, anything to make him forget about the demons that lurked in every corner of the world that he had been born into.

But now, any of those old distractions were futile. Any work he could do to his house just seemed like dusting the furniture on the Titanic. It was all going down, and Kenneth just couldn't find anything to keep his mind off the looming iceberg. He sat at his dining room table, a hand in his pocket along with the two items that always existed there, a black marker and a utility knife. His keys were hung on the wall. He didn't bother carrying his phone anymore. But the marker and knife were always necessary at work, and after some time he noticed their utility in everyday life. Before long, he couldn't leave the house without the two. For the first time in years, he wanted to discard the knife. Sitting in idleness, awaiting death, he could only think about dragging the blade across his wrists. It wasn't in his psychological capabilities to know about an approaching doom. Evolution was a bitch. Organisms weren't made to develop a psyche, to know about the lurking enemies within. To know at birth that everything was temporary was bad enough; to know the names of your organs and which ones were failing you and how quickly they would defeat you was simply too much for the human mind to accept.

His fingers ran slowly up and down the cold steel in his right-hand pocket. He thought about what slitting his wrists would feel like. He walked his mind through every step; the initial surge of adrenaline, the pain, the horrific sight, the realization of the act committed, the panic, the sensation of too much blood leaving the body, the cold, the onset of death, the fatigue, the darkness, the cold, the black, the cold. It was a gruesome thought, but was he not already experiencing the same ordeal on a longer time spectrum?

In a quick jitter, he sprang from his seat and rummaged through the kitchen pantry where he stocked the few board games of the house; a thick layer of dust on each box as none had been opened practically since their purchase. He found a pair of dice and returned to the table.

Five. This was the number in his head. This was his point.

He rolled the dice. *Seven.*

He had recently researched the treatments that he should already be undergoing and all of their outcomes. These treatments were reflected in the ten percent that he received as his hopes for survival.

He rolled again. *Four.*

The most common and traditional treatment of cancer was chemotherapy. With that, he could expect extreme bouts of nausea. He could expect a fatigue that would make any life worth living an impossibility. He could expect basically living in a hospital and forfeiting his life savings to the procedure, not to mention his remaining hair.

Eleven.

There were new treatments, most of them vastly more fruitless than chemo. One of the most cutting edge and daring treatments was based on the most appalling of ideas. The best way to kill a parasite was to eliminate the host. This method involved cryogenically freezing the patient until he or she was clinically dead. After thawing out the body, the cancer would die out along with the patient, and in few instances, they were able to revive the patient. This method would also, as all of the others, involve emptying Kenneth's wallet. None of it sounded as pleasant as dying slowly as he was doing right now.

Nine.

There had to be a time when he would tell Paul, but he just couldn't imagine it.

Ten. Six. Ten again.

He couldn't confide in Paul because they didn't have the relationship built for that type of trust and comfort. He couldn't warn Paul because he just didn't have it in him.

Three.

He felt an overwhelming obligation to tell his son of what was to come, but he just couldn't bear it. Life had already had him beaten down to the ground, and as much as he pushed the thought to the recesses of his mind, he had a certain derision for his own son. The man that Paul was growing up to be was someone Kenneth would not only actively avoid if they weren't related, but someone he would *detest*. This lessened the feeling of obligation, but severely heightened the impact of his own mortality.

Seven. Eight. Two. Nine. Four. Four. Twelve. Six.

Kenneth had one shot at this. Treatment was going to severely diminish the quality of his remaining time and probably not lengthen it, either. Nor would it allow him the luxury of secrecy. Telling Paul what was to come would not only unleash a slew of new problems, but bring the existing ones to the foreground. Kenneth's only real option, therefore, was to continue living as best he could, as nothing had changed other than his ability to let time pass by thoughtlessly, until it was no longer possible.

Five.

It took him seventeen tries. Five. The possibility of rolling a five on a come-out roll was slightly greater than his chance of survival. And it took him seventeen tries.

A red glare danced along the walls. Kenneth looked behind him to see the flare intensified on the window facing the front lawn. Without even looking through the window to see what was amiss, Kenneth threw the front door open to find his mesquite tree completely engorged in flame.

Kenneth let out something between a sigh and a squeak as he raced into the yard. Whether to put out the flames or just get a closer view was debatable. At a closer proximity, the spectacle was mesmerizing, and all thoughts of saving the day and whatever that might entail went up in smoke with the flames that danced overhead.

The mesquite tree was old and gargantuan, so the fireball that it had become was like a burning comet hovering six feet off the ground. The flames rose high above the tallest branches and ascended into the night sky out of view. Kenneth couldn't remember where he left his cellphone. He was enthralled by the spectacle. The authorities must have already been notified by the neighbors because the lights of the fire truck rolling down the street were almost as bright as the fire that was about to consume Kenneth's entire house.

To Kenneth's relief, the firefighters extinguished the flames with ease, almost anti-climactically. A squad car arrived on the scene as the firemen were reeling back up their hose and preparing to disembark. Two officers emerged from the car, both a little too portly and soft to possess the ability of taking down a perpetrator.

"What's your e-mail address?" the larger of the two cops asked Kenneth without the slightest of glances up from his tablet.

"What?" Kenneth replied incredulously.

"Your e-mail address." The officer's droopy eyes, bored and inattentive, finally looked up to meet Kenneth's. Kenneth obliged.

"You'll be receiving a questionnaire concerning the arson. Have a nice evening." The officers were already retreating back to their vehicle, the smaller one apparently only getting out to switch to the driver's side of the cruiser.

"Wait a damn minute!" Kenneth shouted, barely pulling back their attention. "My yard was just set on fire! Get back here and talk to me about it!"

"That's what the questionnaire is for. We'll use your answers for insurance purposes and for any leads."

Kenneth couldn't believe what he was hearing. It seemed as if the entire world had just stopped giving a fuck. He felt like he was in a twisted dream.

"Come back here and do your jobs!" he shouted. "I'm not going to fill out any online questionnaire and you're going to stand here and get the information you need to find out who torched my fucking tree!" Even Kenneth was a little shocked at the words coming from his mouth. He never thought he would be the one to curse at a police officer.

"That's not how this works, sir."

"Well, it does this time."

The three of them stood in silence, dumbfounded. It was going to be up to Kenneth to lead them through a normal dialogue as the two officers were standing perplexed, possibly offended, possibly waiting for commands on how to conduct a face-to-face interrogation.

"Alright," he sighed. "Read me the questionnaire."

"Huh?"

"The questionnaire... that you were gonna e-mail to me... read it to me. You do have a copy of it, right?"

The obese officer sat scrolling through his tablet, eyes blank, wrist bent effeminately, index finger hanging down and sliding across the face of the device. The slimmer officer leaned against the trunk of the car, eyes fixated on the still-smoking mesquite tree, unconcerned and unfazed by the scene in front of him. Kenneth stood impatiently, awkwardly silent in his rage.

"Ah," the officer finally replied. "Here we go." He began to hand it over to Kenneth.

"No, no, no, no," Kenneth said as he held an outward facing palm in front of him and turned his head sideways in disgust. "You read the thing. I'll answer. You record my answers. That's how this works."

"Hmmm," the officer replied dumbly. "Okay, were you at your home when the incident occurred?"

"Yes." The cop took some time to record the answer, then scanned over the next question, presumably to make sure he could pronounce every word before making himself look any dumber.

"So, did you see the perpetrator or his or her vehicle?"

"Of course not."

"Have there been any recent incidents that could be related to this one?"

"No. I mean, yes, actually. Someone bashed my electrical meter to hell." The cop recorded the answer, not the slightest bit surprised nor even interested.

"Have you recently made any enemies?"

"No."

"Have you been having sex with anyone new from your 3-code?"

"What?" Kenneth retorted wincingly. He didn't want to drag it out any longer, so he shook his head and replied another solemn, "No."

"Have you been having sex in any non-recommended or off-brand e-motel?"

"What the hell does this have to do with anything? Someone just set fire to my property and you're asking me what *e-motels* I'm having *e-sex* in?"

"Just answer the question."

"This is e-diculous." Kenneth chuckled at his own joke.

"What it means is," the other officer finally chimed in, "is that some e-motels that don't have The Suit trademark on their startup page are dangerous. You need to veer away from them. Guys will meet girls from the same 3-code and not know that they're old fucks that didn't like the way they were dropped. To get revenge, they'll fuck you in these off-brand e-motels that make it easier to hack the guy's info, usually his address, so she can go fuck up his shit or something."

"Is that really the kind of language an officer of the law should be using?" Kenneth replied condescendingly.

"Look, dude. I know it sucks finding out that you've been banging a bag of crazy. And it sucks serious shit knowing you can't even trust the room where you're fucking."

"And it really sucks knowing you can't even trust the police to do their jobs," said Kenneth.

"You need to show a little respect," the fatter officer said sternly while taking two steps toward Kenneth, looking to engage.

Kenneth's hand reached into his pocket, his fingers once again tracing the cold steel.

"Don't worry about him, Sean," said the other cop. "He's just pissed 'cause he's been fucking some sleaze cheese in a dirt box site. He don't know any better. The dude's fuckin' *ancient*."

Kenneth brushed angrily past the two officers and extracted his hand from his pocket violently. In four quick slashes to the hood of the cruiser as if he were stabbing it to death, in black marker, he drew out a large, bold, and permanent 'E.'

"There you go, assholes! Here's a nice e-motel for you two to go fuck each other in!"

9

Paul had received great praise and even greater compensation for his *Save Our Streets* advertisement. A deposit of four thousand dollars was made to his bank account. He checked it six times before believing it was real. All for two hours worth of work. He looked at the comma in his account balance. 4,798.24. That comma, dividing the thousands from the hundreds, the men from the boys, the careers from the hobbies. He thought of how quickly it sprouted into place and wondered how long it would take for it to multiply. It seemed suddenly reasonable, now that he was employed by the government, now that he had a vastly more prestigious job than his own father. *Fuck you, Dad,* was all he could think.

He logged on to his mother's FlashConnect page, an account that was still active and to which only he knew the password, and messaged his own account.

I'm so proud of you! I loved the advertisement. It was a real eye-opener.

As he typed the words, he knew how pathetic it all was. But after it was posted, it was easily ignored and looked over, just a subtle implication that his mother was still with him and that she did, in fact, know just how awesome he was.

He was also given a new assignment; create an advertisement promoting a law that would instate a mandatory curfew of 8:00 P.M. for all citizens not traveling to or from work.

With memes of robbery, rape, murder, terrorism, and random acts of violence littering every new site and the inability to fathom what anyone would want to do outside after dark, Paul couldn't understand why anyone would oppose the law, so Paul thought of his father. He knew that his dad would oppose it, that he would say that it was an infringement of their freedoms and another tool to make everyone a clone of everyone else, all of the usual rants, and that he would have to use those ideas to create an advertisement compelling enough to sway the most incorrigible; his father.

Let's Suit up.

The message was from Chrissy. It was late and Paul had work to do, but he thought it might do him some good to clear his head before embarking on a new project, so he obliged.

The sex was as frivolous as it was fast. Chrissy wasted no time, advancing quickly, employing various acts of foreplay revolving around pleasing Paul, riding rhythmically to a galloping tempo and giggling flippantly through all of it, overjoyed at every miniscule reaction and subtle moan of ecstasy that Paul issued. Paul lasted all of six minutes and, although Chrissy didn't orgasm, she seemed giddy and content.

"Lay with me," she whispered as he was still finishing his climax.

"Alright," he panted. "Let me wash up."

"No, it can wait this time. Just lay with me."

Paul held an arm around her languidly as he felt completely drained. They stared into each other's eyes silently, Paul's gaze like that of a drug addict fighting off an insistent need for sleep as he was still coming down from the high of sex, Chrissy's like that of an attentive lover, noting every freckle, worshipping every pore, and looking into his black pupils and seeing the eternity that exists in every person that we never seem to notice, all the while being completely alone, literally miles away from one another, lying on their own bedroom floors wrapped in a foamy and robotic full-body wrap, soaking in their own bodily fluids and spooning with the nothingness in front of them like children with imaginary friends.

"I couldn't sleep," she whispered. "I was scared." The word signaled something slightly yet innately jarring in Paul. His eyes opened fully just before surrendering to sleep.

"Scared?" his voice cracked, a few decibels above a whisper. "There it is again. Chrysanthemum the fearless, talking about being scared," he smiled tiredly.

"Don't you get scared? You know, after a long day, you unplug and lay in bed in the darkness, and just feel... alone?"

"Yeah, I guess. I mean, not scared, really. Just... I don't know... lonely."

"Paul?"

"Yeah?" He wondered if she said his name because an important question was coming or just to make sure he was awake.

"Have you ever slept next to anyone?"

"Like, in the RW?"

"Yeah."

"No. Have you?"

"Yes," she replied unabashedly. "You need to try it. It feels so good. It's like, all of that darkness and loneliness doesn't matter anymore. Like you have someone else and so you're, I don't know, a team instead of just a person. It's like they're an extra big blanket that keeps you safe and happy."

Maybe this last sentence was the whole reason Chrissy messaged Paul in the first place. She wasn't really horny. She wasn't really lonely. There were just some things that she needed to say, but Paul was already asleep.

The next morning, Paul sprang from his slumber feeling discombobulated and unclean. The e-motel room he was in was empty, and the time elapsed counting furiously in the corner read seven hours thirty-one minutes and twenty-nine seconds. He ripped off his headset and Suit to find his skin moist and papery from soaking in his own sweat. As he removed his genital compartment, his penis looked sick and lifeless, like a frail man sucking in his first breath after nearly drowning. The smell was enough to make him feel hungover and lightheaded. He quickly hung up his Suit to rinse and cleaned the genital compartment painstakingly.

After a workout and a shower, Paul felt revitalized and clear. He completed his next advertisement, sent it in, and within three hours received another task along with another deposit slip, this time for two thousand dollars. He began fantasizing of how quickly the money was rolling in and what that could amount to in the near future.

Over the course of the next two weeks, Paul had completed several advertisements and had been promoted all the way to the federal government. It was fairly easy, seeing as it was basically one corporation that he was working for. Moving him to national matters was basically just allocating their resources under the assumption that Paul was more fitting for broader issues, but it also meant a potential pay raise for Paul and, of equal importance, doubling his close friend list.

The friend list on any given person's page was merely a list of all the people who subscribed to your page. They could read your posts, follow your blogs, or, in Paul's case, view his advertisements. Paul liked to think of them as the audience for his artwork. They could leave comments, critiques, and creative feedback, they could recommend a person's page to others, and they could tack advertisements for their own ventures to the person's wall, but they could not, however, commence in any sort of one-on-one interaction – no instant messaging, no video chatting, and no fucking. The *close* friend list was reserved for just that. These were the people who had mutually agreed with the page owner to open the gateways between the two to partake in social interaction.

Now that Paul's close friend list was skyrocketing, he spent most of his days bouncing between working on advertisements and fucking new people from various 3-codes, and even some different 4-codes. It was amazing how many girls and guys were lining up to go on a date with him now that he had such a prestigious career, and although his Suit was overused and sticky with the day's undertakings by the afternoon, his nights still belonged to Chrysanthemum. There were nights that she seemed a little more distant, a little fearful of the success of her lover and his growing ego, but that was to be expected. He knew that she would only love him more, that becoming larger than life was sure to bear an aspect of intimidation, but that intimidation would surely be followed by admiration.

The money, the popularity, the sex, they were all making Paul finally feel like a man. All of the uncertainties in his life were slowly melting away, and when the fame that he was experiencing wasn't enough to ward off the feelings of inadequacy, he only need stare into his closet at the large ivory relic; hard, sharp, slightly phallic, the masculine representation of what he had become. It felt like a good luck charm as it had come into his life just as this shift in his career had come about, but it was so much more than that. It was almost haunting, the allure it had to it. There were times when it called to him from his closet as he was working. He would have to take a break and hold it in his lap, caressing the smooth sides, gently prodding and the rounded yet dangerous point. It felt like a murder weapon, like if anyone were to walk in and catch him, it would mean indeterminable consequences, stolen or not. It was his dirty little secret that he was just dying to tell.

His first assignment for the federal government was to create a series of advertisements persuading voters to give one dollar from every domestic tech purchase to go to the salaries of our soldiers. Once again, the idea seemed like such a mindless pitch, but he had a knack for creating that one image that stuck with voters until the question stared back at them from their tablets on voting day. Being that this assignment consisted of multiple advertisements that would be viewed by the entire country, Paul would have to put more time into them, edit a little closer, get better shots, maybe go 3-D. It was going to take some time, but he was sure that the paycheck at the end would reflect his efforts. He went to the refrigerator in his room to fill his belly as he was to be working tirelessly for an indeterminate period of time. His mini-fridge was empty, and he suddenly realized that he hadn't the slightest clue how long he had been locked in his room. Days? Weeks? Months?

He wandered around downstairs like a confused detective trying to figure out what day it was, where his father was, how long he had gone in isolation. Nothing seemed terribly out of place. A pair of black dice with white dots sat on the dining room table, but other than that, nothing was amiss. Then he looked outside.

The mesquite tree that had grown in their front yard his entire life had turned black and leafless. The meaning of this eluded Paul. Had it been struck by lightning? Was this some seasonal transformation that had gone previously unnoticed? Was this a landscaping experiment by his father? Something definitely seemed askew, but Paul, aware of how naïve he was to all things in the RW, couldn't let the recent findings hold any more than face value. He was simply unable to piece them together to see anything other than a vacated house, a pair of dice, and a charred tree.

He went back to the refrigerator to stuff his face with anything that required minimal preparation. His phone jingled in his pocket. When not wearing glasses that would visually alert him of all notifications in a little white box, deciphering his ring tones was akin to translating a language known only to Paul. This particular tone was a multi-party close friend message. He retrieved his phone from his pocket to find that he had been invited to an orgy. He scrolled through the stats of all eight people invited to find that all of them had Attraction Levels over 96 and only one had a Fuck Score under 94. He looked at all of their spin-vids and confirmed what the Attraction Levels already told him.

He had only taken part in one other orgy of more than three people, and the persistent problem throughout the evening was the size of his room. With multiple parties to tend to, one had to be free to move around. Still, he knew all of those involved pretty well and was not embarrassed to have them move to him when they shifted rotation and positions, but this time would have to be different. These were new, elegant, and important people whom he cared to impress – or at least, not to disappoint. He didn't want them to know the modest dimensions of his living quarters. His father obviously hadn't been home in quite some time or he would have bothered him, surely. He must be working overtime, in which case no helicopters would fly him home this early in the day. Paul quickly agreed to the invitation and suited up in the living room.

Paul was the second to enter the e-motel room, the first being another male by the name of Elroy. By this time, the boundaries between heterosexual and homosexual were fundamentally nonexistent. With vast acceptance – and even popularity – of transgenders, polygamists, and bigenders (people who underwent surgery to become hermaphrodites), the smaller boundary lines blurred and vanished. The overwhelming majority of this new generation had at least experimented sexually with both genders, and a slightly smaller majority did so on a regular basis. Paul had partaken in several threesomes with other men and was no stranger to a man's touch. In fact, there were times when a man in the room was a welcomed occurrence. While women were defined by being soft and weak yet animalistic in their passion, the men tended to be strong yet gentle and caressing. Still, standing naked in an e-motel with only another naked man was quite discomforting to Paul, despite Elroy's warm and cordial introduction. Sheila arrived next, silently. She spoke not a word as the three stood in their respective parts of the circle of eight as she squinted her eyes to seductive slits and eyed the two men in the room, a predatory stare grazing their bodies slowly from chest to pelvis, pelvis to eyes, eyes back to pelvis. The others followed shortly after, and all greeted Paul like car salesmen to a lottery winner. They were apparently a preformed group and Paul was the newcomer, making him feel slightly out of place, but confirming his entrance to the socially elite.

As the assemblage awaited the arrival of the last two participants, conversations were had like they were merely the first arriving guests at a dinner party. The banter seemed almost painfully banal considering the events that were about to transpire, not to mention their nudeness. It felt like murderers discussing the score of a basketball game while hacking into flesh with a pickaxe. Paul stood in his place, trying to maintain an aloof smile, as the two stragglers finally arrived. Laura, the blonde woman with the lowest Attraction Level and the highest Fuck Score, shifted the dialogue to business, like a referee announcing the rules before the big game.

"So we have someone new here. His name's Paul." Paul glanced around the room and smiled shyly. "So I'm gonna go over a few things. First of all, all conversation ends when the orgy begins. So if you're gonna talk, it should only be things like, 'harder,' 'faster,' or 'don't put that there,' kind of stuff, got it?"

Paul watched as a few others snickered before realizing that she was aiming the seemingly rhetorical questions primarily at him. "Oh! Yeah, got it."

"Also, everyone is fair game. You can favor some more than others, but you can't deny anyone who wants to fuck you. We don't want anyone having sore feelings, right?" This seemed reasonable – compassionate, even. Paul had been with other men before, but never on the receiving end. The thought would have been a little terrifying, but he didn't even own a penetration adapter for his Suit, so it couldn't feel like anything more than rhythmic pushing.

"And lastly," Laura continued, "when we're done here, if you feel compelled to give anyone a Fuck Score below 95, let them know first so they have a chance to redeem themselves. Give 'em a one-on-one and then judge them however you feel. And some of us do fuck each other outside of the group, so if you're doing it as a follow up because you feel they got a low score, let them know beforehand so they can give it their all. It'd be worth it for you in the end anyway, right?" Paul glanced around the room and noticed that most eyes were on him, so he nodded slowly.

Sheila, the predator, looked at Paul and said, "You got anything you want to add?"

"Nah."

"Anyone else?" Inaudible groans and subtle headshakes.

"Alright," Laura concluded, "let's fuck."

Sheila nearly ran to him, claiming Paul as her first. The others coupled all around them, hands and other unnamed flesh rubbing all over Paul's body. The females all moved about in a different stride than the males as their genital compartments existed between their legs, ostensibly, and gave them a bow-legged stance. Paul was already anticipating the next orgy as this one was all about his performance. He was constantly scrutinizing himself, trying to impress, dying not to dissatisfy, as he focused on one while still diverted some attention to both sides. A hand here. A foot there. Tongue here. Penis there. It seemed like so much work, but at the same time, it was like a complex engine, a moving, flowing life form and Paul was starting to synchronize with its rhythm. And every time the engine moved seamlessly as one, all the cogs reorganized into different patterns and worked to grind together harmoniously. Paul enjoyed the challenge and anticipated the changes. The moans were like an orchestra, the gasoline feeding the machine. Every cry of ecstasy was a pulsing wave, and as they collectively built up toward climax, it felt as if the eight of them were one solid entity, singular in purpose and methodical and elegant in achieving that goal. Laura was bent over in front of him and barreling toward climax. In response, his attention narrowed to her as he thrust with force that bordered violent. Pounding and screaming, he brought her to a roar as others began gravitating toward him to accompany him in his mission. After satisfying Laura, Paul moved onto the next. Others were behind him, fingers on his nipples, tongues everywhere, vigorous prodding at his backside presumed to be various body parts inserting themselves, nearly unfelt by Paul, but bringing others to feral moans. He moved from person to person, satisfying one after the other, feeling like a racecar engine operating in the red zone, all pistons firing and loving the results. His muscles were all drained, but his motions were becoming instinctual, moving faster and faster, the mosaic of flesh before him and the untamed exclamations of rapture propelling him forward, faster, harder.

And then his headset was ripped from his head, the instantly dissolved sensation leaving him dazed and disoriented, suddenly back in his living room, his knees buckling, he noticed that all of the windows had been shattered, and the blackness consumed him as fatigue, physical exertion, profound ecstasy, rapid change in setting, and malnourishment left him unconscious on the floor wrapped from neck to feet in what looked like a connected series of green floor mats.

10

KENNETH'S ROOM ON THE RIG was actually quite similar to the jail cell he stayed in all weekend, only the jail cell was 9x9, had gray concrete block walls, and smelled like stale urine and old lunch meat, while his room on the rig was slightly smaller, had white plastic fire-resistant paneling, and smelled worse.

He stayed in jail for three nights after his little altercation with the police and had ample time to think about his life gone wrong. He was released early Monday morning before sunrise, just in time to catch a chopper out to the rig. Arriving at the rig, little work was to be done, leaving only more time to think.

His first night in jail, he began to wonder how long it would take for his son to come bail him out, but quickly realized that that would never happen. Paul would be locked in his room, probably having virtual sex and therefore tuned out to the world, completely oblivious to the happenings downstairs. Even if Paul did notice the absence of his father, and even if he did somehow come to the conclusion that his father was arrested, Paul would have no means to get to the police station, let alone bail him out.

It was almost more disconcerting that there was no one else in his life that Kenneth could rely on in such dire circumstances. He imagined the guards calling for him, that he had been bailed out, but couldn't imagine a face to go along with the scenario.

Even lying there in his room at his jobsite, the walls were bare. Any pictures of Meredith displayed would only fill him with grief. Any pictures of Paul would fill him with disappointment and failure. When he died, it wouldn't take five minutes for his room to become someone else's, for his job to be bequeathed to another nameless individual, for his existence to be completely forgotten. Maybe sometimes it takes a night in jail with a cancerous tumor eating out your insides to show you exactly how much you wasted your life.

Kenneth was paged on the intercom to report to the head office. This meant report to Bobby, which meant that Kenneth had nothing to fear. Bobby had always liked Kenneth.

Bobby Upshaw was the kind of man who wore cargo shorts and a ballcap to work. In fact, he was the kind of man who more often than not *wasn't at* work. Bobby would go on extended vacations frequently. He would find a deal on a boat that would take him on a road trip to Florida to purchase. Rumor had it that when he didn't show up for a few days without notice, it was due to a drinking binge.

"No family, no responsibilities," Bobby would frequently say to discredit any disdain coming his way for his alternative lifestyle. While he took good care of his employees (and outside contractors, in Kenneth's case), Bobby was a firm believer in leaving nothing behind. He attested to this motto by preaching about how he wanted to make 'buttloads' of cash, and blow every penny. There would be no one in his will and no unchecked boxes on his bucket list by the time his casket entered the ground. Kenneth envied him almost to the point of hatred.

At the same time, Bobby had a good eye for conscientious workers and had limitless respect for hard labor. With that, he took an immediate liking to Kenneth, and thus sealed Kenneth's position at Echo Drilling Company.

Kenneth walked lackadaisically to Bobby's office, recent hardships adding sludge to his step, a new potential assignment from Bobby a flickering optimism in his eyes.

But alas, it was not only Bobby in the head office.

"Kenneth," said Gale Hammerton, "long time, no see, buddy."

Gale was the antithesis to all that Bobby stood for. Gale always donned a name-brand tie along with a gold bracelet on one wrist, gold watch on the other. His jet black hair was slicked back over his bald spot. A light stubble sprouted around his mouth, the beginning of a mid-life crisis goatee. He was always calling people 'buddy' and 'bro,' despite the fact that his buddies and bros all too often had a knife handle protruding from their backs with Gale's name on them. While Bobby was all about substance and experience, Gale was all about flash.

Gale was named CEO of Ferrell Electric, the company that Kenneth worked for, just two years prior. Although Kenneth and Gale had almost no personal nor professional relationship, Gale despised Kenneth. Kenneth had always figured that getting Ferrell Electric the contract with Echo after one service call would have got him in his company's good graces for life, and with Gale's smooth underhandedness, his abhorrence of Kenneth went undetected. Unbeknownst to Kenneth, Paul had started a FlashConnect page for his father, just so people wouldn't find it weird that Paul's dad was completely absent from the web. When Gale first took the reigns of the company, he sent a friend request to Kenneth's FlashConnect page that, obviously, went unreturned. Since then, Gale had no respect for Kenneth. Kenneth may not have been aware of Gale's adversity toward him, but Kenneth had similar feelings for Gale based solely on Gale's lack of substance and the value he placed on meaningless acquisitions, vacuous banter, and fraudulent endearments.

Kenneth looked obviously perplexed at the pair of gentlemen sitting before him, but managed to chuckle, "Whoa! Am I being fired?" as he entered the office.

"Nah, bro," laughed Gale as he slapped Kenneth's back.

"Of course not," said Bobby. "Sit down.

"We brought you in to discuss a big job we've got on the horizon." Kenneth always liked the way Bobby cut to the chase. While out in the field, Bobby would ask about Kenneth's family and home life, but when it came to business, it was just that. "We've just received a contract for some touch and go drilling in India. The initial job should last about six months, but we're hoping that this one will produce other jobs in the area. You interested?"

"Am I interested?"

"Yeah, you know, to be our Johnny on the spot, kind of like how you are now."

"Hmm." He didn't know how to respond. "Well, I've got some questions."

"Sure you do," Bobby laughed from his belly, turning his cheeks round and rosy above his brown beard. "I might've thought twice if you accepted it like that. Shoot."

"Well, first of all, if I went and we... I mean, if Echo got more jobs in the country, would I be obligated to stay beyond my initial contract?"

"No, no, no. I understand you got a family and a whole life here. If India doesn't suit you and you want to come back after a few months, even if the first job isn't finished, just give me a month's notice and I'll get someone to fill in."

"And would I still be working for Ferrell?"

"That's what Gale and I here were discussing. I obviously can't just take you from Ferrell like that, but if you're out there for three years, we also won't be paying extra money to Ferrell just for letting us keep you this long. So basically, if you go beyond the initial project that's supposed to last a tentative six months, we'll hire you full-time, and even after you come back, you'll be employed by Echo. That is, if that's all cool with you?"

Kenneth looked at Gale, who gave an affirming nod. "Yeah, that all sounds good." Kenneth looked down at his lap, knowing that he was going to forget a crucial question. "And what about my son?"

"Yeah," Bobby groaned as he stretched back in his chair and rubbed his belly with both hands. "I thought about that one. Tell you what; if you get on this project with us, we'll hire – it's Paul, right? – well, we'll hire Paul as your helper if that suits the two of you. You'll both be making good money and you'll be together, although you'll be eating curry and praying to cows."

Gale issued a chortle that seemed quite rehearsed. Kenneth giggled under his breath, fearful and exhilarated. "Can you give me a couple of days to sleep on it?"

"Of course, of course. Let me know by the end of the week. How's that?"

"Sounds great."

"And listen," Gale said as the three stood, thus concluding the impromptu meeting, "we'll hate losing you. But you've got to come back and play a round of golf with me and tell me all about the Indian babes, heh?" His laugh was like a ferret, and the way he slapped Kenneth's back was a little too forceful and greasy. His pinky ring struck Kenneth's shoulder blade.

Kenneth was elated. It was something. It was anything other than ordinary, and it was literally thousands of miles away from anything he knew previously. While initially his thoughts were of all of those empty moments that equated to his life finally packing a punch, something deserving of an epic eulogy, they promptly veered off to Narayan.

He ran all over the rig looking for his Indian friend, hoping that he would accompany him on this extraordinary excursion, that he would act as his traveling companion and travel guide, but when he found him, all of those hopes were slaughtered under Narayan's crushing gaze.

"Hey, did you hear?"

"Hear what?" Narayan snorted vehemently. "That your son is a thief?"

"What are you talking about?"

"Something very valuable of mine went missing after your materialistic shithead son left my party the other day."

* * *

A helicopter took Kenneth home that evening, just for him. Bobby knew that he would have a lot to mull over, and he was quite an accommodating boss, but as Kenneth reached his car, his thoughts all did somersaults.

While his reaction to Narayan's accusation had been guilt, knowing that his son committed whatever crime Narayan was accusing him of, he now felt anger. He should have stood up for his son. Paul might be a little backward according to Kenneth's lifestyle, but was he really capable of theft? What a horrible father, to not even grant his own son a breath of doubt, one shred of innocence. He should have punched Narayan in his teeth.

And India? How could he do this to Paul? Paul, who had just gotten over the loss of his mother, who was tied to his room by what might as well be an umbilical cord. He could never adapt to such a drastic life change. It had seemed like a good opportunity to reconnect (or maybe just connect) with his son, but no, dragging Paul to a foreign land to establish a father-son bond could in no way be a fruitful venture. He had to sacrifice. He had to leave this chance for his life to mean something behind to try and find Paul on his own level before he died.

And what about the tree? All this time, he had been so angry at Paul for not possessing the ability to locate and free his father, but he never thought about his own son being in a house that had just been vandalized. Arson was committed in the house that Paul was now living in, and Kenneth didn't even bother worrying about his son's well-being.

He punched the gas pedal. Suddenly, he was sure that something terrible had happened. His baby boy. His baby boy. How had he forgotten what it was like to hold him in his arms? That defenseless infant, rosy face pinched shut, unaware and harmless. Kenneth was supposed to be his protector, his guide into this world of shit, and now his baby boy was home while an arsonist might have burned the rest of the house down with Paul inside.

Kenneth screeched to a halt in the driveway and dove out of the car, almost before putting it into park. The horrors of his thoughts were already manifesting themselves as all of the windows in the front of the house were shattered. *What has happened to my baby boy?!* He was already breathing in sobbing stutters. His fingers were trembling, and he couldn't get a grip on the key to insert it into the lock.

When he finally threw open the door, there was Paul, donning green cushions all over his body, a large, black metallic headset covering the top of his head down to his nose, standing in the middle of the living room, his back arched convexly and his neck stiffly prodding forward with the posture of a geriatric old man, another contraption resembling the one he wore on his head covering his groin as he made deep and spastic pelvic thrusts to the air in front of him, groaning loudly with the intensity and ferocity of a beast, his right stretched out to the side, enclosed fingers bending and straightening, bending and straightening, as if they were motioning someone to come forward, only they were faced downward, apparently inserting themselves into *something,* his left hand slapping the air beside him, groaning and pulsing, thrusting and writhing, like some space-age abomination.

My baby boy.

Kenneth yelled at him. He yelled his name over and over again, but Paul couldn't hear him. Kenneth finally ripped the mask from his face and saw his son's eyes light up in confusion, dazedly looking in every direction, perplexed, but not ashamed, as he passed out in a pool of sweat that dripped down from his neck, slid down the green cushions, and puddled onto the carpet beneath him.

Kenneth peered down at the pool of shame that was his son and grumbled, "We're going to India."

11

TREPIDATION, LIKE AN INFESTATION, HAD nestled into Paul's life seemingly overnight. It was a relatively new sensation. Sure, he had had sporadic bouts with fear, but something sinister had settled in his life, unseen and terminal like a virus.

Paul and Kenneth had found one stone for every window shattered in their home. That, along with the broken meter and the burnt mesquite tree, left little room for the theory that these were all random acts of vandalism. They were being targeted. By whom may have been a mystery to Kenneth. Kenneth believed that if it wasn't someone his son had offended online, it had to be one of Meredith's old friends – or worse, one of her old lovers – who blamed Kenneth for her discontent with her life, which could somehow have been attributed to her early demise.

But Paul knew. There was no doubt. This was retaliation for the stolen artifact. This was from Narayan.

The two of them slept in opposite corners of the house yet in similar cocoons of terror. Kenneth had no idea what to expect from the culprit, but whoever he was, he was determined in his relentless actions.

Paul, on the other hand, was afraid of being found out. The stealing of the rhino horn, the one action in his life that proved he was a formidable and astounding creature, was in danger of being uncovered, in which case he would have no alternative but to return the horn and apologize with his tail between his legs, undoing the one remarkable event in his life, the one thing that set him apart from everyone else.

So after years of every day predicting the day to follow, of the most appreciated tedium, Paul would lie awake at night, fearful of tomorrow.

Kenneth made the India proposal to Paul, at first as an order, then after Paul's resistance, as a plea. The conversation quickly escalated to bellowing insults and a hurled picture frame, the glass shattering and preluding Paul's storming retreat to his bedroom. Paul would not be accompanying his father to India.

Almost more than the drastic shift in setting, the business proposal was abrasively offensive to Paul. Kenneth's audacity to suggest that Paul would want to be his apprentice in the electrical field, fully denying Paul's artistic aptitude (and his marketing career, which was still unknown to Kenneth), displayed how little Kenneth knew and respected his own son.

Paul was growing content with the strangers he and his father had become. In all actuality, they were the greatest of roommates. They left each other to his ways with little interference. Paul thought it a symbiotic relationship as his father paid the bills while Paul offered Kenneth an online personality. Unbeknownst to Kenneth, Paul would periodically update the pages that he created for his father, just to keep him sane.

Now, all of their inadequacies as a functional family were brought into the spotlight, forcing the two to harsh confrontations and greater knowledge of all that they were lacking.

So Kenneth was moving to India. He made it abundantly clear that Paul was not to be allowed to stay at home while he was gone, so his choices were to find a new place or to accompany his father. Paul obviously chose the former, and he did so by means of accepting Chrysanthemum's marriage proposal.

This all, however, was done in Paul's head, as he was not yet ready to share this information with Chrissy. It was a conclusion to which he would have eventually come, but he wanted to arrive at that conclusion by his own agenda.

Monday morning came to Paul's delight, basking in the freedom of an empty house like a cool breeze on his naked skin, although there existed a creeping terror of being alone for the next four nights, sleeping in a house that was being constantly attacked by what could have been a Hindu extremist. Although he knew that Narayan worked with his father and, more than likely, shared the same hours, it would not be beyond logical to think that Narayan could hire other culprits, like that bastard, Chalem, to do his bidding for him.

Paul had yet to start on his campaign for the federal government. He had allotted the next four days to be devoted to this project, but the India argument, the vandalism, they were weighing on him, the gloom following him like gum stuck to his shoe, and he didn't want to begin a new project until he could scrape them from his thoughts.

So he confided in the two things that never failed to dispel any heartache. He sat by his computer, stroking the rhino horn that he clinched between his thighs, while messaging Chrissy to fuck.

She was quick to reply.

Sorry. Gotta go to a stupid funeral. Hate to leave my baby horny. ☹

Paul sat at his chair, bottom half of the Suit already on, the top half draped over the vinyl back support of his computer chair, still stroking his rhino horn like a huge cock, and went through his ever-growing close friend list, deciding who would be the best fuck for the time being. He immediately targeted Sheila from last week's orgy and sent her a message.

Thinking about giving you a 90 on your fuck score. Care to redeem yourself?

Those narrow slits of eyes were already priming Paul for the fornication to come. It was amazing to him how much more the eyes could do for his attraction than tits and ass combined. Within seconds, she messaged back:

Yeah, right. You just want seconds.

Yeah, you figured me out. And how about you?

I want seconds, thirds, and possibly fourths. You ready for a marathon?

Paul was almost the size and rigidity of the rhino horn between his legs. A fleeting feeling of guilt did little to deter his ferocious libido, but presented itself as he realized that this Sheila could possibly be the one to replace Chrissy, if only she had the same key to solve his India dilemma that Chrysanthemum did. It truly was all about the eyes. So many women could fuck him dry, could tell him anything, could do the most decadent acts that would make his head spin almost to the point of short-circuiting his Suit headset, but the eyes were what would grab a hold of him, what would vindicate all of his workouts and tell him just how *good* he was.

He could only pull the left arm of the suit on before getting a message from his employer.

Heard your father will be emigrating to India. You need to abandon your current project and accompany him. Your next assignment is attached. Please respond by the end of the day if you can accommodate us. Completion of this project will be a <u>substantial</u> *pay raise for you.*

The message was cold and heavy, like a lead weight pulling him downward into the icy waters below. There were aspects of his life that were concrete, incorrigible, and immutable – his home, his devices, and now his career – and they were all crumbling before him. He couldn't disappoint his company, but the thought of moving to a foreign country filled with the people who sprouted up in every news meme in front of a destroyed building was unimaginable.

And the money. They underlined the word 'substantial.' There was no telling how much it was, nor what he could achieve with it afterward. He could buy a new house. He could leave his shithead father alone for the rest of his pathetic life. He could finally be his own man.

Before he had too much time to contemplate the implications of the last message or even open the assignment, Sheila was messaging him irritably from the e-motel, sounding as if she was ready to ditch him.

She was just as forceful and even kinkier than last time. Even without the inaugural announcement of the rules, there was no dialogue. She apparently had many upgrades and adaptors for her suit as a virtual table to one side of the e-motel had dildos, whips, paddles, and hotshots laid out like surgical tools.

All of the tools didn't exist in the RW, but many required Suit upgrades to feel the desired effect of said tools. The dildos, luckily, were shaped as such – colorful plastic sex toys. In the virtual world, some would appear as actual male genitalia minus the body, but Sheila, apparently, was not into that. The whips and paddles could be used on both participants, but more forceful swings of each would only be felt in their full caliber if one had a 2033.5X model Suit or higher. The hotshots were like tasers with lower voltages. To feel the effects of the hotshots, an H-series Suit was required, so the 2033.5X model would become 2033.5HX with the H-series upgrade.

Paul had none of these special Suit modifications, but the whips, paddles, and even hotshots could be felt on his end, just to a smaller degree.

Sheila employed all of these tools – dildos excluded – on Paul. He was less than enthusiastic as the India dilemma was now fresh on his mind. His distraction was quite apparent to him as was her acknowledgement of his preoccupied disposition. This troubled Paul further as he struggled to please her, to match her sexual ferocity with his own.

It was only times like these when the sex just wasn't quite synchronizing the way it should, that Paul realized how self-absorbed he could be. Sex was all about proving his worth.

In the beginning, he purchased a Suit because he had to, because if he didn't, he would be the outcast. He struggled desperately, sometimes turning in ten Snippet promos a day to scrounge together the online credits to purchase a Suit. The first girl with whom he fornicated was physically mediocre, but upon his arrival at the e-motel, her eyes lit up and she said elatedly, "Ooh, a muscle man." As phenomenal as the sensations that followed were, nothing would ever equate to that encomium of his physical stature.

He then sculpted his body assiduously. In the e-motels, he perfected his technique and treated the sessions like workouts, pushing his limits and striving to push faster, to bring her to higher orgasms, and to hold his own longer, all for that doting stare, that flattering compliment, or, at best, that fatigued speechlessness that would affirm how truly awesome he was.

Now that his close friends list was growing and his fuck buddies were of higher and higher attraction levels and fuck scores, he saw them more as new challenges than greater rewards.

In other words, his distractions with Sheila were unacceptable.

He finished them both off and made up a lame excuse, promising to double his fuck score tomorrow. She seemed less than satisfied, but hopeful of his promise. They set a time and specified an e-motel before logging off.

Paul removed his headset and went downstairs for a bottle of water.

He couldn't seem to get a hold of his thoughts. While India was the dilemma at hand, there were so many other problems that stemmed from it. His home. His computer. His Suit. His career. His father. His girlfriend. Her proposal.

Getting downstairs, it seemed that the house was in an even bigger state of disarray than his mind. All of the cabinet doors were opened and emptied, cereal boxes and canned goods strewn about the kitchen floor. In the living room, the television set had been bashed in. The front door was still wide open, and all of this happened while Paul was in the house. He couldn't seem to bring his jaw back up to close his mouth.

If Narayan or Chalem or whoever was in the house, he had to know that Paul was home. Why didn't he confront him? For some reason, an unseen intruder was so much more menacing than a fully armed assailant right in front of his face. Paul's hands were shaking, his bottom lip was quivering, and his head whipped around in constant fear of what existed behind him.

A lonely soda can had broken away from a six-pack that was hurled to the floor by the entryway. The contents of it seeped out onto the hardwood floor in a sugary brown puddle, then, as ominous as a ransom note, Paul noticed the vague brown circles on the carpet that began just short of the stairs, the coke footprints that bounced from left to right on each step and somehow went unnoticed on his way down. Someone had been upstairs.

Paul followed the footprints slowly, timorously, to the only door at the top of the staircase. His bedroom door was still open, and the footprints didn't stop at the threshold. While the brown spots grew fainter and fainter as the soda wore from the soles of the intruder's shoes, two definite spots had soaked into the carpet, side by side, two inches apart, in the corner of his room, where the intruder had stopped to take notice as Paul stood in the center of the room fucking Sheila.

Paul was crying fearfully.

Somewhere deep behind his trepidation, behind the feeling of being bound and blindfolded as someone tickled him with a machete, a different fear sprang to life in a quick jolt.

Paul ran to his closet and looked deflatedly at the spot on his shelf where the rhino horn used to stand.

12

"You know when you wake up from a nightmare," said Kenneth, "and you're so relieved that it wasn't real. You're so thankful to be back to your life and not in the one you just came from. And then you go back to sleep, and the same nightmare continues?"

Narayan nodded solemnly.

"That's how I feel, only when I wake up, I'm still in the nightmare, and when I go back to sleep, a new hell just gets tacked on to the one before. It keeps multiplying and multiplying, and I just can't get back to reality." The image of his son thrusting in that twenty-first century atrocity was still glowing caustically in his vision, like when you stare at a lamp and it glows in green every time you close your eyes, only this light was eating away at his brain like an acid burn. He was thankful he finally had a friend in whom he could confide. He told Narayan every sordid detail.

Narayan had apologized for accusing Paul of stealing from him, although he was still convinced that it was, in fact, Paul who stole the rhino horn from his bedroom. No matter how wronged he felt, Kenneth was one of Narayan's very few friends in this country, and he could swallow his pride. Given the present conversation, Kenneth was as confused at his son's motives and priorities as he was.

"I always wanted a daughter. None of this would have ever happened if we had a daughter."

"I don't know," responded Narayan. "I wouldn't want to imagine what the female version of those suits looks like."

Kenneth shuddered at the thought.

"Sons are always a mystery to their fathers," he continued. "It is nature's puzzle, how the father always bears a stronger connection with the daughter and the mother with the son, and then when the son grows older, the father wants him to be the man he is, and they never are. Every difference between the man that they want them to be and the man that they really are only adds distance between them. But every father has that idea of playing sports with his boy. It is just so quickly slaughtered and replaced by the son playing video games while the father mows the lawn."

Kenneth marveled at Narayan's insightfulness, let alone his English. It was amazing how a man with no children could so easily put his life in a paragraph.

"There is something else we need to talk about," Narayan said gravely. Kenneth's self-pity quickly turned to attentiveness. "Very few people enter my home. I'm not saying your son stole from me, but someone did, and there are very few suspects. The item that was stolen is, well, very, very valuable. If your son does have it, he could stand to gain a lot of money and power, dangerous levels of both."

Kenneth was dazed. "What the hell was it?"

"A rhinoceros horn."

"What?"

"A rhinoceros horn. You see, twenty years ago, the Vietnamese would pay top dollar for the horn of a rhinoceros – around $300,000. It was believed that the powder made from the horn had the ability to cure cancer. Over the following few years, more and more rhinos were killed with very little being done to stop it. The trade was so common that many of the Vietnamese were also using the powder as a drug, as well as a cure for an ordinary hangover. But organizations like PETA disrupted the rhinoceros poaching and the problem all but vanished. Very few rhinos were hunted over the following decade, but three years ago, a very important political figure in India was diagnosed with cancer, and rumor has it that the powder from the rhino horn cured him. So once again, men around the globe have been seeking rhinoceros horns for trade, and being that there are far fewer rhinos in the world now than there were twenty years ago and there are more organizations attempting to control the situation and making them more difficult to obtain, the price has gone up.

"Now, I don't believe that your son would have the connections to sell the horn to any foreign medical organization and get the millions that it is worth, but billionaires do tend to see a rhinoceros horn as an elitist symbol. They'll use it as a paperweight just to show their worth. I am fully confident that he could find one of these men online and make a good chunk of money that way."

Kenneth didn't know where to begin. As soon as the words 'cancer' and 'cure' were mentioned, his thoughts went to extending his life. But he had to think about his son. Owning something of such value had to be dangerous, especially if they were to enter a country where it was more acceptable and highly sought after. The money, the cure, the danger; it was too much to absorb.

"I've got to ask, Narayan," Kenneth finally retorted, "how are you so calm about losing something so valuable?"

"At first, I wasn't," he chuckled. "But I've always felt uneasy about owning something as such. It was obviously obtained illegally. It is quite plain that it is a crime against nature. And to tell you the truth, I have seen it as a sort of curse, a bad luck charm. Ever since it came into my possession, things have not gone so great for me. I was sent here to south Texas – no offense. But here, I have experienced more racism aimed at my people, and now my people have been targeted by the entire country, it seems like. I was almost relieved when I found the horn missing. Now it is gone, and look, already I am returning to my homeland with a new friend."

Kenneth caught the next chopper back to land and zoomed home to accuse his son of robbery.

When he arrived, he raced upstairs, not oblivious to the mess in the house, but ignored it nonetheless, and barged into Paul's room. Paul was still standing next to his bed, eyeing those two footprints, imagining a mysterious intruder watching him fornicate. How long did he stand there?

Kenneth was unmindful of his son's petrified state as he went straight to the closet and tore apart its contents.

"Where the fuck is it?!" he shouted. Paul still wore the blank expression one would wear after witnessing unspeakable horror – not shocked or scared, but lifeless and drained. "Where is it, you little shit?!"

"What are you talking about?" Kenneth mumbled.

"You know damn well what I'm talking about! The horn! Where's the rhino horn?" Paul didn't have the energy to feign offended or act like he didn't understand.

"It's not here."

Kenneth turned his attention to his son, grabbed him by the shoulders, attempting to shake understanding into him. "Where is it?! Where?!"

"I don't know."

"WHERE?!!"

"I don't know! I don't know! I don't know!" Paul screamed in quick bursts before crumbling in sobs. It had been years since Kenneth had seen his son weep, and the image was enough to jar him back to composure.

"Listen," Kenneth finally said with an alarmed tranquility. "I need this, I need it back. You don't understand, but it could save me."

"Dad," Paul responded, his eyes, wobbling with tears, finally raising to meet his father's, addressing him as 'Dad' for the first time in months. "I want to go to India with you."

It was enough to subdue Kenneth for the moment.

Beyond the pressure from his job to accompany his father to India, Paul was just terrified. The marriage proposal, the job, the acts of vandalism, it was a whitewater current when Paul had been content living in still water for so long, but none of it amounted to the fear of those two footprints. And not Chrissy, not his job, not Sheila could provide him with the sense of safety that his father could. As much as he loathed his father, he couldn't stand to see him leave.

"I want to go with you."

That was it. He committed to finally changing his life in the most drastic of ways, to move across the ocean to an unknown land, sure to be as far different from the one he was living in as possible, all the while not even checking his latest assignment, which read:

> *President Mayank Kapoor of India is protecting groups the U.S. has targeted as Hindu extremists and responded with hostility to our request to turn over said groups to ensure the safety of the American people. Create a series of advertisements persuading the American people to go to war against India. Use the utmost discretion.*

PART II

ALTHOUGH EVERY SHADE OF THE color spectrum was presented on every sign, every building, every vehicle, the entire country was enveloped with the sandstone beige color of dirt.

Walking the streets of New Delhi was like a bombardment on all of their senses. Car horns were loud and constant, like twenty different submarine commanders barking orders in Morse Code. A whirlwind of scents blew by like a dust storm carrying the smell of fried food, livestock, jasmine, and always, always shit. Every building looked like the face of a brittle skeleton – dirty, holes instead of windows like hollowed eyes, and on the brink of collapse. Cars, taxis, rickshaws, cycle rickshaws, auto rickshaws, bicycles, scooters, and motorcycles were a constant threat battling them to the outsides of the street and toward the buildings on either side, winding around and through one another with no sense of order. Traffic clashed together with the chaos of a smashed anthill, yet flowed like a breathing organism. Cows with white fur painted in blue and pink spots and adorned with yellow flowers moved at their own pace through the pandemonium like a diver through a school of fish, their languid movements magnified by the mayhem around them. Dogs and macaque monkeys trailed in their wake, but with much more spastic movements as the world did not stop for their species. The ground was mottled with garbage and fecal matter from an array of different animals, humans included, as even the barefooted would trudge through the squalor unconcerned. And every image was seen through the foggy lens of New Delhi pollution, a perpetual smog hanging over the entire city.

Kenneth found it humorous that back in the states, he viewed a collared shirt and khakis as classy, as someone of importance and wealth, yet in India, nearly every male was wearing a long sleeve button up, and they all looked penniless. Perhaps it was the sandals. Maybe it was the dirt, the surroundings, the smell. Maybe on his television back home he had only seen one version of the dark-skinned man.

But Paul, however, quickly identified their attire as pitiable as he recognized not one name brand.

Kenneth was like a child seeing an amusement park for the first time; his eyes lit up and his mouth agape, gawking at this new world to which he had emigrated. Everything was new and entirely different from anything he had ever known. Living in a world for decades where human interaction was slowly becoming extinct, his introduction to this over-populated and bustling country was like holding his breath for minutes, then having an air compressor violently fill his lungs to the point of bursting. It was like using all of his senses for the first time.

Paul, on the other hand, was rapidly questioning what he had gotten himself into. Physical contact was entirely foreign to him. Although Kenneth was an affectionate father when Paul was a toddler, Meredith was quickly coaching Paul to be the man *she* wanted him to be, and Meredith was more about expressing her love by posting a family photo online than a hug or a kiss. By the time Paul was six, the touch of another human was strange and unfamiliar, a feeling substantiated by his life online.

But in Delhi, he was in such close proximity with every other person in the vicinity. There was no such thing as personal space in this country.

Bodies were brushing by his shoulders. He would have to turn sideways to inch past dormant cows. Fighting off insistent beggars who would follow him for blocks was almost cardiovascular. The smell, sight, sound, and touch of every other person was being incessantly and forcefully shoved into his face. He felt like he was being submerged in a garbage dump, feeling around for the least toxic areas, trying to avoid the wet corners. He wanted to cry. He felt helpless. Every time a stranger came in contact with him, he felt like he was up against the ropes taking jabs to the gut, knocking his breath from his body. Every time he saw a vacant shop, he wanted to dive inside to escape the crowd, yet no store had more than three feet of walking space between shelves loaded with breakable items, and Paul was carrying and wheeling more luggage than could fit in most of the houses he had seen since their arrival.

Rajeev, their assistant/driver/translator, was escorting them to their new domicile. Most of their belongings had been previously mailed there. The van they would be riding in wouldn't be ready until tomorrow, so Rajeev met them where the airport shuttle dropped them off in Paharganj, a short walk from their new home.

They arrived at their bungalow feeling filthy and exhausted, Kenneth exhilaratingly so, Paul the opposite.

The house, contrary to its outward appearance, was quite nice in comparison to the rest of the town, despite the stone flooring. Two plain yet cozy and separate bedrooms were adjoined by a common bathroom. The small yet functional kitchen wrapped around to a living room. A small television set was perched upon an antique brown cabinet. On the small end table next to the blue denim couch stood a card.

Hope you like the place. If you need anything, just ask
Rajeev. Don't be bashful, that's what he's there for.
-Bobby

"Wow," said Kenneth, forcing the volume to Paul's range, "that's really nice." Paul offered back nothing in return other than disgusted scowls at their current living situation. Kenneth wanted to show that they were being well taken care of, but quickly aborted trying to comfort his son as he was inconsolable in every way that Kenneth was ecstatic.

There was already no walking space in Paul's room as every inch of spare floor space was occupied by his luggage. The Suit had a special, metallic transporting case, the likes of which were more than common around the airport and added tranquilizers and tar to the already crawling pace of airport security. The endless amounts of designer apparel stuffed in three different suitcases suddenly seemed unnecessary as Paul wasn't sure he would ever want to wear anything worth more than fifty bucks in the grubby streets of India.

During the two months it took to pack up the house and get all of the visa and travel arrangements in order, Paul cleared some things up in his life. He had some questions about his next assignment. His nameless boss informed him that Paul would have adequate warning time before the vote came about so that he would have time to evacuate the country. They wanted him in India to get some first-hand footage that may be used against them, something more than the memes that all Americans had already been desensitized to. They didn't have a specified amount of advertisements they were asking for, but they stated simply that they preferred quality to quantity, although both were appreciated. They didn't need to emphasize the discretion issue because not only was Paul completely aware that disregarding any of their wishes would result in immediate termination, but he also knew that giving away his motives would additionally be giving away his safety. It obviously wouldn't be the smartest idea to make it known that he was in India to act as a spy and a gambit for inciting war against their country.

Paul pacified an angry Chrysanthemum with the promise that they would marry upon his return. She wasn't thrilled with her boyfriend moving to a country that they were consistently warned against, but it would at least kickstart her plans for stability, and in the meantime, the distance meant nothing in the online world – or so they thought.

Paul's discontentment for his new residence was multiplied as he realized that his room only had one electrical outlet, thus negating his entire way of life and half of his luggage. He would first have to locate and use an antiquated power strip, a feat that – given his initial impression of the city – was next to impossible.

Paul threw a tantrum and screamed his condemnation for his new home at his father, but as of late, Paul's rants were beginning to lack in enthusiasm and stamina as Paul felt like he was floating away in open water and Kenneth was his only lifeline.

Kenneth responded with promises to alleviate the situation, that Rajeev would find all that he needed and that they were well looked after, and finally ended on a note imploring patience.

"Just enjoy the change in scenery. Why would you want to fly across the ocean to plug into the same e-motel you were in back home?" The statement was painful for both – to Paul for the idea that he would want to do anything outside of his room in this godforsaken land, to Kenneth for merely using the word 'e-motel.'

Rajeev, who looked more perturbed than intrigued by the drama unfolding in front of him, patiently yet agitatedly awaited a dismissal after showing the home (that was three times larger than his own) to the new family, until Kenneth asked him to retrieve a random assortment of groceries – fruit, bread, toilet paper, shampoo, soap, bottled water, soda, paper towels, and if it wasn't too much trouble, ice.

"I think you'll find that the house has been stocked with all that you will need," Rajeev answered in a pleasant tone, his face expressionless and apathetic to their needs.

"Oh! I'm sorry, I didn't even –" Kenneth fumbled as he felt around his pocket for a tip. He pulled out five hundred rupees and held it in Rajeev's direction, still quite unsure of the exchange rate. "Thanks for everything."

Rajeev mumbled an insincere offering of thanks and hurried back into the chaotic streets of Delhi, not bothering to tell Kenneth that tipping was not customary in his country.

2

Rajeev picked Kenneth and Paul up the following morning, along with Dan, Eric, Leonard, and "Roach," all of whom were transferred from the same Texas branch of Echo Drilling and all of whom lived in the same community of bungalows. Kenneth had worked with all four of them for years, yet knew nothing about any of them.

It was to be a forty-minute drive to work for the week and different every week after. Although Bobby introduced the drilling sites as 'touch and go,' they were more like what Narayan referred to as 'mobile-permanent.' These were much smaller than the offshore rig that Kenneth was used to, but still as large as a small city block. The structure was supported by a steel exoskeleton that anchored into the ground. Endless wheels lined the perimeter of the rig as well as underneath various parts of the center, and when the time came to move, the steel would unhinge from the ground and hydraulically lift to floor level, giving all of the weight to the tires. The structure was not meant to move long distances, but basically to prod around a large area to find the optimum spot for drilling.

Kenneth and Paul were to spend a week at this location to familiarize themselves with the motors, panels, and wiring and do any preliminary electrical organization before moving on to the next rig. Kenneth gathered that there were thirty-eight units that they were to oversee. He already had that feeling that the job would last much longer than six months. He worried about Paul.

Paul was trying his best not to make eye contact with Rajeev in the rearview mirror. He knew that if they connected eyes, Paul's expression would undoubtedly convey the contempt he held for Rajeev after going to bed hungry as there was no food in the refrigerator, showering with only water as there was no soap nor shampoo in the bathroom, and wiping his ass with pieces of a paper bag as there was no toilet paper. Still, Paul was glad to have someone other than Narayan act as their ambassador and butler for their stay in India. While Kenneth had been verbally expressing his excitement to visit his new friend's home country for the weeks prior to departure, they had not yet seen Narayan.

Rajeev was silent as he navigated through the chaotic traffic with ease and the disposition of a man on the verge of sleep. Kenneth was practically bouncing in his seat with merriment as he scanned the passing scenery. Paul, silent in his rage, joined the other four in peering down at the device in each one's lap, scanning memes and updating FlashConnect pages.

Upon arrival at the rig, Kenneth felt right at home, despite the half dozen brown faces staring at him in disapproval. But among the faces was a familiar one, one not smeared in disgust.

"Svaagat hai!" Narayan exclaimed as he forcefully shook Kenneth's hand, combining the Hindi language with American customs. "Welcome!" His face was plastered with enthusiasm. The same greetings were extended to Paul, but in a muted fashion.

Narayan immediately began showing the two of them around. All of the motors were identified and their purposes explained, yet none of the jargon was expressed in terms Paul would understand. He stood behind his father, at first trying to look important, then trying to look attentive, then finally settling on bored. Only Paul seemed to notice all of the other workers, obviously natives, watching them with the appearance of a child looking on as a stranger abused his mother, helplessly livid. Paul felt vindicated in his job – the marketing job, that is – and couldn't wait to complete his task.

Every other sentence, Narayan would peer over Kenneth's shoulder at Paul as if he was going to explain his introduction in terms he could understand, but his quick dismissal at Paul's apparent confusion confirmed that he was only glancing over to ensure that Paul wasn't sleeping on the job or stealing from the jobsite already.

Narayan left quickly, claiming that he was busy in the lab, never alluding to where this mysterious lab might be, with promises that the three would reconvene later to celebrate their safe arrival in his homeland.

Kenneth quickly put Paul to work. Their first order of business was to address the pile of SO cord coiled up like an endless snake, no head nor tail visible, just miles and miles of abdomen. Each cable ran from the main electrical panel to one of the motors via a giant tangled ball pushed to one corner. Kenneth decided, although not in their scope of work, that it would be beneficial to identify where each cable was going, label it, and support it in a way where it would be isolated from all the others. In case of an emergency, this would make it easier to identify problems and fix any motors that may have gone down.

It was also a tedious task. First, Paul was to untangle the large tumbleweed of black cord into some sort of identifiable order. Next, he had to cut endless pieces of galvanized unistrut at the same length with a bandsaw, a task that first entailed stringing out an extension cord, setting up a tripod vise, and hauling over ten foot sticks of unistrut in heavy bundles. After cutting each piece, it was to be filed down and sprayed with cold galvanize to prevent rusting. Kenneth would then assist him in mounting the unistrut pieces, installing springnuts and square washers, bolting in standoff supports, then tie-wrapping each cable all the way from the panel to its assigned motor. Each monotonous task was at least an hour of repetition with very little reward. Ninety minutes in and Paul was ready to quit both of his jobs and retreat back to America.

If the tedium of the job wasn't enough, the piercing looks from the native workers would have made anyone feel unwelcome to the point of never returning. The heavyset Indian worker was insistently working in Paul's space, doing whatever he could to offer a gentle nudge, any gesture to show that he didn't approve of Paul's arrival on the jobsite.

Kenneth, although appearing oblivious to the entire situation, took notice of it all. He noted the way his son was less than intrigued at his profession. He watched as the other workers bullied with their eyes and subtle gestures, and he gleamed proudly as Paul went about his work unfazed by the insolent behavior.

The two of them worked together, father and son, mounting all of the unistrut and supporting the cables. Kenneth was more than ecstatic. Paul was falling asleep with boredom, sweating in the dry heat.

"Is this all you do all day?" Paul finally asked, agitated and fatigued. "When does all the cool electrical shit come into play?"

"You wanna see some cool electrical shit?" Kenneth smiled mischievously as he issued the third curse word he had ever spoken to his son, the first not spoken in anger. "I'll finish up here. You go look busy and try to figure out which car belongs to that fat asshole that keeps bumping into you."

Paul did as he was told. Both father and son were glowing; Paul with the first enthusiasm of his new job, Kenneth with his first bonding experience with his son in over a decade.

After half an hour of surveillance from the edge of the platform, Paul caught their target retrieving something from the glove box of his dirty white car. Paul went back to assisting his father until all the native workers retreated to a corner for what appeared to be break time. Paul and his father scurried over to the truck with a long piece of wire, giggling and tiptoeing like children toilet papering a house.

With the speed of an experienced prankster, Kenneth opened the unlocked door, ripped open the fuse box, and ran a wire from the brake sensor to the horn, wirenutting both ends.

Within seconds, the job was done, and the two trailed off as if they were surveying the land. After ensuring that they completed their crime without witnesses, they went back to the job at hand. All of the wires had been neatly isolated and supported. All that was left was to go through and write the motor number on each cable in a white paint marker.

"Do you understand what we just did?" Kenneth asked his son. Paul shook his head with an impish smirk. "Now every time he hits the brakes, the horn will honk. Even with the way they drive in this country, he's sure to piss some people off on the drive home today."

All evening, Kenneth was elatedly satisfied with his new job alongside his son, even after he overheard Paul talking to his girlfriend online, telling her of his new shitty job. The entire venture, shamefully, was based on a selfish decision. Kenneth was not looking to restore any remnants of a relationship with his son by coming to India, just restoring any remnants of a life he had left.

Kenneth thought about when Paul was three and he broke his arm on the monkey bars. He picked up his frail boy, arms thin and brittle like twigs, one of them bent like a question mark, as he frantically sprinted back home with his crying son in his arms, screaming at Meredith in startled sentence fragments, informing her of the emergency. They rushed him to the hospital, holding a tablet in front of his face while the nurses wrapped his misshapen arm. Paul screamed as they showed him cartoons, desperately trying to distract him from the pain, from the trauma of watching strangers bend and twist his already broken arm. Meredith giggled at the frivolous attempts they made, showing him pictures of him minutes before the accident, both arms mockingly straight. Kenneth cried.

In the end, as Paul's incapacitated body, weak and lifeless from painkillers, lay in an oversized bed with an oversized cast on his tiny body, as his sleeping face somehow looked so much older even though it was dwarfed by the bed and all of the machines surrounding him made for adults, Kenneth felt like a father. Possibly for the first time. Every moment of the ordeal was torturous and traumatic. Every second bore with it a new trial filled with pain and fear, and with every trial, Kenneth lost a little of himself and lived only for his son. He felt his fear, his pain, his confusion at all the horribly new sensations little Paul was experiencing, and by the time it was all over, they did it. Kenneth and Meredith. They succeeded. They faced tragedy and came out with only a lime green cast that they would later sign in permanent marker. It was like that initial fear the day Paul was born, the anxiety when parents bring their first newborn baby home for the first time and realize that they are clueless, like those terrors never truly wore off until that moment. It was then that Kenneth realized that he could really *be* a father.

Sitting in their new bungalow on the outskirts of New Delhi, Kenneth had that same feeling. It was going to be painful, but they might just make it. It may not have been the greatest of places to raise a family, but he was ready to start, even if it was eighteen years late.

3

PAUL WAS LATE GETTING UP the next morning. Kenneth yelled at him, but Paul's body was sore, and he felt like he never wanted to get out of bed again. The fatigue seemed natural as it was the longest Paul had ever spent in the sun. The muscle soreness, however, was almost shameful to Paul. He prided himself on working out and being more massive and muscular than all those around him. It seemed that manual labor worked different muscle groups than those targeted by bench presses and skullcrushers. Paul thought about the fat Indian man whom they pranked the day before. He wondered if they would get into a fight. He wondered if the muscles he had worked out for so long would prove advantageous in a brawl. He wondered what getting beat up would feel like.

He stayed in bed until Kenneth's screaming was more irritating than his own thoughts.

After being berated and coerced out of bed, Paul spent the good part of his morning hacking up New Delhi pollution. All air that hadn't been processed by an air conditioning unit and dehumidifier was foreign to Paul's sheltered lungs. The pollution of India was more than just a contaminant; it was poison.

Although he would never admit it, Paul's first day on the job had a profound effect on him. All of the sensations he had been experiencing were completely new. He had sweated through a workday. He had used his body to complete a task. With his father narrating every minute movement of his body, Paul had begun learning a new trade. They had played a practical joke on a stranger, and all of this was done in close physical contact with dozens of other people.

Paul thought of the fat man; his haggard appearance, the warts on the back of his neck, the bags under his eyes, that mouth stretched in distaste. Paul would also never admit that every time that man nudged his body into his own, Paul had to hold back the tears, swallow them like a thick ice cube that stretches the esophagus, praying that his father wouldn't notice. It wasn't so much the fear of confrontation or the terror of all things new. It was just the feeling of that body against his own, unknowing of its intentions, flesh against flesh, words and facial expressions somehow inadequate, pushing all of his hatred or his irritations or his love that fluttered fractions of an inch beneath his warm exterior into Paul.

Paul thought of all of those sensations rolled into one gigantic ball, so massive that it could plow over any other emotions previously felt. The smell, the taste, the fear, the burning sun, the salty sweat, the gritty dirt, his father's smile, the warm belly of the fat man, the pandemonium of the crowds outside the van, the subtly distasteful glances from Rajeev, the aching muscles, the roaring motors, the drive home thick with fatigue and achievement, all of those together could leave some of his greatest sex and his ever growing close friend list squished flat to its underside as it mowed over his past.

Still, thinking of that colossal and formidable sphere of yesterday becoming mundane and plowing through his future was unthinkably terrifying.

Paul hid behind his sunglasses and watched a snippet in his left lens as they boarded the morning van fifteen minutes late, Kenneth uttering apologies to four co-workers already lost in their devices and a driver unwavering in his apathy.

The fat man was waiting for them at the rig, already livid and shouting, waving a blue wire in their direction, two of his friends attempting to hold him back. Kenneth and Paul approached slowly, guardedly. The other four dropped their devices to their pockets momentarily, gawking at the scene.

Paul quickly, slyly, pulled his phone from his pants pocket and switched it over to his breast pocket, the eye of the camera peeking over the top and recording the hysteria before him.

Narayan, luckily, showed up to play mediator, exchanging quick and heated words with the fat man, faces an inch apart, Narayan's tone a more collected sort of anger. The fat man was subdued and taken to a ground level facility near the rig. He didn't come back the next day.

For their remaining time on that site, the other native workers lost their odious dispositions around the foreigners, looking at the Americans like prison wardens, accepted dangers that they were forced to coincide with. Kenneth couldn't wait to move on to the next site. Paul was enjoying it. He felt superior in all realms, and they didn't even know the hell that was to follow them, the trail of carpet bombers that would wipe them all down to nothing in Paul's wake. He was never religious, but right then, Paul felt like God.

Paul trudged through the following days as there was little work to be done. Kenneth showed him how to take amp readings and what they meant. They inspected panels and made slight rectifications. It wasn't long before Paul was nostalgic for the monotony of cutting unistrut.

When the clock inched toward quitting time, they sipped coffee and watched the horizon. Kenneth liked to glare out into nothingness and imagine what existed beyond. Paul merely saw the nothingness. But even in silence defined by their polar opposite trains of thought, there was a camaraderie, a kinship previously unfelt by either of them. Little work was done. There was no reason for congratulations on a job well done. There was no accomplishment highlighted by the retreating pink sun, so only the silence enthralled them. It tied them together and finally freed Kenneth from struggling to find the words to bring the feeling to the foreground, to put a pretty label on the moment and show that once, they were indeed a family.

The workweek came to a sort of anticlimactic finish as their workload never spiked and made way into the weekend, Paul's first weekend from his first regular job. It felt different than expected, as everything does. It was a little less dramatic, like a high, whether from a drug, fame, or love, that is so anticipated that its effects aren't realized until their absence. Paul reached the weekend feeling like something else needed to be done, like he was stealing his paycheck as nothing seemed concluded.

Nothing was gained. That may have been true for his new job, but quite the contrary for his former. Paul spent his first hours of solitude away from responsibility on his computer, modifying the video footage he took of his would-be assailant, the fat man who was presumably now unemployed.

Paul cut away the men restraining him. He cropped the video to ensure that the two faces behind the fat man were in clear view. They went unnoticed at first glance, but their silently wrathful expressions made the fat man look almost pacified.

As Paul played with the video, highlighting all of the rage and discarding anything that would take away from how revolting and lethal the man looked, the artistic aspect felt just like making his promos for the snippets back in high school. He named an emotion and exemplified it in one image, cutting away all the fat, presenting it in its rawest and most abrasive fashion to the point where one picture would stick with the viewer for days. He wanted to tattoo his name to the world.

And the setting made it all so much better. Back in his room in Texas, he was safe, alone, in the fortress of anonymity casting down judgment without consequence, but here, he was naked and vulnerable. He was a rogue operative, a spy armed only with a camera. No one knew his agenda other than a nameless employer, just like every secret agent snippet he had ever seen. If he could accomplish his task, if his advertisements could incite a war, Paul would need no further vindication of his worth. His finished product would stand taller than any rhinoceros horn, his online status would far surpass any fuck score he could obtain. He would be the Supreme Bad Ass.

Paul finished his project with some narration that modeled much of what he had seen on older news memes. The message had never changed, but it was up to Paul to make an image adhesive enough to stick to the viewer until election day. He reviewed the video one last time, staring directly into the eyes of that fat fuck, feeling like the commander of a victorious army as his enemy was boxed in his computer, helpless and contained, waiting to be shipped off to America where, just like the prisoners of war, he would be tortured and interrogated until giving the information that would put the rest of his nation in the crosshairs. His furious eyes gleamed back from the computer screen, the warts on his neck slightly enlarged and the wire in his hand replaced with a revolver.

Paul sent off the advertisement. He logged on to his mother's old FlashConnect page and sent himself a message. Instantaneously, her face smiled back on his own page next to the words, *You are doing such a good job!* Paul smiled back at her before closing his laptop and joining his father and Narayan on the patio in celebration of their first weekend together.

4

"I MUST ADMIT," KENNETH SAID CAUTIOUSLY, unveiling a thought that had been gnawing at his brain like a piranha, "I don't know how you're so calm about losing the rhino horn. You say it was worth millions?"

"Yes. Probably," Narayan responded placidly.

"That could have been your retirement. It could've been anything. That kind of money could've gotten you anywhere!"

"It could have." A group of children ran past alongside the patio where they resided. They giggled and yelled as they stampeded by, some stopping to ogle Kenneth's white skin and light eyes.

"Then I don't understand. I'd be losing my mind over it."

"Look," Narayan said, somewhat exacerbated, bending over and resting his elbows on his knees with a deep exhalation. "First of all, I don't know what I would have had to go through to sell it. I am not in touch with the type of people who could make that transaction. And more importantly..." Narayan trailed off as if holding back a painful piece of information.

"What is it?"

"I didn't want to bring it up, but it was that afternoon at my house, you know, when we poured the dye on each other and your son, well..."

"Lost his shit."

"Yes, then. He was so upset over a shirt. A *shirt*. And I just realized how *evil* money is. We worry about it, we die for it, we kill for it. Everyone is trying so hard to get ahead, to work at a job they hate just to make more money, all the while blind to the fact that they are losing their lives. Their happiness goes right out the window in the great pursuit of money.

"So yes, I could've 'lost my shit,' as you say. I could've confronted your son and Chalem, accusing them both. I could've called the police. And in the end, I would've lost a friend and more than likely gained nothing. Even if I had it right now, even if I had the money that it is worth, what could I do with it? Buy a helicopter? Quit my job? For what? What would it all be worth? Even if I quit my job to pursue my own happiness, I would only be denying myself the right to associate with the one friend I have made in the past few years."

Kenneth blushed. It had been a while since he had a heartfelt conversation with a friend. Or had he ever had one?

"Well, I appreciate that, but—"

"No," Narayan interrupted. "You don't understand. I cherish our friendship because it is so uncommon these days. You see it, and I see it, but everyone else, they are all blind to it. No one communicates anymore. There are no more experiences to be had. I have suffered watching this by myself for so long that I forgot what a treasure real friendship is. I have known Chalem for some time, and I do miss him. But we need new friends. We need constant interaction to gain new perspective. And it seems that in this world, new friendship is much rarer than a rhinoceros horn."

As if on cue, Paul opened the door to the patio and ended the conversation. Kenneth and Narayan both applauded gleefully, cheering for the man who just completed his first week of work. Although it felt like nothing of the sort to Paul, Kenneth had every reason to see this as a rite of passage, his son entering into manhood.

"So how does it feel?" Narayan asked, giving no implication as to what 'it' was. Paul responded by shrugging his shoulders, partially out of embarrassment, partially out of a lack of a response, and partially out if his still present contempt for Narayan.

Things had most definitely changed. They were on the opposite end of the globe. Careers had molded new designs for all present. But still, behind Narayan's deep-set eyes, Paul saw those two brown footprints in soda, ominously peering back at him. With all of the new threats and triumphs encountered, those footprints were fading, but part of them, he knew, were ingrained into the fabric, never to be washed away.

It seemed that all of them had something to forget. Narayan was trying to forgive Paul for his crime. Kenneth was trying not to remember his son thrusting away in the middle of the living room. And Paul was trying not to remember those footprints. While amaranthine thoughts as such could never be completely erased, one could shove as much as possible to the foreground to dulcify them.

So they drank.

A bottle was passed around. Toasts were made. The three of them made a triangle that if spun in one direction bore the color of friendship, nemeses in the other direction, but under the light of inebriation, all was warm and amiable.

Kenneth didn't even grimace at the sight of his son partaking in alcohol consumption. In fact, he was encouraging him. It was a peace offering, a gesture that stated from here on out, they could just be friends. A father couldn't punish a fully grown son, but merely steer him in the direction he sees fit – and only when the son asks for such advice. These are the words that neither of them knew how to say, and so they poured poison down their throats in hope that the message would be conveyed.

A young woman adorned in a pink pavada meandered by their patio, which existed without a physical border. Her slow and seemingly directionless strides made her curiosity obvious. When her presence caught the attention of all three of them, she stopped and spoke to Narayan in fast and bouncy Hindi, like the tires of a speeding truck on a gravel road. After a rapid interchange, Narayan finally said, "Well, go on. Speak to them."

She eyed the two foreigners with a look that somehow bordered both fear and confidence. "You are Americans?"

"Yes," they answered in unison, Kenneth with an amused chuckle.

"Welcome."

Her skin flowed like caramel from her neck to her chest, barely made visible from the opening of her pavada. No collarbone nor wrinkle interrupted the flow of her skin, just a smooth, silky layer of flesh gently twisting and turning with the shape of her body. Her eyes were impressively large, irises so dark they weren't discernable from her pupils, sclera like an infinite cloud and whiter than a morning snow. Her eyebrows were like rolling hills, stretching the horizon of her brow and gently connected with a soft layer of fine hairs on the bridge of her nose, smeared in red with the paint of the bindi. Her lips were full and, like her eyebrows, stretched wide and flat, offering a welcoming disposition, like arms outstretched awaiting a warm body to embrace. Although imperceptible from the short distance between herself and the men at the table, a fine layer of black hair like those of her unibrow lined her upper lip, hairs that brought her shame, hairs that she would stare at in the mirror for hours, promising herself that one day she would use her father's razor despite the people who would notice their disappearance and mock her efforts.

"Come," said Narayan. "Sit down. What is your name?"

"Riya."

Narayan explained to the two non-Hindi speakers that Riya had been studying English her entire life, but never had any use for it. She learned that the neighboring community was to be occupied by an American company and was enthusiastic at the prospect of finally conversing in English.

"So explain to me," said Narayan, "why is a beautiful young girl like you wondering around by yourself and talking to strange men?"

"I only live right there," she replied, gesturing at the dilapidated houses across the way. "And I told my father that I would come talk to you. He doesn't speak English, and he is curious about the new company moving in and what they are doing."

"Well, you can tell your father that we are here to find more petroleum for his country."

"And keep the money for America?" she riposted unapologetically.

"No, no, no," Kenneth responded this time. He had learned enough from Narayan as to the mission of their endeavors here. "Sure, our company will make some money from the deal. But the idea is to put permanent rigs here in India that will continue to produce oil for you forever. And all of *that* money goes to India." She seemed satisfied with that answer. "But all business aside," Kenneth continued, "I'm going to get some more drinks. Narayan, could you come help me?" Kenneth glanced in Paul's direction and gave him a furtive wink. The gesture was something far greater than any offered by his own father. Paul, however, was more than terrified at the prospect of being alone with this girl, so the token went unappreciated.

Narayan gathered cups and began filling them with ice as Kenneth watched through the window as his son, ostensibly, was enjoying his first real courtship. Never would Kenneth have thought this overseas move to be so advantageous on so many levels, but glaring on as Paul tucked his head in an awkward shame and Riya giggled with that wide smile of hers in response, something was finally clicking.

Outside, Paul felt quite differently. Riya was beautiful and exotic, but every girl who was not displayed on his headset could be deemed 'exotic.' The virtual third dimension had always seemed every bit as good as reality, but its flaws were quickly exposed in the presence of a beautiful woman. Every ounce of her beauty was a direct ratio to the level of his trepidation.

Paul twitched nervously. He rested his right foot atop his left knee, but no, that didn't feel right, so he quickly let it fall back to the ground before hoisting his left foot atop his right knee. Nothing felt natural. He pawed at his head and neck, scratching with no itch, yearning for some place to put his hands. A layer a sweat encapsulated his body. *Is this how it is supposed to feel?* Paul wondered why anyone would seek out this feeling, if it was, in fact, normal. Maybe Paul was just inexperienced. Maybe he was – inversely proportionate to his sexual virility online – terrible with women.

He kept the small talk alive with one-word answers and shy smiles as Riya questioned him of his life back home and his relocation to her country. *What was that smell?* Her skin permeated the air with an unknown fragrance, something that The Suit could not replicate. *Was it sweat?* Surely, no sweat could smell so intoxicating. It wasn't sweet. It was dark and haunting, almost smoky, a scent like the melody of a song that stays in your head all day but you just can't remember the chorus.

"So, we're neighbors now, huh?" Paul finally said.

"Yes, apparently."

"Do you have a Suit?"

"Do I what?"

"Never mind." He felt so out of place. His fuck score had gotten up to 94, but it just didn't matter here. Riya couldn't check his FlashConnect page and see that he had a popularity rating of 98%. He couldn't add her to his close friends list where she could read a stream of comments confirming his sexually elite status. He didn't know what to do next.

Riya seemed to sense this as she announced her departure and asked him to wish a goodnight to his father and Narayan for her.

"Will I see you again?" Paul asked desperately.

"Sure. Just look that way." She pointed at her house, laughed, then followed the direction of her finger.

Kenneth stopped Narayan from taking the drinks to the patio.

"I have to ask," said Kenneth, deterring Narayan from the flirtatious scene outside, "how bad is it, being an American in this country?"

"What do you mean?"

"I mean we've been getting a lot of bad vibes at work and around the city. This Riya girl is acting like her family is suspicious of our motives here. I feel like Americans might not be too welcome here."

"Well, everyone does know about the arrests made for so-called Hindu extremists. That doesn't sit very well. Nothing in the Hindu faith could possibly support these acts, and so we, as a people, feel like we're being framed.

"And as for you and your job, any time a foreigner comes to India to work, it is presumed that he is taking work away from our people. But still, Indians are a loving, welcoming, and forgiving people. If you get to know them, they will all be your friends. Just look at how you and I started. So really, I think you should be more concerned about that."

Narayan made a gesture to the door where Paul sat with Riya, but she was already getting up and returning home.

5

ENNETH AND PAUL HAD ALREADY begun setting precedents that would predict their different ways of life in India. Paul would call Rajeev and send him out two or three times a day to get him snacks, batteries, power adapters, headphones, soda, socks, deodorant, toothpaste, tissues, or – just in case – condoms. Kenneth, on the other hand, enjoyed going out by himself to retrieve any groceries he might need. He had no map, no direction, and no knowledge of the Hindi language, but he figured he had nothing but time to walk around the city until he stumbled into a grocery store. Gestures and body language surely could go far enough to make ordinary purchases.

Even better than grocery stores, Kenneth would only find outdoor markets. Produce was displayed on the dirty ground, rats and monkeys strategically positioning themselves on rooftops and in dark corners, waiting to make a quick snatch of an orange or leaf of lettuce. Cauldrons were filled with murky white liquid, stirred laboriously by shirtless men who just got done bathing next to their cooking supplies. Small gas grills sent sizzling smoke into the clouds of pollution above, foreign smells emanating from unidentifiable delicacies.

Kenneth decided to go for an early lunch before attempting to purchase any vegetables from a street vendor.

He found a restaurant overlooking an intersection, and sat at a counter facing the window. The view below was like looking at the ocean from a satellite in outer space. Different currents pushed in different directions at different speeds. Auto rickshaw taxis squealed their horns as they pressed through the slower pedestrian traffic. Bodies were pushed to the outer edges as some stray waves of playful children darted through the vehicles, oblivious to the imminent death blaring its horn and refusing to find its brake pedal. In the cul-de-sac of an intersection was the eye of the storm. The perimeter was lined with booths and street vendors pedaling used clothing and fried chicken. A cow trudged lackadaisically through piles of garbage next to a toddler wearing only a shirt, squeezing out a bowel movement in the middle of the street before gallivanting fervently from shop to shop, pecker bouncing proudly with every unsteady step.

Kenneth ordered the biryani, completely unaware of what the dish entailed, as was the same with every other listing on the menu with the exclusion of butter chicken, to which he knew two ingredients. Fortunately, biryani was a rice dish that tasted delightful. Flavors previously untouched by his taste buds infected his saliva and emanated from his breath. Belches were pleasant reminders of the meal for the rest of the day.

Kenneth enjoyed his biryani while entranced by the images of the streets below. *Have I really come this far?* His life was like a twisted fairy tale, something to be enjoyed vicariously, not first-hand.

"Holy shit! Another Canadian!" The voice boomed from across the restaurant as its source cut across the dining area. It was like a skeleton plowing toward him. He had a shaved white head, black leather wrist cuffs, and a pinched smile punctuated by two holes, each the circumference of a plum, stretched around thick circles of plexi-glass, thickness growing toward the center and shining out grossly magnified images of his clenched molars. The holes in his face were large enough to toss a golf ball through without hitting a rim and pinched his smile narrowly so he looked like he was always getting ready to interject.

"No, actually I'm—"

"French-Canadian?" the skeleton interrupted. Fake pinched smile and wide eyes suggested that this was a statement of advice and not a question. "Me, too!"

The skeleton sat next to him and ordered lamb curry.

"I'm from Oregon," the skeleton mumbled under his breath. Kenneth couldn't make eye contact as he was transfixed on his molars opening and closing with each syllable, the glass from his plugs bent so that his teeth were visible from every angle. "But it makes it a lot easier for everyone if you just say Canada. And word of the wise, don't say French-Canadian again unless you're prepared to speak some French."

"But *you* said French-Canadian."

"Mui." The skeleton chuckled with his mouth as wide open as it could get, his chortles thick and raspy. "So what are you doing here?"

"I work for a company that's drilling for—"

"Vacation?!" the skeleton interrupted. He issued a subtle wink before continuing. "Me, too. Been here for six months and I'm not sure if I'll ever leave." He motioned to the window in front of them. "You can't find this shit in the ice hole of a country we're from, eh?"

Kenneth didn't know how to respond, so he stuck his hand out and introduced himself. The skeleton did likewise and identified himself as Justin.

To Kenneth, Justin was just on this side of intriguing, his appearance pushing him closer to the borders of disgusting, intimidating, and avoid at all costs. But more important than the holes in his face, Justin was out here all alone, even more so than Kenneth, and he seemed to know the rules of the road. Not only was Justin a potentially valuable acquaintance as he knew all of the Dos and Do Nots of India, but he had the willingness and fortitude to make it all the way here. That kind of audacity and curiosity put him a few tiers above the rest of the people Kenneth knew back home, and so, as difficult as it was, Kenneth looked past that skeleton grimace and the superhero wrist cuffs.

"Been to the Taj yet?" Justin asked.

"The Taj?"

"Yeah, you know. The Taj Mahal. Neither have I." Justin had an annoying habit of asking questions without waiting for answers. "Been six months, and I haven't seen the wonder of the world that's right around the corner. So I was thinking about it and decided if I don't go now, I probably never will. Headin' out next Saturday. Care to join?"

"You want me to…?" Kenneth was having trouble keeping up.

"Yeah, man. 'Nother Canadian in these parts don't come often. We should stick together, you know. Beautiful building, I've heard. But really, come on, how beautiful can a *building* be?"

Kenneth accepted the invitation and exchanged phone numbers before leaving the restaurant. He hadn't thought about the Taj Mahal. He hadn't even thought about meeting another American who wasn't attached to his phone. As Narayan said, new perspectives were always necessary. A new friend on an excursion to the Taj Mahal sounded like just what the doctor ordered.

That night, Kenneth got food poisoning.

It started with light bouts of nausea as he lay in bed scanning the television for anything in English. A fart came with a warm and wet sensation. An alarmed Kenneth went to the bathroom to investigate, but before he could find out if he ruined his boxer shorts, he was puking violently into the toilet. Chunks of biryani floating in an orange bile stared back at him, forever ruining the flavor for Kenneth. Beyond the nausea and the stomach acid burning at the back of his tongue, Kenneth was sad and wistful for his new favorite Indian dish that he would never be able to eat again.

Then came the diarrhea. Wave after wave tore at his waistline for excruciatingly long minutes before exiting his system. He began puking on the floor in front of him as he was scared to stand from the toilet. The smell of bile and feces burned the nostrils, as acidic as it was repugnant.

He was warned of this sort of illness upon his arrival in the country. Food poisoning was a normal occurrence for a foreigner in India. The bright red blood in the toilet was not.

That first week in India, Kenneth allowed himself the luxury of forgetting about his disease. He bathed in the newness of it all. He basked in his new job, his new friend, his new relationship with his son. He even convinced himself of the idea that the mind was the most powerful muscle in the body, and this newfound positivity could do more for his health than any advanced form of treatment, that his happiness could force the cancer into remission.

But after seeing that blood swimming among the brown fecal matter, Kenneth noticed all of the symptoms that he had blinded himself to. He had lost a few pounds. He face seemed to have aged; wrinkles underlining wrinkles underlined his eyes. His skin had a jaundiced yellow tint to it, a slight variation in color unnoticed by most and possibly only his imagination, but to Kenneth, he was a six-foot tall banana. The physical evidence of the turmoil inside him was a harrowing reminder of the racing stopwatch counting down to his final breath. This was not something he could wish away, something he could ignore, something that a friend and a new home could fix. This wasn't something he could face alone.

The next day, after he composed himself and was able to hold down some fluid, he had Narayan accompany him to a doctor.

The clinic, although small, was surprisingly clean in comparison to the squalor that existed just outside the front door. Narayan advised him to tell the doctor that he was only visiting on vacation. Although Echo supplied all of its employees (and subcontractors) with Indian health insurance, Narayan explained that even uninsured health care was extremely cheap in this country and he would probably be better received if no one knew he was living and working here.

The doctor wore jeans and a tee-shirt beneath an unbuttoned white lab coat, one sleeve rolled up higher than the other. His gray hair was dyed bright orange, yet not completely. It wasn't discernable if they were highlights or just a haphazard dying job.

"Hindi?" was his only introduction. No handshake, no hello.

"No. English."

"No English! Me, no English! Only Hindi." He was somewhere between outraged and confused as how to conduct his job with the language barrier. His following soliloquy in perfect English suggested the former.

"If I go to your country, I won't speak Hindi, will I? No, I will speak English. So why do you come to my country and not speak Hindi?"

"I'm only on vacation."

"Oh!" His mood took a drastic one hundred-eighty degree turn. "Vacation! Okay, okay, okay." He then went silent, poked randomly at his keyboard, and eyed his computer screen for a lengthened, awkward period of time. He would occasionally break the silence with an exclamation of "Bingo!" or "Bong!" The onomatopoeias and western exclamations were meant to make him sound more American, a notion that seemed absurd after his appalled impression of Kenneth the monolingual, and when he finally issued a coherent phrase, it was even more daunting. "Broken spine."

"What?"

Doctor Mulukutla turned his monitor to face Kenneth. It displayed an x-ray of another patient's spinal column. One of the vertebrae was cracked. Doctor Mulukutla seemed very pleased.

"Normal. Normal. Broken. Bong!" he said while tracing the spine with the butt of his pen. Kenneth was speechless. After acknowledging the tragedy of the unknown and possibly paralyzed patient with a confused grimace, Doctor Mulukutla finally addressed Kenneth's ailment.

It resembled his last doctor visit when he was investigating the disc in his back. He was given a brief oral interrogation by the doctor before depositing blood and urine into plastic containers, only this time the questions were interrupted by the doctor's utterance of random cities he had visited in the United States. When asked about any other medical issues, Kenneth lied. He spoke nothing of his cancer.

He thought it odd that he couldn't even tell a doctor. He couldn't tell Narayan because he wasn't sure what would follow. Once he opened that door, there was no telling what would spill out of it or if he could ever close it back up. That sort of intimacy between friends was unheard of in this era. Confidants were those who posted to a change in status on a FlashConnect page. It was something that Kenneth missed and yearned for, but still felt strange and shameful. If he were to relay that sort of information to Narayan, their relationship would be permanently modified. Whether Narayan was repelled or drawn in by Kenneth's confession, their friendship would either end or be brought to a much more intimate level, both scenarios less than desirable. More than anything, Kenneth just didn't want to admit that he was dying. He had yet to speak the words out loud, and admission of his fading health would somehow make it real.

Even more than speaking of his cancer, blood tests and further medical investigation would bring his disease into the unforgiving light of reality, and so he chose not to disclose this information to Doctor Mulukutla.

He suddenly wondered why he was at the doctor at all, but his diagnosis yielded him an answer; he wanted an easier answer to the blood in his stool. He wanted it to be completely unconnected to his cancer (something that he would have known was the exact scenario, had he followed up on his disease) so that he could once again let the cancer retreat to the background and go all but forgotten.

With the description of Kenneth's condition and blood and urine test results offering no leads, Doctor Mulukutla attributed the blood to internal hemorrhoids. Kenneth asked what might have caused them and if there were anything he could do to avoid them in the future. Doctor Mulukutla was less than helpful.

He shrugged. "Too much coffee, too much naan…" The doctor then slapped his thigh with a "Ha!" like he had had an epiphany. "Too much women. Last night, how many women you…?" He thrust his fist down and up three times.

Kenneth brought all four fingers on his right hand to meet his thumb in a circle. "Zero."

"Bingo! There's your problem."

With that, Kenneth was sent on his way. He thought of the last time he saw a doctor. He thought of reading his diagnosis on the screen of his phone. Maybe this wasn't such a bad alternative.

140

6

PAUL AWOKE THE NEXT MORNING feeling emasculated. He had always had pride in his sexual prowess, but the night previous had been the first dent in the monument he had built for himself. He tried to give himself reprieve with the explanations of the game being entirely different than the one he had known, that he would soon excel even in the RW, and that Riya was an Indian. What her nationality entailed wasn't clear, other than the fact that she was the enemy.

Rajeev had finally been able to accommodate his need for a power strip, and for the first time since his arrival in the country, Paul had the means necessary for sex.

Despite the time difference, Chrysanthemum was awake and ready.

Paul geared up and entered the virtual world to a hauntingly familiar image; himself.

Paul in the passenger seat of his father's pickup truck, Kenneth behind the steering wheel, fraudulent moments of father-son bonding taking place in random seconds pieced together over years. An automated voice read words written by Paul, urging him to vote for the Save Our Streets campaign. It was Paul's first advertisement, and the first piece of his work to finally be streamed. The election was this Friday, and although Paul was almost nine thousand miles away, he was still registered in Nueces County, Texas. Therefore, local election advertisements would still be brought to his system, even when on the other side of the globe.

Watching his work, remembering the clothes that he had to painstakingly delete and transform, making the video look like one seamless clip, feeling the fatigue from pulling an all-nighter to get the ad done, Paul felt proud and accomplished. He felt famous. The money received was a testament to his talent, but it was intangible. Seeing himself on screen gazing out the window of the truck before getting blown to Kingdom Come by an explosive hidden in a pothole, that was the ultimate trophy affirming his greatness.

Other implications, however, quickly dissolved his elation. Although this was a local election and the advertisement wouldn't be presented to anyone outside of his 3-code, it was online, and therefore, publicly available. If anyone in New Delhi were to come across this video, it might not look great for him.

Paranoia quickly got the better of him. He remembered the fear back in Texas when the acts of vandalism were getting more frequent and personal. The most terrifying aspect was the facelessness of the culprit. He was invisible, unseen, and unknown.

But now, with the prospect of the government releasing the work he provided before evacuating him from the country, the culprit would then be *everyone*. The entire nation would be the villain, every person aimed at destroying him. And then he thought that in another light, *he* was the culprit, and the rest of the world would be seeking to take him out.

He had to rid himself of these thoughts. Fear was parasitic, and the more he fed it, the more it would grow. It was one video, a video that wouldn't be seen by anyone within thousands of miles. He had to cut off the parasite, and he knew the best way to wipe a slate clean was with some dirty sex.

Chrysanthemum had lost a little more weight and gotten a new tattoo. Just as Paul, most of the surface area of Chrissy's body was inscribed with ink, mostly numbers and web addresses. Written vertically down her ribcage beneath her left armpit were a series of ones and zeroes, still rough, almost peeling off in fresh, black scabs. The eight digits equated to 361, Chrissy and Paul's 3-code, in binary code. Paul made no comment on her weight loss nor her tattoo and commenced to pounce on top of her.

The sex was passionate and quick, although Chrissy seemed slightly despondent. She didn't eye his muscles like usual. In fact, her eyes remained closed for most of their time together. When they made eye contact, she seemed to be looking *beyond* him. It seemed that although the internet made the miles between them arbitrary, the distance had had an effect. Figuratively and literally, they were having sex from opposite ends of the world.

Once again, they began their pillow talk without rinsing out their respective Suits. He told her about seeing his advertisement in the outer shell of the e-motel and yearned desperately to inform her of his mission in India and why seeing that advertisement elicited such fear, but issued restraint. Chrissy, all smiles again, asked about India, if he had seen any explosions yet or if anyone had tried to kill him. The questions were posed in sincerity and coincided with most modern Americans' view of India, yet they lacked the tone of concern that Paul had anticipated. He told her of how horrible it felt to be constantly touched by every other pedestrian, but that he now only left the house when a van awaited him. He told her of the hardships of starting his life over from scratch, even if he was to return in a few months. Chrissy seemed disappointed, like crowded streets didn't bear the intrigue of whizzing bullets and car bombs. Paul wanted her to feel what he was feeling, for her to understand the profoundly different experiences he was taking on and the pain that they entailed, but it was like a movie that she had gotten bored with.

Just as his anger rose his body temperature a degree or two, he realized that he didn't know anything about *her* life. He knew what she had posted on her page - her age, her hobbies, the names of her pets - but he didn't know the intricacies that made up her day, who cooked dinner in her family, if she liked to shower before going to bed or when she first woke up, if her parents ever hugged her and, if so, what it felt like. Their talks mostly revolved around popular memes and Self Stations (internet channels that presented someone's life from his perspective, filmed from a tiny camera on his glasses and broadcast live twenty-four hours a day) that they both enjoyed. It seemed that if someone else's life wasn't a quick joke or as instantly gratifying as an explosion, it didn't matter. Everyone else was merely a platform to broadcast your own life. Paul felt this way, too, but for once, his life was something that *really needed* to be heard. It was something substantial that shouldn't be ignored or passed over, and though he had every podium, platform, and microphone previously unavailable to him, people may listen, but would never understand. He posted short video clips and still frames tagged with witty slogans from his daily life and received ample feedback on his page, but no one truly understood what it meant to be so utterly alone, as helpless and lost as a shark in a bathtub.

He finally understood that the only way to gain true empathy was to become a team, to adjoin his life to another's, and with that, he may feel safe and important again.

"You'll still marry me when I get back, right?"

Chrissy's eyes were downturned crescent moons as her tightened cheeks squeezed her eyelids together, her smile tightly subdued.

Paul, feeling icky from the sentimental dialogue and the drying semen in his Suit, opted to exit the e-motel. He bid his farewells and made promises for a future rendezvous before disconnecting his headset and peeling off the upper layer of his Suit. He shut down the genital compartment, all the sensors immediately retracting away from his penis, and carefully pulled it away from his pelvis. Just as his flaccid member flopped gracelessly out of the carbon fiber housing, he noticed a large pair of bright eyes peering up above his windowsill.

His pulse pounded in his face and neck, beating to a rushed tempo of humiliation. His cheeks buzzed with the sensation of a sleeping limb as the sweat on his forehead turned to ice.

Even when his father caught him having sex in the living room, he didn't feel any sense of shame. Sex was something mundane and expected. Not owning a Suit would have been shameful, but using one regularly was quite the opposite. His body was fully covered. Nothing of his or the other party's was exposed. In all actuality, Paul had secretly wished that his father could've seen Sheila and Laura and the other girls in the orgy. He wanted his father to know the kind of girls that he was capable of getting. Instead, he blacked out on the living room carpet, but still, nothing of the situation bore a reason for shame.

But this, *this* was shameful. It wasn't so much Riya seeing his naked and limp penis, but it was her seeing his penis coming out of *The Suit*. It was an item that he struggled for months to afford to buy, an acquisition that he loved to flaunt, a suit of armor that he adored wearing, that he would never attempt to conceal, but here, in this country, it suddenly seemed necessary to lock this part of his life away. It wasn't the sexual aspect of it all, but it felt more like being the rich kid in the poor part of town – which, essentially, was what Paul was now. He needed to hide his expensive possessions and affluent lifestyle. Everything that made him popular back home made him the outcast here, and while he wasn't seeking to impress, watching his worth plummet in Riya's eyes was somehow devastating.

He quickly ripped the rest of The Suit off his body and threw on some clean clothes. He ran to the back porch expecting to watch as she fled the scene with the horrific shock of a witness of a gruesome murder, but instead found her sitting calmly at his patio table, eyeing him confidently. Paul anxiously attempted to maintain eye contact, but his gaze kept dropping to the ground.

"Do you always spy on people?" he finally muttered dejectedly. Riya ignored the question.

"What was that thing?"

"It's called a Suit," Paul replied while sitting down, feigning comfortable. "We use it to have sex."

"But no one else was in there with you."

"I know. We use it to have sex online, you know, with people far away."

"Then it's true."

"What?"

"We sometimes hear rumors that Americans don't touch one another. You don't hug or kiss and you stay inside all day, every day, completely alone. We usually don't believe it, but we hear that you grow your babies in a lab because people don't want to touch each other to reproduce."

"That's ridiculous," Paul responded, though knowing that the first half of the statement was true and wondered why it sounded like such a bizarre way of life to her.

"I want to see it."

"See what?"

"The Suit," she responded. "Show it to me."

Paul led her abashedly to his room, feeling like he was walking willfully into a trap. What benefit could be gained, he wondered, by obliging her? His Suit was still full of sweat and semen and had had enough time for the smell to really permeate into the room.

Crossing the threshold, he pointed in The Suit's direction, hoping that she didn't opt for closer inspection.

"I don't care about that," she said as she moved in close. Her forward facing palms landed gently on his chest before gliding up over his shoulders and curling around his neck. Paul reflexively flinched and backstepped into the wall, but Riya proceeded forward. That same scent from last night now pervaded his nostrils, promising to linger throughout the day, taunting him. Her breath was warm on his chin, springing billions of goosebumps across his body to life. His knees began to give way, but his hands surreptitiously clutched the doorway behind his back, offering him support. Her nose tickled the tip of his own as she breathed into him. *This is wrong,* he thought. Every sensation felt illegal, immoral, something that surely bore the steepest of consequences if anyone was to witness. He wanted to back away farther, but the wall pressing into his spine offered no escape. Her separated lips danced across his own, her tongue gently probing and retreating, once, twice, three times. His actions bordered retreating and mirroring her own actions, the combination of the two surely resulting in awkwardly frenetic movements of his lips and tongue, nothing that would be deemed pleasurable on her end.

Her face gently drifted away from his own. "I just didn't want my dad to be able to see," she whispered. As if in reverse motion, her hands slid back down to his chest, then withdrew, as did she. "And I really thought you needed to see what someone else's touch felt like."

With that, she left Paul to himself, hanging his Suit up above the bathtub to rinse out, watching the steady drip of his bodily fluids exit the toe, and seeing it for the first time as lacking.

ENNETH HAD SPENT THE NEXT week at a new drilling location repeating last week's tasks. His son was much more efficient in his job, performing tasks without assistance that he couldn't complete the week previous. They still sat and watched the sun turn from yellow to pink at the end of the day. Kenneth still longed for a motor to go down or a part to come in that they would need to replace so real work could be done, because with real work came the opportunity for real bonding, but still, every morning Kenneth had to do all but pry his son out of bed, and every evening he had to go home and shower next to a drip-drying Suit.

On Thursday, Paul didn't even make it in to work. Kenneth was tired of being responsible for holding up the van from an on-time departure and no longer had the stamina to coax Paul into getting up, so he left without him. This was surely a blessing to Paul, and it was a pestering itch in Kenneth's mind for the entire day, denying him any sense of satisfaction.

By Friday, Kenneth had the taste of the weekend dripping from his teeth, and while bonding with his son had been the most fulfilling of rewards last week, he had no intention of inviting his son to accompany him to Agra with Justin.

Kenneth left early Saturday morning and didn't bother telling Paul where he was going.

"So why *didn't* you bring your son?" Justin asked as Kenneth admitted his guilt in the matter. The bus – unlike most in India – was air-conditioned and quiet, a rare ambiance that begged Kenneth to unleash his worries to the ears of a new friend.

"I really don't think he would enjoy it. He's more of a computer kid, if you know what I mean."

"I totally get ya. But he's gotta break away from it some time, ya know? That's why we're here anyway. This is a pretty hard place to keep to yourself." Justin took a breath to take in the passing nothingness away from the city that streamed by his window. "But you're still a good dad, man. You're still here worrying about him. So in a sense, you're still with him. It's not until you stop thinking about him that you truly fucked up."

"I guess that's one way of looking at it," Kenneth chuckled feeling slightly mollified. "And what about your dad? You've been here six months, right? How does he feel about that?"

"Fuck if I know, man!" he cackled. "The man's kinda like your boy. Ma pissed off about three years ago and so the old man got himself a Suit. Pays top dollar where he can go to those sites where you modify your self-image, makin' him look all Hollywood instead of the fat, hairy asshole he is, bangin' out top notch pussy all day – or at least other fat, nasty bitches that have the gear to make 'em look like top notch pussy! Haven't talked to him much since he found out how to use the sex tech and all."

Kenneth didn't know how to respond, so he simply said, "I'm sorry."

"Nah, nah. Don't be. I'm happy for 'im. If that's all his desires are, all he needs to be fulfilled, then he's livin' the dream, I guess. Me, I'm a little different. Gotta see what else is out there, and seein' it from a screen never did me right. But if he were a more attentive father, I might not be as inclined to up and fuck off to India, ya know? So I guess this is the only way it could work where we could both have our fills without infringing on the other's. I still love 'im, but we work better apart, I think." He had a melting pot of an accent. Dropped consonants and random idioms were like souvenirs from all of the places he had been in only twenty-three years of life.

Kenneth watched outside the window. How quickly the scenery could go from total anarchy, people on top of people, buildings on top of buildings, to just nothing. He wondered how far they would have to go outside the city before the pollution lifted and visibility cleared, but it never came.

As six hour bus rides with new friends go, the first hour was spent with seemingly vacant chatter, probing to find out if the other was a person he'd want to spend further time with, itching to bridge the gaps of awkward silences, then finally succumbing to introspection and window gazing. Kenneth employed every ounce of restraint to keep from gawking at the transparent plugs in Justin's cheeks, but came up short, eyes reverting to those shiny, round magnets.

As the road neared a bridge stretching across a wide river, Justin became anxious, whipping his head around looking for landmarks. At the end of the bridge, they reached a stoplight where Justin dragged Kenneth to the front of the bus and ordered the driver to open the door. The driver barked back some angry Hindi. Justin pushed his way through the shut door, the hydraulic hinge pushing back almost to the point of snapping. The driver's tone kicked up several notches. Kenneth pushed nervously against Justin's back, awaiting the driver to pounce from his seat and attack. Justin shouted a quick, "Namaste!" without turning his head.

The two of them followed the current of the water, Kenneth in tow as Justin kept peering around, not quite lost, but definitely unsure of his whereabouts, hot onto a trail that he didn't disclose to Kenneth. Kenneth thought it seemed unnecessary as the Taj Mahal had to attract an ample amount of visitors, so going against the flow seemed counterintuitive.

Macaques lined both sides of the river ahead, some skirting the banks of the river and getting their feet wet, the younger ones wrestling wildly, but most perching stoically like gargoyles, eyeing the intruders and guarding the entrance to some imaginary relic beyond. The people commixed with the primates, indifferent to one another's existence, but out here the ratio shifted, the monkeys outnumbering the humans and offering a more unstable atmosphere. Back in the market streets of Delhi, monkeys were mostly unseen, clinging to heavily wooded areas and rooftops, inhabiting the city streets only for a quick swipe of an apple or open bag of chips before scurrying off, forever aware of how quickly they could be exterminated. But along the banks of the Yamuna River, it was the pedestrians who kept a vigilant eye on their surroundings, mindful of the eyes upon them and how quickly the mood could change and they could find themselves overpowered.

Kenneth stepped heedfully, curving his path through the thick grass away from the larger of the macaques. Justin seemed to plow right through, unmindful of the monkeys and their curious stares. Kenneth followed suit, even as Justin stepped directly over a man with skin like leather, somewhere between states of consciousness, lying flat on his back, eyes closed, mumbling incoherently, painfully, as flies swarmed all around his face, his hands motionless and helpless to swat them away.

"That's one problem with this place," Justin shouted without turning his head. "You come to see things that you could never imagine back home, but a lot of it you don't want to imagine, and you spend more time trying to forget."

The people as well as the monkeys began clearing off as they approached vaster areas of nothingness. Only the still water, the green grass, and the banks lined with washed up garbage existed ahead. Trees polka-dotted the horizon beneath the brushstrokes of white, a smog that seemed to accompany the morning sky quite aesthetically. Justin pulled his phone from his pocket and stared down at its face while he walked, occasionally fumbling his steps over unforeseen variances in the terrain. He appeared to be following himself on a satellite map. Kenneth was more fascinated than perturbed.

Before long, they arrived at a small group of trees huddled together and isolated from any other vegetation as if they were telling a secret. Inside the hidden circle made by their collective trunks existed a jungle green, two-seater kayak stocked with two oars.

Finding the kayak was an unexpected surprise for Kenneth. He was beginning to grow restless. The hike alongside the water in the arid Indian heat produced a thick layer of sweat that encapsulated his entire body. It accumulated in the soggy marsh of his butt crack. The sensation was not unfamiliar to Kenneth, but he suddenly feared a repeat of the previous weekend, that blood would discharge from his anus, stain his pants, and leave him a humiliating six-hour bus ride to a clean change of clothes. He wanted to stick something down his pants to check for remnants of blood to ease his mind, but he packed no such item in his backpack. He thought briefly about using his fingertips, but the hygiene, the smell, and the thought of getting caught in the act deterred him. He tried to nullify his fears, but every sodden step dyed his thoughts red.

They set the kayak out onto the tranquil water and began paddling.

"How did you find this thing?" Kenneth finally asked. Justin replied only by shaking his phone like a baby rattle in Kenneth's direction. "I thought you weren't into all that."

"I'm not," Justin replied. "I mean, I'm not into all the bullshit that the rest of the world's into. But there are some good uses, ya know? There are other people like us, and these little machines make it easy for us to hook up and pass along info, like this here kayak. Ya can't dismiss it all as shit, as much as you'd like to. Some good can come out of anything. Besides, we're bypassing the lines."

Kenneth would be lying if he said he wasn't a little disappointed. He liked not owning a computer and using his phone only for making calls. It was difficult and frowned upon, but he also wanted his friends to have the same ideals.

"I gotta ask, did it hurt?"

"Huh?" Justin finally turned his head from the front of the kayak.

"Those holes in your face. How did they do it?"

"Well, it kinda sucked. They're not stretched. They said that would permanently fuck up my face." Kenneth chuckled under his breath at the irony. "So they had to actually cut them out, then cauterize the wounds. It hurt like a bitch!"

"So why did you do it?"

"It was just something different, ya know? I wanted to be different than everyone else, and I wanted to feel everything that no one else felt, even pain."

"I don't get it."

"Don't get what?"

"Well, you got a procedure done that's been done all over the world to make yourself different. No offense, but I've always felt that it's what you do that makes you different, not how you dress. I shouldn't say anything, because you're probably the most unique person I've ever met, and you're doing more than anyone I know. I guess the fashion part of it all just never really made sense to me."

Justin grinded his teeth, an action made visible through the looking glass on either side of his face, possibly in a seething reaction to that last statement, or maybe just chewing on the thought. He set his oar down, scooted his ass toward the front of the kayak, and leaned back as the Taj Mahal drifted around the bend.

Kenneth was transfixed by the glowing white marble as the sun's reflection momentarily blinded him. The smooth roundness of the dome and the cylindrical minarets were flawless. The pointed archways were outlined by Arabic calligraphy laid in shining jasper and black marble. The sheer perfection of it all was mesmerizing. Kenneth thought about the endless hours of labor from innumerable sweating bodies, the fathers, sons, and grandfathers who lived and died building this monument. He thought about all of their work living on for centuries and centuries to come, their blood and sweat soaked into the ground below and marking their immortality. He thought about Justin and his father, how they had left each other to their own lives, continents and oceans between them, but content with how they had grown apart. He wondered how to let go of everything that existed between himself and his own son. It seemed that there wasn't anything substantial to hold onto and so much to cut adrift, like once the tie was severed, there wasn't anything that made them part of the same family other than the code in their DNA. He had to find something beautiful and eternal, something to replace all of the hatred, the arguments, the distance between them before cutting the line and floating away with the current.

"Not bad for a shitty building, eh?" Justin smirked, fully adopting the Canadian accent that he assumed in this country.

SHE KISSED HIM AGAIN THE next day. He immediately extended his hand toward her crotch, a gesture which earned him a ferocious slap to the face. His cheek stung with the intensity of a chemical burn, a feeling made miniscule in comparison to his pride. She sprinted lividly to her house. Her frizzy black ponytail bounced hurriedly, waving an angry goodbye. Paul peeked around the side of the house, confounded and belittled by her wrath. He watched intently as she ran with the stride of an Olympian. His gaze followed her all the way to her doorstep, where he first saw her father. His enormous belly stretched his undershirt to its breaking point. A receding hairline and a bald spot attacked his little remaining black hair from both sides. The furrowed eyebrows and angry scowl that he just witnessed on Riya's face was embedded in her father's. His eyes shifted from his daughter to the house where she just ran from. Paul quickly hid from his stare and retreated to his bedroom feeling certain that he would be the next target of 'Hindu extremism.'

Lo and behold, Riya returned the following day virtually unfazed by Paul's sexual misconduct. They discussed the misunderstanding (normal dialogue now a possibility for Paul, although Riya still did most of the talking). She said that she knew that forming any relationship with someone of such a vastly different culture would be complicated, but they needed to understand their differences, the first of which being that Hindu women place a strong value on their sexual integrity.

But Riya was a modern woman. While her mother had gone to her wedding bed a virgin, Riya, at the ripe age of nineteen, was no stranger to a man's touch, and although she held modern views, the family and society that she grew up in were still quite traditional. Her father needn't know about her romantic life, not unless she wanted to be fitted for a chastity belt, and therefore, she explained to Paul, her father didn't even know about his existence – at least, not in its entirety. She visited his house every day after her work on the farm under the pretense that she brought the American man an English newspaper on her way home for an extra fifty rupees. As for the white boy her father had seen on the man's porch, he was merely a work colleague who rode home with the older gentleman, who sometimes stayed at the house for a cup of tea before walking the rest of the way to his house.

Paul was still stuck on the word 'relationship.' He had every intention of losing his RW virginity to this girl, but his motives steered well clear of anything deemed a relationship. His final thoughts before sleep every night were of his promise to marry Chrysanthemum upon his return to Texas and what that would entail. Although he existed in the real world now, the RW back home was another universe and still elicited the deepest fears in him. India, for all Paul was concerned, was practice. Just as he experimented with girls outside of his 3-code to prime himself for Chrissy, his entire life in India was training him for the married life where he would be responsible for all errands that existed off-screen, sex included. Although Chrissy was far from his thoughts during his time spent with Riya, at the very most he would view her as his first RW sexual experience, nothing more. On the days when he couldn't expel her scent from his nostrils, it was only because it was a sense unoffered in the virtual world. When he made love to Chrissy and would suddenly see Riya's bright eyes staring back at him, it was only because he had yet to see Chrissy in real world dimensions. He didn't deny that he enjoyed their time together, but it was on the same level of enjoying a video game. After all, they both knew of the racing clock that counted down to his imminent departure with every meeting.

Every evening they enjoyed a fifteen-minute date, usually spent playing an ongoing game of chess (something that Paul was proficient at from endless hours of online play). Riya had a beautiful chess set, the pieces carved out of onyx, which Paul loved to run his fingers over. He would always be the first to strike, just so he could hold that initial pawn in his hand and caress the smooth edges of its perfectly spherical head.

They probed one another (Riya much more than Paul) with trivial questions, like two feral animals circling and sniffing, determining the potential threat and possible kinship. They were both curious of the other's upbringing, although Riya was more vocal about her curiosities. The two were almost from different eras in time – Paul the futuristic spaceman, Riya the cavewoman. While India wasn't untouched by the wave of technology that divided humanity into the isolated space pods that were each person's computer as in America, their society wasn't yet irreparably altered by it. She had heard of the wealthiest of individuals owning Suits, but had never fully comprehended the idea before Paul's arrival. Many people had accounts on social media, but checked and updated them with the frequency that most would floss their teeth. It was only a tool, not a way of life, and Riya viewed this social transformation as regression, and therefore, they both viewed each other as the Neanderthal.

The two investigated one another's backgrounds like scientists entering a new ecosystem and studying a new species. The eons between them gave a heightened appreciation of all they had in common. Shared interests were akin to digging up a time capsule and finding a picture of yourself.

The exoticism of their vastly different backgrounds and the points where their incongruous lines crossed created an oddly suiting environment for a blossoming romance.

Kenneth was well aware of these secret meetings that they would share and would make himself scarce, though he loved catching furtive glances at his son experiencing his first love, so he thought.

On the weekends, Kenneth would usually go off with Justin somewhere – to the spice market, to the Red Fort, to the Lotus Temple, or sometimes on longer trips to Jaipur or Agra. During his outings, Paul would usually spend the day in The Suit, if not with Chrissy, then with Sheila or someone from a different 3-code. Though one day a week, Riya would find time to sneak away and share an extended meeting with Paul, often catching him in The Suit.

Riya was intrigued, and a little revolted, by Paul's addiction to this synthetic form of lovemaking. It was a habit that she intended to break him of and a custom that deserved studying, but Paul saw things in the opposite direction. His life in The Suit was his reality, while Riya was just a supplement, and Kenneth felt satisfied enough with the time shared with his son at work and watching him court a woman who didn't exist inside a monitor to venture off with Justin, a figure who was becoming more and more like a son to him, because it was just so much easier with someone who shared his ideals. Given their implications about the people they lived with, Kenneth, Paul, and Riya could have just as easily been complete strangers.

One Saturday, Paul found himself in the bustling streets of New Delhi. After countless efforts to get Rajeev to find him a magnetic hard drive in which he would return with antiquated thumb drives, external hard drives, and in one case, a computer mouse, Paul was left to his own devices.

Gearing up for the expedition differed little from psyching himself up for a good workout. He donned the appropriate clothing (in this case, jeans and his cheapest long sleeve to avoid direct contact with passersby) and got his blood circulating by breathing quickly and heavily, shaking his hands as if to dry them, and jumping up and down.

There was a slow saturation into the madness as his house existed in a nook tucked away from the pandemonium, or at least as hidden as could be in a city as such. Still, nothing could prepare him. Facing the streets of Delhi was equivalent to going into battle.

He hadn't the slightest clue where to begin, but the randomness of the shops suggested anywhere was as good as any. He passed a gift shop, a chicken stand, a travel agent, and a secondhand clothing shop, all adjacent and in that exact order. All were open to the street lacking a front wall, and Paul began to wonder how they locked up at night. His thoughts quickly retreated to self-preservation as a dog barked angrily behind him and another homeless woman clung to him for two blocks.

When the chaos of it all became unbearable, Paul would turn off the main street. The alleyways would narrow as he would often find himself face to face with a drooling cow blockading the side of the road not covered in garbage and feces, and Paul would be forced to turn back.

On one occasion, he ended up in a more residential area, walking past housing units cramped so tightly together they might as well have been lockers. Children scurried up and down stairs. Women washed clothes in the walkway. Paul walked right next to a family yelping jubilantly as the father figure chased the youngest into the alley before picking him up, lifting his shirt up to his chest, and blowing his lips on the boy's belly making fart noises. The scene appeared traumatic and violative, the man's lips on such a tender area of a child no more than two. Paul wondered if he should notify someone, but the rest of the family seemed elated by the spectacle, so he thought better about it. Adolescent boys at the top of the staircase glared at him, as did everyone, and shouted,

"Wrong way!" Paul bowed his head in shameful acknowledgement and turned on his heel.

As Paul returned to the main street, a fragrance sailed with the wind and found its way to his nostrils. It was entrancingly familiar, sweet yet fuliginous. He could almost see it, blurring the air in ambiguous waves. He followed the faint trail of smoke back to a tiny cone on a wooden shelf in a souvenir shop, the bottom of it a deep maroon, the top gray ash, the two colors divided by a thin line of glowing orange, a miniature volcano the size of an adult thumb spewing out the scent of Her. Riya.

Paul mindlessly entered the store, careful not to knock over the endless rows of wooden elephant figurines and bronze Durgas with arms spread out like arachnids. Without any cordiality, Paul addressed the shopkeeper by pointing at the burning cone of incense and said, "I want this. This one. How much?"

Unlike the very few Indian men Paul had come in contact with, this one returned the inquiry with an open smile and cheerful eyes.

"You like that one, my friend?" He reached under the counter and rummaged through drawers before extracting an identical cone and placing it into a brown paper bag and extended it in Paul's direction. "Have this one."

"How much?" The man closed his eyes lightly, stuck out his bottom lip, and shook his head. Paul didn't know how to react to this. He kept waiting for the next sales pitch, but it never came. He stood dumbly in the middle of the store before reversing out the door, his expression still perplexed and his show of gratitude never mentioned.

Although slightly moved by the gesture, Paul was somewhat disappointed. He wanted to buy several as he planned on burning them frequently, but felt too awkward to turn down the offer or ask for more. He knew how difficult it would be to find that exact flavor again. And given his sense of direction – or lack thereof – he would never find that particular store again.

Suddenly, the magnetic hard drive escaped Paul's mind as his agenda took on a different shopping list. He walked in shop after shop and scanned the merchandise. Some shop owners were warm and welcoming even after he left empty-handed. Others were not. Paul scoffed at this method of shopping. It would all be so much easier if he could return to his old life and peruse the items online, but the goods for sale in these shops were items that he would never find on any internet shopping site, nor would he want to. The thought of someone actively seeking to find a rosewood Buddha or a miniature rickshaw made of copper wire gave Paul a chuckle. The most revolting looking foods were scattered among tiny porcelain tea sets and gold-painted pocket watches, and everyone was bustling about, proving that the shopkeepers were actually making money off all of it. Paul felt like he had gone back in time.

The one benefit of this manner of shopping was the ability to test the merchandise. Paul realized this as he finally spotted what he was looking for; perfume. He sampled bottle after bottle, but none supplemented the scent of his incense, the combination intended to equal the scent of Riya.

"For a special lady?" the man behind the counter with missing teeth inquired. Paul ignored him and sampled another bottle. By the twelfth fragrance, his nostrils felt numb. The thirteenth, however, held a potion that entranced him just as hers did. It may not have been exact, but it was close enough.

After a harrowingly reckless auto rickshaw ride back to his house, Paul returned with a cone of incense and a bottle of perfume with no label. The magnetic hard drive was long forgotten. Riya was waiting for him.

"And where were you?" she asked with a smile.

"Shopping."

"In the market?" Paul nodded, terrified that she would ask what he bought. "And what do you think about my city?"

"It's nice, but…"

"Yes?"

"The people. Some are so nice to me, but a lot of them hate me just for being white."

Riya's eyes dropped to the floor as she nodded slowly in recognition.

"We are a very warm people. The ones that you say are nice, that is us. But as for the others, I understand them, too. We see what you say about us, the things that you accuse us of doing. And then you all come here to work and take money away from our people." Paul looked as if every word was targeted at him. "But see, these are all just details. They are distractions from who we really are. I know you and I choose to spend time with you, not because of where you are from or what your job is, but because I enjoy your company. We are all just people. We are all trying to find our own happiness, but everyone gets so caught up in everyone else's pursuits, worrying about who is infringing upon whom, that we forget to see everyone as a mirror of ourselves."

"And what about your father?"

"What about him?"

"Does he hate me – or would he hate me just because of where I'm from and what my job is?"

The corner of her mouth and her left eye squeezed toward each other in a facial tick.

"He is confused. He is a man with a lot of anger. And sometimes he treats me poorly because he is afraid of the world and what it will do to me. You see, women are held to a different standard in India. My actions reflect on him and my family, but more importantly, they have the ability to scar me for life. He knows that I must maintain a certain dignity so that my future may be secure. Sometimes, it is very easy to ruin your life in this country. But I love my father. I just see things that I feel he does not understand, so I choose not to disclose those parts of my life to him."

Later that evening, Paul took a lighter to the pointed end of his incense cone and let it burn in the corner of his room. He used the palm of his hand to waft the air toward his breath. He sprayed the perfume toward his cracked open window so that the draft would circulate the fragrance around the room. With all of the lights out, he pulled his bicep to his face, pushed his lips onto the skin of his upper arm, and kissed. His tongue lapped up the taste of flesh, the hint of sweat sitting just beneath his pores. He smelled his breath emanating from the saliva on his arm, the scent mingling with the incense and the perfume. He thought about her. He thought about Riya, but only because that was the only face that he associated with those sensations. He moved to his other arm and began again, imagining he was kissing her lips, her naval, her thighs. While the taste of skin could only be tied to her, one day that same taste would grace his tongue in the form of Chrissy, or possibly even Sheila.

He met Chrissy in an e-motel and made slow, passionate love to her while the perfume still sifted through the air, while the smoke from the incense acted as another modification to his Suit, an adaptor that he had created himself. At times it was Chrissy staring dotingly back at him, at others it was Riya's wide and soulful eyes. As he mounted her from behind, he opened the top of his Suit to reveal his shoulder and went back to kissing his deltoid and savoring the taste. The smells of his spit and his skin blended with the fragrances permeating the air, almost as they did when he kissed Riya. He reached for the bottle of perfume, surreptitiously feeling along the baseboard as he was blinded by his headset, and sprayed one more mist to the air in front of him.

He felt as if he had plugged up the holes in his Suit. All that it had lacked, he had now fulfilled, and Riya, all of her intimidation, that feeling of empowerment that she exuded, the feeling of inferiority when she was near, her exotic disposition, her calm and confident gaze, those huge eyes that Paul would get lost in for eternities, they were all suddenly disarmed as he now had the ability to recreate them.

Once the session was over, Paul went to his computer and put together his second advertisement. He sifted through all of the footage he had taken of Riya from the phone in his breast pocket, mostly from their meeting earlier that day. He pieced together everything that she said about her father, words like "anger" and "confused," phrases like "treats me poorly" and "scar me for life," and sentences like "It is very easy to ruin your life in this country." By the end of it, the ad was dripping with misogyny and abuse. It was all made so much more direct and real by the shaking camera proving it to be real amateur footage of a native in the country proposed as the enemy. Paul wrapped it up with a voiceover stating that, *"We are not out to destroy a nation, but to protect the innocent in our own country, as well as theirs."*

As he submitted the advertisement, he actually believed it. He believed that the innocent would be spared and only those deserving of punishment would receive it. He believed Riya when she said that people got lost in everyone else's pursuits and that we could love people for whom they were and not *what* they were. Paul believed that he could keep performing his job and being friends with Riya, and that the two would never conflict with one another, because they were just two people who enjoyed each other's company, and everything else was just details.

9

BRIGHT RED BLOOD AND WHITE foam filled the sink. Kenneth had just finished brushing his teeth to find that his gums were bleeding profusely. He had always had poor gums and would occasionally find a little pink in the toothpaste when he would spit into the sink, but this time, the red was overpowering the white like a strawberry sundae. He showed his teeth in the mirror in a painful grimace and saw two different spots where the blood pooled in the corner where the gap between teeth met the spike of the gums. He hadn't flossed since reading his diagnosis from his cellphone screen. It wasn't a conscious decision, but every time he reached that part of his agenda and the floss was peeking at him from beneath his razor in the medicine cabinet, it just seemed pointless. The task had always been tedious and annoying, and now the act would have been akin to buying popcorn during the final credits of a movie.

But it wasn't the flossing (or quitting flossing) that Kenneth was thinking of. It was those final credits rolling, ending the film of his life.

Whether or not the bleeding gums could have been contributed to the cancer inside him, Kenneth was now panicking. He couldn't deny the pain in his abdomen that was growing stronger every day and now moving around to his back. He couldn't pretend that the pounds were coming off because he was working harder and the cuisine was healthier. His time was coming. And he wasn't ready.

Kenneth wasn't prepared for his death in all of the ways that he should have been preparing. Many people don't see their final scene approaching, and therefore aren't able to make preparations, but Kenneth had the luxuries of being able to make ready his family and organize some sort of financial plan for the future without him, although they didn't seem very luxurious to Kenneth. He had procrastinated these duties that would entail facing his mortality and admitting that he was dying. He postponed these responsibilities until it was so late in the game that he felt like he deserved to ignore them and enjoy his final days as best he could.

But more than anything, Kenneth felt *panic.* No matter how long you are warned of your own death, when it comes, you always feel like life is slipping from your grasp. Kenneth struggled desperately to clench on to life, to not let it leave, like he had some remaining song to be sung, but it slipped through his fingers, and just like when he was a kid and he broke Mom's special vase, he watched it fall in slow-motion, in disbelief, as his world shattered into a thousand shiny pieces, each one screaming at him that he was dead. It was a panic like none before, frantically searching for some doubt or some way out, but the curtain was closing, and the more he clawed at the velvet drapes, the more they spun around and entombed him.

Narayan had begun picking up Kenneth and Paul for work that week as he had just purchased a car. His car was white and ordinary, somehow already coated in a thick layer of dirt. Seeing his friend's new car depressed Kenneth. It was a symbol of permanence, a sign that Narayan was preparing for the long haul and would not be returning to the United States. It only dispirited him further to realize that neither would he.

Paul sat in the back with his sunglasses on despite the overcast skies. His aloof expression suggested he was watching another snippet. Kenneth sat in the front seat and tried not to notice Narayan studying him every time the traffic let up enough for him to veer his attention in his direction. He wondered if it was his morose disposition or his gaunt and jaundiced face. It didn't matter. Nothing did anymore.

When they reached the jobsite (a new one for Kenneth and Paul), Narayan asked if there was any work to be done that Paul could complete unassisted.

"You know the drill, right?" Kenneth asked. Paul nodded slightly and exited the vehicle without a goodbye. Kenneth worried that the bond they had made was only felt on his end, or possibly worse, that he had done something to break it, but in reality, Paul just assumed that his father would be accompanying him soon enough. Perhaps Kenneth was overanalyzing things, but overanalysis seemed unfathomable as he had eighteen years to form a relationship with his son, eighteen years had gone with nothing between them, and he only had days to compensate for the thousands that were lost.

The door shut behind him. Narayan took some time before driving away to scrutinize his best friend. He put the car into gear and asked what was the matter. Kenneth, unexpectedly, burst like a balloon. His somber face erupted with such sudden and violent sobbing that Narayan almost thought that he was hurt, like a bullet had just whizzed through the door and caught him in the gut. Narayan didn't attempt to console him from across the front seat of the car while driving, but rather drove to his house, a seven-minute drive from work, to provide him with some much needed solitude.

In American standards, Narayan's house was mediocre. In India, it was a mansion. Stepping into Narayan's house felt like walking into a portal to another dimension, to another time, and for a brief moment, Kenneth thought he was already dead. It wasn't lavishly decorated or fashionably designed, but all of the furniture just seemed new and clean, two adjectives that were rarities in that part of the world.

In a fleeting moment of mental clarity more than likely brought on by malnourishment and oxygen deficiency, all of Kenneth's thoughts and worries melted away in an instant, and were replaced with one all-consuming image - the rhino horn. There was no other excuse why Narayan could afford this opulent lifestyle. He had to have gotten it back. Maybe Paul really did steal it, thus explaining all of the acts of vandalism on their home and the ransacking and burglary that came along with it. It was certainly feasible that Paul took it from Narayan and he took it back, and while the wealth would mean that he sold the horn, he remembered Narayan telling him that it was worth one hundred dollars *per gram*, so it was possible that he merely sold *part* of it.

"So what is the problem?" Narayan's eyes showed true concern. It was a look entirely unfamiliar to Kenneth, something that reminded him of childhood, of his parents, of a love now foreign to him.

"Could you get me a cup of water, please?" he squeaked out. As soon as Narayan left the room, Kenneth tore it apart. The time for subtlety was long gone. In the short time it took Narayan to pour a glass of water, Kenneth had torn apart a chest, emptied three drawers, and was racing back to the bedroom. When Narayan found him, Kenneth was swiping picture frames off dresser tops, the frantic searching quickly dissolving into sheer destruction.

Two cups of water fell to the floor. "What is the meaning of this?!" Narayan shouted.

"Where is it?! Where the fuck is it, Narayan?!"

"What?! What?!"

"The fucking rhino horn! I need it, man! Where the fuck—"

His arms got suddenly heavy and the darkness swarmed in from all directions. Kenneth fell to the ground, weeping like a baby, balled up on a pile of broken glass and pictures of Narayan as a boy that he had just thrown to the floor. A stringy trail of saliva and snot dripped down to a photograph of Narayan in Kenya, a small line of blood entwining with the spit and mucus.

"I'm dying, Narayan." His eyes looked up at his friend, big and pitiful, wet and desperate. "I'm fucking dying."

"What do you mean?"

Kenneth's eyes dropped back down to the glass beneath him. "I've got cancer. I don't think I've got much longer. I just thought… I don't know… I thought maybe you had the rhino horn, and I could…" Kenneth couldn't complete the thought, but Narayan fully understood.

And then Narayan did something unheard of. He hugged him.

He crawled across the broken glass, shards slicing into his palms, and he wrapped his arms around his friend and wept softly with him.

For a moment, everything was okay. Kenneth was so enthralled in a warmth he had long forgotten about. He had fought against the world for so long that he had forgotten what he was fighting, and really, he just wanted to be *touched*. How could something so celestial and necessary as a hug go extinct? He didn't think about the world and the war that he had waged against it just then, but if he had, he would have thought that he wanted the entire human race to feel what he was feeling, to experience the pain and panic and loss that he had, to know what real misery feels like, then to lose it all in one gesture of human compassion, and then just maybe everyone would forget why they gave up their humanity for a quick high. Maybe everyone could love again. But he wasn't thinking about that. He was just thanking God that he had a friend.

"I think there is something you need to see," Narayan spoke softly into his ear. "There is a place that we must go. You, me, and your son. We should leave right now, and we won't be back for a couple of days."

ENNETH SAT BETWEEN HIS SON and his friend on a propeller plane.
He felt much better, physically as well as psychologically. The pain
in his gut had subsided and he even had a healthy appetite as he
found an American pizza chain restaurant in the airport and devoured two
huge slices of cheese pizza. Although his fear of death and knowledge of it
lurking around every corner had not been nullified, they were preceded by
the enthusiasm of a new excursion and the warmth of being sandwiched
between two of the only three people in the entire world whom he genuinely
loved.

After a one-hour flight and a half-hour taxi ride, the three of them
arrived in Varanasi.

Even after living in the country for more than a month, the shock of
Varanasi took the breath out of Kenneth like a battering ram to the gut.
The squalor, the people, the monkeys, they had all multiplied. Every person
who passed by was a postcard for bizarre. A shirtless man wearing only a
thin orange loin cloth, hair in filthy clumps, forehead painted white and
divided by a red line extending from the bridge of his nose to his hairline. A
toothless woman carrying a burlap sack the size of an armchair on her head
walking barefoot through cow shit. A man with skin the color of coffee, just

a shade lighter than black, with dredlocks down to his ass, a white powder covering the entirety of his naked body. In every one of the hundreds of faces that passed by at any given second, Kenneth saw a novel story to which he couldn't begin to fathom.

The garbage upon garbage upon garbage made it so they didn't even notice the brightly colored buildings that made up the skyline. Metal canopies extended over both sides of the street and were riddled with rust, holes, and macaques.

The monkeys of Varanasi, although vastly outnumbered by humans, were much more audacious in their actions. They constantly ambushed the markets with aerial and ground strikes and were chased away by men with painted faces wielding wooden canes.

Occasionally, a man in a long-sleeve shirt and slacks would pass by, and it was he who would draw Kenneth's attention. It was the ordinary Indian man who stood out in a place like Varanasi.

"The first thing that you must remember," Narayan spoke loudly over the mobs of people, "is that everyone you see is just like you. We are all human, and we all have the same basic desires to attain happiness and avoid suffering."

Paul clung closely for safety. If the overwhelming new setting wasn't quite enough, the tour guide spouting off life lessons like they were parading toward the afterlife was almost enough to jump into his father's arms and have him carry him like an infant.

Farther in, the roads turned to alleys. Kenneth could almost hold his arms outstretched and touch the walls on either side. The narrow streets made avoiding walking directly in feces and wet garbage a challenge. Passing painted people and fresh piles of cow dung were obstacles constantly pushing them to the walls to avoid them. The monkeys swinging by overhead and glancing down with a calm ferocity in their eyes seemed to push them down from above. Sometimes a cow would block their path, nose against one wall and rump firm against the other. There was nowhere to go, and the alleys were not in a grid format as the normal layout of a city should be, but solid and twisting lines offering no detours. In other words, turning around wasn't an option. They could either squeeze by or slap the tail end of the cow and intimidate it into moving, neither of which Kenneth nor Paul thought themselves capable of doing. Luckily, their Indian guide would get the mammoth creature moving so that their only worry was walking through its filth.

Paul incessantly yearned to question their purpose for being there and plead to return to Delhi, or better yet, America. Although the filth and drastic downsizing of his personal space still got to him, Paul no longer cringed when rubbing shoulders with a passerby.

The alleys became more and more narrow. The crowds around them became fewer until they were completely alone. Suddenly, as if funneled into the vastness of the ocean, the street opened up completely as they looked out onto the Ganges.

A wide staircase with tall steps that chipped apart the joints in their knees with every step down spilled out to the flat and gray water. Both banks of the river were lined with colorful yet faded buildings. The skyline was cluttered with stacked rows of asymmetrical rooftops in no apparent order, like they had been building on top of buildings for centuries. Gazing down the river, Kenneth watched the edges of the water that were dotted with brown, the banks with blazing yellow, as waders cleansed themselves with the healing powers of the Ganges and fires burned at every ghat.

A confused dog ran wildly past them, his head whipping from side to side as a small monkey clung to his back, the image drawing their attention away from the river and slowly into the crowds that gathered and passed languidly along the wide walkway running parallel to the water.

Narayan held an upturned palm out toward the Ganges. "People from all over the planet spend their lives journeying to get to where you are standing. It is the holiest place in the entire world."

As they plunged through the crowd and gained distance toward the first ghat, the eerie source of the glowing fires became clear.

Every five minutes, another corpse wrapped tightly in bright orange cloth was paraded down the stairs and set atop a pile of firewood. Holy men who looked to be even older than the ancient buildings that they emerged from would unwrap the bodies, exposing the head of the cadavers. They would rub oil on the face of the deceased and scan the face with their hands as if they were doctors performing a routine physical on a patient they weren't aware had already expired. The faces of the dead, although superficially no different than the lively faces of those around them, were hauntingly inanimate and drained. The facial features identical to those of a living specimen bore no personality. Wipe away the identifying human traits – the nose, eyes, ears, mouth, and fingers – then toss them into the water, and they could easily be mistaken for driftwood. The subliminal transformation that death took over the body was horribly unnerving.

The jaws of Kenneth and Paul were gaped open and frozen. Kenneth's arms hung heavy at his sides. Paul's left hand was clutching the camera phone in his breast pocket.

As the inspections and preparations of the body were finished, the head was wrapped back up in the white cloth that existed beneath the orange, and the corpse was set ablaze. The orange glow of the fire reflected hauntingly from the eyes of Kenneth, Paul, Narayan, and an ever-watching camera lens.

"Like I was saying," Narayan continued from his earlier speech, "people come from all over the world to *die* here. We Hindus believe in karma. If a person does not learn the lessons taught in his life, he is condemned to repeat those lessons through reincarnation. But whoever dies in this river, whose body rests beneath the surface of the water you see in front of you, his soul is expelled from the cycle and attains moksha, and will live in eternal splendor."

"Where are all of the women?" asked Paul.

"Women are not allowed at the cremations. They are much more emotional, and tears and sadness will draw the soul back to this plane, when their mission here is to depart to a new one. So you see, death can be a joyous occasion." He eyed Kenneth compassionately. "Although you see it in all its horror, right in plain view here, the real journey is the one that you do not see, and it is the greatest and most beautiful journey a soul can take."

Paul wanted to scoff at this remark. 'Beauty' didn't belong here. The naked and filthy men, the burning flesh, the trash and feces left no room for beauty. These people may believe in the unseen, in spirits floating away from these bodies, but in the mist hovering just overhead, Paul only smelled the stench of rotting flesh and shit.

Another body was carried down the steps and laid down ten feet in front of them, away from the spaces allotted for cremations. The lump beneath these sheets was much smaller, and as the holy man unwrapped the cloth, the smooth, pale face of a young girl no older than eight was revealed.

Her lifeless face void of wrinkles, unstained by the harshness of time, choked Kenneth with tears. Death was such a malicious and heartless monster. It tore apart the cruel and the innocent, the young and the old alike. Everyone coincided with a terrible beast, did their best to forget about the boogeyman that lived in every closet, but just when you thought it was safe to be happy, he poked his head out and ripped your life apart without any remorse or concern. These men here knew it. They tossed the ashes of bodies into the river and said that it was a doorway to a better universe, believing anything to make them forget that the beast would come for them next.

The beast was stalking Kenneth, constantly reaching out to him, ready to shred him to pieces like the others before him.

The little girl was wrapped again and tossed aboard a small rowboat. A solitary man dressed in all white accompanied her as he gave one push to send the boat into deeper waters. He turned at the waist and held a hand to the water. From it scattered a crumpled handful of white lily petals. He turned again and repeated the process three times. The lilies gently scattered, the ones farthest from the departing boat spread wide, those closer still held tight to the boat, creating a white 'V' stretching across the Ganges and pointing at a small rowboat carrying a dead girl.

Her weighted body slipped from the side of the boat and sank with a quickness that knocked the wind out of Kenneth. Narayan saw the distraught look on Kenneth's face and how deep he sank with that little girl.

"Come on," he said. "Let's go get some dinner."

As they retreated from the scene feeling everything but hungry, Kenneth watched as a little boy of about five years wearing a dirty white tee-shirt, stained jeans, and no shoes played carelessly directly between two burning corpses. His bright, innocent eyes that had already seen so much more than most men of eighty were fixated on the sky above. His tiny hands worked the taut string of a kite with calculated movements that only come with experience. Up in the cerulean sky, a crimson diamond fluttered in the wind, its long tail winding with the smoke of sandalwood and burning human remains.

That night, the three of them sat on concrete steps amidst a densely packed crowd comprised of painted faces, dredlocks, skin smeared with human ashes, wooden beaded necklaces, mangy beards, jewelry sifted from the ashes of the bodies, and a hundred other faces that Kenneth and Paul never thought they would see in their lifetimes. Five men in orange robes with white sashes that draped over one shoulder and wrapped around their waists kneeled on five separate altars and held candelabras blazing into the night sky. With choreographed movements, the five slowly brought their respective flames in large circles around their bodies. A barefoot man with glasses and dressed all in white walked back and forth in front of the crowd and acted as the hype man, encouraging the spectators to clap along with the music that lacked any sort of rhythm or tempo.

This was the actual funeral. While the family members who orchestrated the cremations acted without emotion, as if the entire ordeal was strictly business, now was the time to mourn or rejoice. This was the bon voyage party for the three-hundred souls that were all disembarking to a nirvana to which thousands of candle-wielding, clapping spectators wished them off.

Kenneth was peering at his son. Paul had relinquished much of his uneasiness around the crowd and seemed intrigued by the entire spectacle, from burning to bon voyage, but lacked any sort of natural human emotion or sympathy, completely desensitized or just oblivious to the death that surrounded him. It was one of many fears that rode the repeating carousel in Kenneth's head, the one that reminded him that he was leaving behind only one person, and that boy was in no way prepared for the crushing weight of life. His entire career as a father was spent supporting that weight above his family, keeping them safe, but he forgot to teach his son how to carry that weight once he was gone, and now it was too late, and Paul would soon be flattened.

"The last thing I wanted to show you," Narayan continued with his sporadically resumed speech spanning hours, "was that when you die, the biggest fear is being alone. But as you can see, we are sending off three-hundred souls at one time, and this is only one city in the world. You will exit with thousands of others, all there to comfort one another, as you enter a realm much more beautiful than this one."

Kenneth had to commend him for trying, but it just wasn't working. Sure, the entire process did possess a twisted sort of logic and sublimity to it, but he couldn't get past the image of that little girl plummeting into the ashy water. While they sang and danced, watched the heat rising off waving torches carrying her to her heaven, Kenneth only saw a little girl who should be off flying a kite far away from a field of cadavers, a little girl that was sitting at the bottom of a dirty river probably being torn apart by catfish the size of marlins. He hadn't the slightest idea whom she was in life, but Kenneth wanted nothing more than to bring her back, and worse than his inability to do so, she was pulling him down with her, that murky fate to be his own in a few more rotations of the earth.

"I hope some of this helps you, my friend," Narayan said.

"It did," Kenneth lied. "Thank you." Kenneth looked at his son, then back at Narayan. "I need something from you."

Narayan's eyes were fully attentive, as if the mobs of people surrounding him had suddenly melted away.

"When I'm gone," Kenneth whispered clandestinely, careful not to let his son hear, "I want you to look after Paul."

Narayan looked confused and slightly disappointed. He looked around Kenneth's head to see Paul lost in his phone, earbuds tucked into his ears. "You mean, you're not taking him back to America?"

"I don't think I want him to go back. This is the first time in his life that he has experienced...*reality*. Everything that we have back home... I don't want it for him. I... I don't know."

"I don't think that is a good idea, Kenneth."

"Why not?"

"I was going to tell you this before your... sickness," he skirted around more abrasive terms. "But I'm growing weary about our agenda here. The company has me testing the ground samples, but not only for oil. They have been instructing me to also test for neodymium levels."

"Neodymium?"

"It's a rare earth element that is used in making magnets, specifically for computers and lasers, along with a long list of other products. For decades, China has owned more than ninety-seven percent of the world's neodymium mines and has had a monopoly on the industry. But there are rumors that these mines are running dry. I believe that America, in their constant rivalry with China, is looking to take over the industry by claiming the mines in India, the ones that we are creating."

"And how would we do that? We can't just take them over."

"By war. You've seen the media frenzy over Hindu extremism. Well, look out at these funerals. Our religious doctrines are... I don't want to say selfish, but... *unconcerned with others*. We live to learn our own morals and attain our own heaven. As I told you before, there is nothing in our beliefs that could be taken as moral grounds to commit murder. So, I believe that this rise in 'Hindu extremism' is just a platform to launch a war. The American economy is in its lowest state since the Great Depression. With this electronic sex phase, the birth rate has gone into such a decline that the country can't support itself. Nothing catalyzes economic growth quite like war, and that initial spike can be sustained once America is the world's leading supplier of neodymium. And possibly worst of all, your government has lost all burdens of responsibility with your new election system. First they will get the American citizens to vote *to* go to war, and then any collateral damage will be at the blame of the American people."

"But Echo will get us out if the declaration of war goes to election, right?"

"I don't know. We may work for Echo, but as far as the paperwork is concerned, we have technically been subcontracted out to an Indian corporation. It is basically up to the American government, and they have two possible alternatives, assuming that my theory is correct. One, they can bring us back to the states before the fighting begins, hopefully discrediting any claims of their true intentions, then ship us back when things have calmed down and suck all of the neodymium from the ground. Or two, they can try to kill us in the first strike, deny their knowledge of our existence here, and destroy all evidence of their geological findings prior to the war."

Kenneth sighed heavily, trying to soak in all of the information. It seemed that there was always so much to contend with that he never had any time for himself, and for that, he was strangely thankful. Any new burden, even that of a world war, was a distraction from his impending doom.

"So what you're saying is, I *shouldn't* keep my son here."

ALMOST MORE SHOCKING THAN THE burning corpses Paul had spent the past two days gawking at was his pining for Riya. His time spent in Varanasi was blanketed in the shadow of her absence. Paul's life spent in the boundless confinement of the virtual world released him of the burden of understanding the sorrow of *distance*. With a phone in his pocket and a computer and Suit always close by, he was never far away from anything nor anyone, but the fifty hours spent away from Riya taught him that he might have been – for the first time in his life – experiencing love.

He found himself giggling at the sons sprinkling sandalwood on their fathers' dead bodies before setting them ablaze, confounded by the idea that even a corpse on display could remind him of the woman in his life. He thought about their vastly different cultures, her growing up amidst these bizarre customs, him growing up in a Suit, and how much they *disdained* one another, and that disdain somehow made it work. He had been with single-dimensioned girls who were mirror images of himself for so long that maybe he needed something entirely different.

He thought about the last advertisement he had sent in, the ethereal icebergs that were her eyes surrounded by her dark forest of eyelashes and thick eyebrows, staring into the camera and telling of the horrific man who was her father. While Paul was beginning to regret submitting that particular advertisement, he was still ambivalent about pursuing his campaign to wage a war against the nation. *We are not out to destroy a nation, but to protect the innocent in our own country, as well as theirs.* It was a slogan that he chose to believe. The war was a retaliation against the crimes committed against his own nation, and America, in its infinite wisdom, would seek out the culprits and bring freedom to the masses. Riya would be safe – safer, in fact – once America had rid her country of the evil that lurked just around the corner. When it all began, if the battle got too close to her back yard, he had fantasies of bringing her back to the U.S., them finding a place together, fulfilling all of those dreams that Chrissy had laid out for him against his will. Maybe it could work.

Arriving back at his house in Delhi, Paul sat on the patio, the gesture equivalent to waving a flag signaling a potential rendezvous. Despite his choking through the past two days without one of these patio meetings, Paul had become afraid of conveying all of his twisted emotions to Riya. Disdainful adoration and such. They weren't the easiest ideas to pitch, and existing in the RW for the past six weeks had made his inability to communicate abundantly apparent.

As his confidence plummeted, he longed for the rhino horn. Seeing it peek out of his closet like a miniature scale of the summit of a colossal mountain was indicative of his manhood.

Paul sat at his computer and searched the internet for images of rhino horns, the ambiance of the room being a pathetic sort of nostalgia.

The first image that he found of a rhino horn was surrounded by a broad red circle divided by a diagonal slash marking its diameter and cutting the rhino horn in two. The site was dedicated to stopping the illegal poaching of endangered rhinos and urging people not to buy any product made from rhino horn. Perplexed at what products those might be, Paul searched further only to find endless sites claiming that the solution to curing cancer existed in the phallic artifact that Paul cherished so dearly, the icon of the first epic moment in his life, the prize that was stolen from him. Various countries in southern Asia, namely the one that he resided in, were using powder from the horn in experimental medicines to combat cancer.

Suddenly, it all made sense. His father was dying.

He thought about those words: *You don't understand, but it could save me.* That's what his father said when he first interrogated him about the horn. And Varanasi. Narayan was like a tour guide to Death. The whole trip had seemed like a threat as Paul was still sure that Narayan knew he took the horn. With the same level of certainty, he knew that Narayan had gotten it back.

Just as when his mother died, Paul was hollowed out, numb and vacuous. The imminent loss of his father was indifferently cataclysmic. He acknowledged the weight of his discovery, but couldn't bring the feeling to his core. Just as at his mother's funeral, he tried to cry, to feel anything, but failed.

Worse than the fear that he was void of emotion was his selfishness. Reaching down into his soul, grasping for any natural emotion that should coincide with loss, he only found the disappointment of knowing that his father's condition would ultimately bring distance between himself and Riya. He would have to be spending time at a hospital, a funeral, possibly America, all places that wouldn't bear his newfound love.

He knew these reactions were abnormal and cold, but he could only despise himself for feeling them. He couldn't deny them.

And so once again, his self-worth nosedived and he lacked a rhino horn – literal or metaphorical – to comfort him.

He messaged Chrysanthemum and specified an e-motel to convene in, the action meant to alleviate any feelings of self-loathing, but felt as a betrayal to both Riya and Chrissy. He now knew that he would not be entertaining any plans of pursuing the mundane family life with Chrysanthemum, and worse yet, his plans may just entail eloping with an Indian woman and immigrating her to American soil.

Riya had buried herself deep in Paul's head like a carnivorous earwig, trailing all of his thoughts with her infectious scent. Her presence behind his eyes would be as obvious to Chrissy as the smoke that lifted off the pinnacle of his conical incense and filled his room. Paul was never very good at masking his emotions.

He quickly messaged her with an ambiguous excuse. Unsatisfied, he messaged Sheila and coordinated a different room and time after receiving a green light on the proposal.

His incense already burning, Paul began spraying the room with perfume and tongue kissing on his shoulder, which emerged out of the open corner of his Suit. For a split second, he exited his body and watched himself from an outer perspective, doused in women's perfume and kissing himself. 'Pathetic' didn't have enough syllables to describe the setting. All of these actions were engendered to recreate Riya and destroy the hold she had on him, but instead, they did the inverse. Although it heightened his sexual experience, it only strengthened his desire for the real thing.

He watched an advertisement persuading him to vote against a proposition to dismantle monopolizing corporations based on the idea that free enterprise was what made the country great. He didn't give a fuck. Still, he saw the ad for what it was worth: his competition. And the fact that he didn't give a fuck stated that the advertising representative did a shit job.

Paul entered the motel and was greeted by Sheila's milky, round ass staring back at him as she looked over her table of sex tools, deciding which to employ first. As she sensed his arrival, her head turned and her dark eyes peered through loose strands of hair, her predator eyes peering through the thicket, hungry to pounce on her prey.

She turned her body and took one step in his direction before he was unplugged.

The monitor lifted from his head, and Riya's eyes were inches from his own. While she was not ignorant to the fragrances that clouded the room or the green cushions that entombed the man in front of her, she selflessly chose to ignore them completely, not allowing the slightest of twitches to her eyelids, anything to convey her distaste and catalyze any fear or shame in Paul.

Paul's vocal chords were frozen. His fingers twitched with the likes of the coffee jitters, aching to reach out and touch her. The slap that proceeded his first advance on her weeks previous thwarted any further effort on his part. He knew that he should be doing something, saying something romantic, touching her body in places that didn't elicit violent reactions, but he just didn't know what, so he chose to remain nervously motionless.

Riya undressed him slowly, her graceful pace not only for heightening desire, but also slowed by her ineptness to conquer all of the seals that contained him. She pulled one arm free, then another, her eyes dancing across his tattoos, then her hands did the same. All ten fingers ice-skated gently across his skin, swerving sharply, barely making contact, gliding slowly toward his pelvis, then turning back and tickling his ribs. Her face moved into his. He opened his mouth for the kiss, but it never came. She moved down lower, off to the side, her lips grazing his cheek, moving around to the neck before landing. Soft kisses were stepping stones leading to his ear. Her tongue lapped at the lobe, soft at first, then gained pressure. It spiraled slowly inward, tickling just shy of making him flinch in reflex, just enough to make every hair stand erect, perched firmly atop any of the ten thousand goosebumps across his body. Her exhalations made sensual by the saliva coating his ear made every nerve in his body fire in ecstasy. A warm, breathy voice whispered, "Take the rest off."

He bent down spastically and ripped the Suit from his legs. It was the most naked he had ever felt. He had met so many women, first impressions made without a shred of clothing, but nothing had ever felt like this. It wasn't just the fact that it was now taking place in the real world, but that it was *her*. It was someone who knew him. Sure, Chrissy knew Paul pretty well, but that all happened *after* the sex. This felt different, almost wrong, almost incestuous, like their kinship somehow put her off limits, but it was that taboo that made everything feel so vulnerable and deep.

She backed away, just enough so he wasn't poking her, as he was already rigid. Her eyes stayed with his as her fingers continued to dance. They wrapped around beneath his arms and scratched gently down his back before ending at the top of his buttocks, then once again, turning sharply. They wrapped back around to his front side, just above his waistline before slithering down his thighs. He could feel his pulse all over his body like it was about to burst out of his skin. Her fingers drifted closer and closer, teasing him, then wrapped lightly around his firm member, starting at the base and spinning back and forth like a metronome, sliding up to the head, then off, shrinking away like a crucial part of a spaceship drifting off into space, Paul the astronaut staring helplessly out the window, readying himself for the crash. Her hands went back to her sides, then she turned and walked out, waiting for him to dress himself and meet her on the patio.

He thought to question her, to beg, to plead for anything more, but he knew that she was teaching him, and despite the insolubility of questions that she posed, he was still glad to be her student.

He turned to retrieve a pair of underwear from his dresser and saw the dark silhouette of an ominous figure in his window. Paul jumped back in reflex. It was Rajeev. The two connected gazes, Rajeev's eyes as sharp as razor blades. His stare couldn't have been more obvious if he tattooed the words on his forehead. *I've got you, now.*

12

From the roof of the hostel, the midnight streets of Delhi looked like a Christmas tree tent on December 26th. Like the morning after a party. Lights hung in parallel strands over the street, revealing the filth and emptiness, the feeling of a chaos gone to bed as the streets still vibrated with the bustling crowds that had finally gone home. Paper food wrappers from the chicken stands blew by past sleeping cows. Rickshaw horns that were a ringing in the ears hours earlier now came in short, sporadic spurts. Men congregated in dark corners, refusing to surrender to the time.

"Main tumse pyar kartha hoon!" Justin shouted from the edge of the rooftop at no one in particular. A group of men down below glanced up in his direction, then dismissed the interjection.

Justin and Kenneth sat with their legs dangling, three stories between the soles of their shoes and the ground. Justin opened a metal lunchbox with a cartoon dinosaur on the front. From it he extracted a joint and lit it up. Kenneth wondered what else could reside in that little lunchbox. Although barely large enough to fit a couple of sandwiches, it seemed like Pandora's Box, like a character as enigmatic and bold as Justin would only carry it around if it had enough drugs to brainwash a civilization. Justin sucked deeply on the joint. Even in the dim orange light, Kenneth could see the smoke fogging up the windows into Justin's mouth. It was oddly transfixing.

"So where else ya been?" Justin grinded out the words while holding the smoke in his lungs.

"What do you mean?"

"India. America. Where else?"

"That's it," Kenneth smiled while taking the joint. The two had been partaking in marijuana use over the past couple of weeks, a new endeavor for Kenneth. It was a hit-or-miss operation for him. Sometimes the high would make him forget about all that had gone wrong in his quickly expiring life. Others, it would make him nervously aware of all the interworkings in his body and make him fidgety, constantly rubbing his skin and imagining things going wrong beneath it.

"Aw, man! You gotta get out, bro! So much you needta see!"

"Like what?" he questioned while sucking on the joint. "Where've you been?"

"All over, man. Just got here after doing two months in China. Don't bother with that place, though. Concrete jungle. Buildings and pollution, chicken feet and discos, blah blah blah. Like here, but not cool. But man, this place is fuckin' wicked, right? Like another fuckin' world!"

Kenneth knew just what he meant. It was difficult and disgusting and terrifying and confusing, but the people everywhere without a care, the way everything was shoved in his face, although tiresome, it was so rewarding. It was life on steroids. It was all of those things in life that we try to hide come out from the shadows to haunt us. Even if Kenneth were to live forty more years, he might spend them all right where he was sitting. Blowing marijuana smoke into the night sky, sitting next to a new friend overlooking a vacated market in New Delhi, it didn't seem like such a bad idea.

And then it all went to shit.

Kenneth choked on a hit from the joint, the smoke burning like acid inside his lungs. He coughed and hacked, intensifying the fire within. After a minute when the pain subsided, the high set in with an intense first wave.

The lingering burning inside suddenly sprang nerves to life that didn't previously exist. He was feeling his respiratory system do its job. He could feel the air move down his trachea, cilia springing to life and acting as filters. He felt the oxygen moving down into his lungs, tunneling through bronchi, filling the alveoli and moving out into the bloodstream. Though separate systems, the oxygenated blood now moved to the cancer inside him that was interrupting the flow of blood, hogging it all to himself like a fat kid at a birthday party eating all the cake.

He began clawing at his skin, feeling like it was detaching itself from the flesh, like his body was dying before his mind. This was going to be one of *those* highs.

A sharp pain arose from his abdomen. Whether it was the weed or the cancer was indecipherable, but his pain was made well apparent to his buddy next to him.

"You alright there, homey?"

Justin. Why hadn't he thought about him before? He was a man who existed off the grid, a man who could obtain a box full of drugs in a foreign country. He was like the guy in prison who had the connections on the outside, the man who could get you what you need. He was the one who could find a rhino horn. He could save Kenneth's life.

"Yeah, yeah," he coughed again. "Listen, I've got a strange proposition for you."

"Ooh." Justin rubbed his palms together enthusiastically. "This sounds good."

"Do you think you could find something for me? It's something pretty strange and probably difficult to find, but I just figured… I mean… You've found weed in India, so I just thought…"

"Weed in India?!" he laughed heartily. "Get on any rickshaw and you can get weed in India! Hell, they practically throw the shit atcha!"

"Yeah, well, anyway. I need you to try to find something for me."

Justin's eyebrows went up to solicit detail.

"A rhino horn."

Justin's chin dropped to his chest as he blew a dejected stream of smoke from his nostrils. His tone turned deeply morose. "You must be in bad shape if you're askin' me for a rhino horn, eh? What is it, man? Cancer?"

"How did you know?"

"Saw a documentary on the rhino horns once. I know what they use 'em for. You fuckin' dyin' or what?" Kenneth nodded gravely.

"Aw, shit," Justin mumbled. "I'm fuckin' sorry, man. How ya feelin' about it?"

"I don't know. I mean, I've got good life insurance and Paul will be financially set for a long time. I guess I'm… I don't know."

"I didn't ask about your insurance, man. How do ya feel about dyin'?"

Kenneth broke down into tears. His body shuddered so bad with his whimpers that Justin brought him down off the ledge and onto the flat surface of the roof. He wrapped his muscular arms around Kenneth and held him like a child while he ran his tear ducts dry. Justin's breathing matched his own, even shuddering slightly with Kenneth's weeping. Using only his lips, Justin still puffed on the joint while he ran his fingers through Kenneth's hair. It was a profound gesture. It was something maternal and feminine, something two men would never do to one another, but it came naturally to Justin, just as smoking on the joint between his lips was involuntary. The two actions together defined Justin as a person more than any profile page on a social media site could ever convey.

Kenneth felt naked and vulnerable. He felt the masculine fingers running through his thinning hair and knew that they shouldn't be there, that it was shameful, that if anyone opened the door to the roof right now, he would probably make up a series of lies to explain their position, while Justin would probably punch anyone in the face who would try to ruin this beautiful moment. As much as he had feared death for so long, dying right there on that rooftop in Justin's massive arms didn't feel like such a bad thing at all.

After Kenneth had fully dehydrated his body from crying, Justin released him from his grip.

"You know, man," Justin said, "I might have somethin' that could help you with all this. I mean, not something that could cure you, at least not *medically* speaking. But I've got somethin' that could help you come to terms with what you're facing."

He went back to his dinosaur lunch box and removed two twenty-ounce water bottles filled with a murky liquid, so gray it was almost black. He handed them to Kenneth.

"It's called ayahuasca. It's totally natural – comes from a tree root. In fact, the chemical element is naturally occurring in the human body."

"What does it do?" Kenneth asked while unscrewing the cap.

"Whoa! Whoa! Don't drink that, my man." He probably wouldn't have as the smell was pungently repulsive. It had an earthy scent, like a marshy sludge mixed with mint and human waste.

"I thought you said it could help me?"

"Yeah, but not now. We gotta set up first."

"What do you mean?"

"It's a ritual. This shit ain't just a drug. You gotta respect it. Tribes in the Amazon have been doing it for centuries. It's a spiritual healer, a psychiatrist, a portal into other dimensions. At first they would just give it to soldiers who were dying, somethin' to help 'em come to terms with death and all. But they started havin' these ceremonies and fuck if these dudes didn't become the most enlightened and peaceful guys in South America.

"Now it's spread all over the globe, but it still manages to stay under the radar. But it's gotten just mainstream enough for 'em to make documentaries on it and shit. There are churches that use it to help people find God. People travel all over the world to help solve their psychological bullshit. A few hours on this shit is like a decade of psychotherapy. Scientists believe it's the key to evolutionary shifts, like on the long-term chart of our species, this is the shit that can make us jump from apes to free-thinking, computer-usin', skyscraper-buildin' sons of bitches. Just imagine, like this is the shit that makes X-men! Proper use of this shit and we could all be like fuckin' Magneto – more enlightened beings, at least." He chuckled an ominous laugh.

"I don't think moving things with my mind is really going to help my situation."

"Nah, man. You don't understand. You will *see* shit with this, shit that is real and unfathomable and beautiful. Shit that will let you see that death is just a part of something greater, and I ain't talkin' about angels flappin' their wings and all that. It's bigger."

"And how do we 'set up'?"

"We can do it tomorrow. I finally found a guy that's got a plot of land – Indian guy. Real good dude. It's gotta be outside, and it's gotta be nighttime. What d'ya say? You in?"

Kenneth could feel his clock counting down, and it was definitely now counting days rather than weeks. For something like this to present itself now seemed almost fateful, although Kenneth still had a hard time believing in fate. If he were to die doing a psychedelic drug on a ranch in India, it would at least be better than dying while smoking a joint on the roof of a hostel, and after crying in Justin's arms, feeling his empathy embrace him, feeling him take on his pain as his own, Kenneth thought that he would really like Justin to be there when he died.

13

RAJEEV'S FACE WAS SMOOTH AND brown like toffee. He was neatly groomed and freshly shaven. Despite the heat, he always wore a black leather jacket to show his elite status, emulating western culture, and he always wore a look of contempt and emptiness reflecting his career of serving the westerners whom he despised.

Riya had seen him as she went around back. Although she knew she had been caught in the act, she walked up to where Rajeev and Paul were locked in a dead stare and asked obliviously, "Is Kenneth home?" while holding yesterday's newspaper that she retrieved from the coffee table on her way around back.

"Go home, Riya," said Rajeev without taking his eyes off Paul. She tried to get a look from Paul. She wasn't looking for consolation or a lie telling her that it wasn't as bad as it was. She just wanted him to know that they were in it together. But Paul didn't break eye contact with Rajeev. He didn't watch as she ran fearfully back to her house.

"So what the fuck do you want?" Paul asked wrathfully once Riya was out of earshot. He had never liked Rajeev, and for some reason, his father's cancer heightened his distaste for Narayan, Rajeev, and Riya's father. The origin of his abhorrence of Narayan was obvious – he still believed that he had the rhino horn that could save his father, but wasn't giving it over. That, somehow, made the other Indian men who got in his way even more dislikable by association. He didn't even know Riya's father. Paul's racism, it seemed, was targeted, sharp, and illogical.

"You fucking Americans," Rajeev sneered through clenched teeth. "You come here and take our jobs, take our land, and then you think you can take our women?"

"Maybe it's just that you all do shitty work, you trash your land, and beat your women, so they all just kind of flock to us when we get here." This wasn't the direction the conversation should be moving, Paul knew. Rajeev held all the cards. Paul wasn't in a position to intimidate, but he just couldn't help it. It had been a while since he felt like a man.

Rajeev was well aware of this himself as he turned to exit, saying, "I think I'll go and have a quick talk with your neighbor. He might be interested to know where his daughter has been going every day."

Paul caught him by the arm, sweaty fingerprints quickly evaporating from the black leather.

"Wait," Paul asked calmly, defeated. He didn't want to bargain, but he had no choice. "What do you want?"

Rajeev looked around the room. Every wall, it seemed, was lined with gadgets. In America, the bedroom would have looked scarcely stocked with tech products and lacking. Here, it looked like a laboratory.

"That," he finally responded. He pointed in the direction of The Suit with a trembling finger, undeterminable whether the twitches were the product of fear or anger.

Paul chuckled softly. Who would want a *used* Suit? The thought was disgusting. When demand so greatly outweighed supply, sweaty and cum-filled origins went by the wayside, Paul guessed.

"Take it." Paul was wealthier now than he had ever been, and his *substantial* pay raise for his current project still hadn't shown itself in the form of an electronic deposit slip filled with zeroes. He could buy a hundred Suits when he got back.

Paul graciously loaded him up with the Suit, the headset, the genital compartment, the Suit-issued lubrication, and all of the cables and connectors. *Good luck figuring all that out,* he thought. He envisioned Rajeev naked in a corner, half-Suited, shoving the USB connection in his ass, filling his headset with lube.

Rajeev hauled the cumbersome load out to his van and threw it into the back seat where Paul would usually sit on his way to work.

"Hey!" Paul yelled before Rajeev could get in the driver's seat. "We're out of condoms! So, you know, when you get a chance…"

"Fuck you," he grumbled before speeding off. Both felt like the victorious parties of the altercation.

Paul hastily went to his laptop and remotely deleted the hard drive and disconnected his profile from his Suit. Otherwise, Rajeev would have had access to everyone on Paul's close friend list. He thought about Sheila awaiting his arrival with a table lined with whips and hotshots to see an angry and out of place Rajeev walking around the e-motel like a blind man with his headset on backwards.

As he logged onto his FlashConnect page, he saw three messages from Chrysanthemum.

What is going on with you? I'm worried. I feel like India is changing you.

And then:

You know what? Fuck you. You tell me you want to marry me, then you ignore me? You wanna know what I think? I think you're turning into one of those terrorist fucks over there. Maybe you don't have time for me because you're off bombing buildings and shit. Well have fun with that, dickhead. Next time you want to message to fuck me, just stick your dick in a bowl of curry.

And finally:

I'm sorry. I love you.

While his initial reaction was damage control, seeking the right words to lure her back and put himself in her good graces, he lacked the motive to do so. After watching public cremations, inching toward his first RW sexual encounter, the newfound knowledge of his father dying, and being ambiguously blackmailed by his chauffer, he just didn't have room for Chrissy's drama.

He decided that Riya and his father deserved all of his attention (or at least, his attention divided into two equal parts), and therefore, he needed to cut Chrissy loose.

It was distilling to find it so easy to discard someone who had been so crucial to his existence for so long. It wasn't so much the cutting-off-the-fat aspect, but just that something he had feared for so long didn't have the painful sting that he had been avoiding. It was quite calming, in fact. The opposite was true for his father. Perhaps Kenneth fell into the category of 'fat' in Paul's life, inessential and distracting, but he was still his father. He was his only parent left, his only connection with the past, the last member of his family.

Chrissy, however, was not.

He decided to video call her from his laptop since he lacked the means of meeting her in an e-motel. While being nude while breaking up with his girlfriend of one year didn't strike him as odd or awkward, entering an e-motel was always done with the anticipation of sex, and he didn't feel right giving her the false hope, even if he *did* have the means.

Video chats, like e-motels, were still preceded by government-funded election advertisements, and gearing up for the most confrontational phone call of his life, Paul, ironically, was greeted by Riya.

She stared back at him and told in clipped videos that her father was an evil man who ruined her life, in so many words, before a narrator read Paul's words and urged him to vote to save the countries of India and the United States of America from terrorism by voting to go to war. And just before it ended, Riya's eyes pierced into the camera lens, her voice containing an extra contralto behind it, shifted an octave down as she hauntingly warned, "We will ruin your life in this country."

The screen went blank, then revealed Chrissy's face, looking ready to strike, eyes already teetering between crying and scowling, ready to beg for him back or tear him to shreds.

Paul stared blankly from the other end. His eyes were glaring off to the edge of his screen, slightly averted from her stare, mouth barely open, terrified. It was on. The message was out in public, waiting to be seen by all. America was pressing to wage war against India, and the spokesperson behind the message of battle was an unknowing Riya.

Why wasn't he informed? His employer should have given him ample notice to exit the country before these advertisements went public. Although the messages were only to be broadcast to American citizens, to think that the potential victims of the propaganda wouldn't receive it just short of instantaneously was asinine.

We will ruin your lives in this country. That wasn't what she said. Did he really end the ad with such a haunting message? Or was it modified? And if so, by whom? The moment he asked himself these questions, he realized how easily soluble they were.

Chrysanthemum spoke on the other end, her tone perplexed and accusatory, but Paul couldn't make out a word through the ringing in his ears.

What did all of this mean? Why the fuck wasn't he notified? Normal issues hit hard with their advertisements three weeks before they went to the polls, on average. Something as substantial and potentially catastrophic as war would surely make its way to viral ads months before the election, unless the country wanted to strike quickly. Covert battle tactics were made somewhat archaic by the evolution of Fair e-Lect as those battle plans were to be voted on prior to execution, thus negating any covertness they might have had. The longer that the ads ran prior to election was just more time for India to prepare a counterstrike.

If he was seeing this now, so was Chrissy. So was the world.

He suddenly wondered if he had mistaken her fearful tone for one of anger and accusation. Maybe she was pleading for him to come home, to escape the catastrophe to come, but it was too late. He had already hung up on her.

That, he thought, was one way to break up with your girlfriend.

He tried contacting his employer, but he was offline, a first since Paul had had him on his contact list. He sent a series of messages, some enraged, some desperate, all exactly what was expected, asking why this was already going viral and he was still in India, when they would be evacuated, why he wasn't notified.

Although he now existed behind enemy lines and had just essentially broadcast himself to the world as being a spy for America, his primary concern was Riya. He wondered if there were any way to explain this, if there was any positive spin he could put on such a cataclysmic event where he wasn't the scum of the earth. He had to try.

But as he rushed toward her house, he saw that his troubles were still escalating.

Rajeev's van was parked outside Riya's house as he had apparently just circled the block after departing Paul's home. Outside the back door, Rajeev and Riya's father were engaged in a clandestine conversation, one that even from such a distance, its magnitude and severity were more than obvious, as Riya's father's gaze slowly shifted up and followed Rajeev's outstretched finger that was burning a hole in the center of Paul's forehead framed perfectly in his back window.

14

THE CEREMONY BEGAN JUST AFTER dusk.

In the time spent waiting in nervous anticipation, she entertained them with memories of her last experience on ayahuasca.

"She showed me all of the most traumatic events in my life. She laid them out in front of me. I was bawling like a baby. Justin had to hold me and puke for me to get me through it. But then, it was like I had these haunting memories stored inside me for so long, and once she showed them to me in a specific order, in the perspective of the grander scheme, they made sense. They were *necessary*. And I was at total peace. I've felt so much better since. And with the time remaining on my journey, after all of the hard work was done, she asked me if I wanted to see other life forms in other galaxies – her other creations. We travelled light years and saw completely foreign beings, but my time was up, and I returned to this plane of existence."

Kenneth asked the more obvious question. "Who is *she?*"

"Oh, sorry," she giggled. "Mother Ayahuasca."

He decided to let the rest of his questions go and attribute them to a religion based on superstition and psychedelic drugs.

They were at Ishaan's farmhouse just outside the city. He was a timid and amiable native, a friend of Justin's, who didn't speak much on account of his self-consciousness with the English language. Aside from Ishaan, Kenneth, and Justin, there was the only female of the group, an *actual* Canadian by the name of Nora. She looked like someone Justin would befriend, mostly on account of the colorful tattoos that covered the majority of her body. Dark eyeliner extended her eyes toward her hairline on both sides, giving them an inauthentic Asian quality. Her face had an intriguing sort of welcome to it, like a dubious smile, eyes somewhere between warm and manipulative, like arms so open that you rush in to hug before noticing the daggers in her hands. Kind of like Justin. And like Justin, her initial impression made was quite warm and affectionate, but without the ramblings of an insane person. Kenneth liked her immediately.

All four of them had brought sleeping bags as the ceremony was to take place outside on the ground, but the unforeseen rainstorm brought them indoors.

The farmhouse was actually two houses connected by a sort of skywalk, an open vestibule on the second story covered by a tin roof. This was to be the alternative setting now that sleeping on the ground was no longer an option. The narrow walkway had just enough room for four sleeping bags with 'vomit bowls' next to each and the two ice chests full of supplies. According to Justin, performing the ceremony inside was highly dangerous as the spirits weren't free to come and go, that they would feel contained, and that nature was an integral part of the journey. Kenneth wanted to scoff at this and push to move the festivities indoors as the ideas of 'spirits' and 'journeys' were a little too whimsical for his tastes, but he decided to keep his mouth shut. Justin and Nora scrutinized the location for the better part of an hour, standing by the ledge and judging the visibility of the skyline, scanning the adjoined attic space that would be their bathroom, and looking for spots to post their perimeter markings before agreeing that it was their best viable option. Nora was apparently an ayahuasca veteran, as was Justin.

As they all started laying out their respective sleeping bags, the tension began to mount. Kenneth could feel his veins pumping extra loads, covering him in tingling sensations and a cool sweat.

They were each given a white ceramic bowl to contain their regurgitations and shown the makeshift toilet over a bucket lined with a black garbage bag in the attic space for when the ayahuasca diarrhea came on. This part concerned Kenneth.

"A huge part of this," said Justin as the sun descended toward the horizon like a countdown, "is expelling negative energy. You might do this by farting, puking, shitting, but it's all good. You're getting rid of all the negative shit you have stored inside you, like a physical and psychological cleansing. Every little bit you get out will make your visions less terrifying, so don't be embarrassed. We're all friends here. And Nora knows," the two shared a knowing look and a chuckle, "I've done the most embarrassing shit, so trust me, you can't do any worse than me."

"What did you do?" asked Kenneth. Nora and Justin both belly-laughed, Nora to the point of bringing tears to her eyes.

"Last time, I apparently stripped down naked in front of a bunch of people I had just met that day, ran around shitting myself and jacking off on one of the girls there. I don't remember a fuckin' thing, but I felt great the next morning, aside from the shit all over my ass!"

This was much bigger than Kenneth had anticipated.

"Are you fucking serious?"

"Yeah, man," he laughed. He was unloading the contents of the first ice chest. A headlamp wrapped tightly around his forehead illuminated various items in front of him – two coffee mugs, twenty hastily rolled tobacco cigarettes, a box of breath mints, a bell, a digital music drive, a speaker, four purple wildflowers, eight candles, four stones the size of dictionaries, three lighters, and ten water bottles. The liquid in eight of the bottles was transparent, the last two filled with the gray matter that Kenneth had smelled the night previous. "But don't worry. That was just 'cause we did it indoors. Like I said, man, being outside is crucial. I just wigged out 'cause I was locked in a box, ya know? You'll be cool, though."

"Are you sure? I'm starting to freak out a little."

"Don't worry, bro. I'll be here to help you. You're mind is gonna go on a bit of a journey, and it'll show you some shit that you don't like, and some that you do – that you *really* do. But if any of it gets too intense, just tell me and I'll help steer you through it. Remember, you can control it. So if the shit you're seein' is too fucked up, tell it to show you somethin' else and it'll listen. And I'll be there to make sure you don't injure yourself or anything."

"Injure myself?"

"Sometimes your body doesn't quite work the way it should and some people take some nasty spills, but I won't let you go anywhere alone."

"So what you're saying is, I might be puking and shitting and walking like a drunk person. I'm a little concerned, mostly about the shitting mixing with the inability to walk correctly."

"Seriously, man. Don't worry. I'll be there to guide you. Even if you're shitting and you need some help, just call for me. I've helped a couple of other dudes shit while journeyin', so don't feel ashamed."

"But aren't you going to be doing the ayahuasca, too?"

"I've got to, man. That's the only way we can connect. If I didn't, you probably wouldn't even be able to ask me for help."

Nothing had even begun, and Kenneth already felt like he was drowning.

Ishaan was sitting in the corner watching the dialogue, but probably not understanding anymore than fifteen percent, still smiling like he was trying to make a good impression. Kenneth wondered if *he* knew what the night had in store for them.

The sun retreated beneath the horizon, turning everything to a violet shade of black. The constant beating of raindrops on the concrete below made everything seem darker, more dangerous, ensuring that any light grumbles of pain and uncertainty would go unnoticed. Justin lit the first cigarette and blew puffs of smoke on all solid objects in a large ellipsis surrounding their sleeping bags and bathroom. Nora trailed behind him with a burning piece of sage, climbing up on the railing to ensure that the smoke touched the ceiling above them, then bending down to blow the smoke down toward the floor. Nora and Justin then identified the cardinal directions and started at the north corner, which happened to be the railing just in front of Kenneth's sleeping bag where he now sat with his legs crossed in the yoga position. Nora placed a purple wildflower on the ledge next to a lit candle while Justin closed his eyes and muttered a long prayer in an unknown language. When the prayer was done, he lit the new cigarette pinched between his lips and blew cloud after cloud of smoke onto the flower. After doing this for the better part of a minute, the process repeated for the stone. He prayed to it, blew smoke onto it, then placed it atop the flower on the handrail.

When the process began again in the attic/bathroom that represented the eastern corner, he summoned Kenneth to witness.

"I'll do this one in English so you understand, cool?"

Kenneth nodded nervously.

The two of them squatted next to a flower the size of Kenneth's pinky finger. Justin closed his eyes soulfully and began the prayer. His voice was just above a whisper, heavy with sincerity and purpose.

"Flower. You are delicate. You are colorful. You are beautiful. You have grown from our Mother Earth, fed by the water from the heavens above. You are life. You are beauty. Show us the beauty that exists in the world.

Show us all that is good and nothing that is harmful. Show us the way to enlightenment. Show us all that is positive. Show us love. Show us beauty."

He blew the smoke on it, then had Kenneth do the same before placing it on the ground amidst a temporary toilet, a hot dog grill, and other random items that you would find in an attic in the middle of rural India.

"Rock. You are hard. You are strong. You are the Earth. You are the beginning of all things. May you surround us and protect us. Act as our guardian. Allow all that is good to enter, and nothing that is harmful. Keep us safe as we strive to find our true purpose. Help us become one with the Earth. Keep fear away. Allow love inside. Show us strength."

More smoke. Kenneth blew only one puff this time as his mouth was dry and he was already about to vomit from nervousness. He retreated to his spot atop his sleeping bag provided by Justin while Justin and Nora finished the south and west corners. This part of the ceremony took forty minutes and six cigarettes.

Then it was their turn. Nora held the burning sage and held it a couple of inches from her skin and let it glide over the entire surface of her body, using her other hand to waft the smoke under her arms, behind her back, under her legs, and around her neck. She looked like she was bathing, and essentially, she was, only she was bathing in a spiritualism that Kenneth just didn't quite understand. When she finished, she held the burning sage in his direction.

"Sage?" she asked, as if it was a matter of preference. Kenneth wanted to refuse for fear of looking foolish as he wasn't sure the purpose of this ritual, but at the same time, his fear was consistently escalating, and he figured he could use any protection he could get, even if it was rooted in a fantastical belief system that he still wasn't sure about.

He took the sage and stood, mimicking the movements he just watched Nora make, only he didn't take quite as long, anxious to pass the burning torch on to a seemingly aloof Ishaan. Ishaan and Justin bathed in the smoke, Justin taking twice as long as Nora. Then Justin, still with the headlamp around his forehead like something between a miner and a mad scientist, asked everyone to stand.

All four faced the east as Justin spoke the first words in the past hour that were above a whisper.

"Spirit of the East, Brother Eagle, be with us. Fly us high so our prayers can reach the creator. May we have eyes as strong as yours. May we see the Earth as you see it. May we see the path that we must take. Give us the courage to walk that path. Brother Eagle, be with us." Nora rang the bell as she and Justin bowed, Ishaan and Kenneth following suit. Kenneth was about to dry heave in fear.

The four shifted ninety degrees to the right.

"Spirit of the South, Jaguar, be with us. Let us have your heart as we journey out into the unknown. Let us feel compassion for all creatures of Mother Earth. Let us use our hearts to their fullest capacity, even when we're afraid to use them. Jaguar, be with us. Show us love."

Ring. Bow. Turn.

"Spirit of the West, Brown Bear, be with us. Allow us to heal. Allow us to connect with one another and help us to connect the physical, mental, and spiritual so that we may know our places on Mother Earth in life and in death. Heal our bodies. Heal our minds. Bring light, joy, and awareness into our hearts. Brother Bear, be with us."

Ring. Bow. Turn.

"Spirit of the North, White Buffalo, be with us. Allow us to let go of our failures. Let us see all that is wrong so that we may learn from it. Help us to journey safely and to return to the physical realm with gained wisdom. White Buffalo, be with us."

Ring. Bow.

"And now we will state our purposes, what you wish to seek in your journey. I'll start.

"I wish to guide our newcomers into the spiritual realm, to act as their shaman and protector, to keep them safe from fear and guide them to light, love, and beauty."

He then nudged his chin in Kenneth's direction.

"I... uh... I wish to come to terms with my own mortality and to gain understanding of powers unseen." It didn't feel like enough, but anymore would have brought forth another weeping session.

Ishaan gave his soliloquy in Hindi, possibly to hide his broken English, possibly to hide his intentions.

Nora looked at Kenneth with grave concern. She sensed the journey that laid before him. She saw something powerful and potentially destructive, and knew that she must abandon her own intentions.

"I also wish to help the newcomers and protect them as they walk difficult paths and pray that those paths lead them to ultimate beauty." Her eyes never came off of Kenneth.

The four of them sat with legs crossed at their respective sleeping bags, no words uttered, Kenneth's eyes bouncing around for anything calming to look at, anything to distract him from the magnitude of this ceremony. He felt like he went to the airport to fly back to Texas and instead was instructed to board a spaceship bound for another galaxy. He had no idea what he was getting into, but he was already strapped in as Mission Control had already begun the countdown.

T-minus ten...

Justin worked in the only light available as the candles offered little in the way of illumination as the constant breeze kept them at the smallest flame possible before extinguishment. He poured the dark liquid into a coffee cup, almost all the way up to the brim, and extended it to Kenneth.

"Cheers,"

Nine...

Kenneth downed the contents in three large gulps, each more revolting than the one before. He had previously identified the smell of the liquid as swamp water mixed with mint leafs and feces, and it tasted even worse, but similar. He exhaled vehemently, bringing the taste back with every breath. He swallowed and gulped, swallowed and gulped. Anything to keep from vomiting.

Eight...

Justin pushed the box of mints his way to rid himself of the taste. He chewed four of them to no avail.

Seven...

The cup was filled and drank. Filled and drank. And then it came to Justin. He gave Kenneth a clandestine wink before chugging the same disgusting liquid that he had a few minutes before.

Six...

To Kenneth's dismay, he was only half finished with the ingestion portion of the ceremony. It seemed that there were two bottles for a reason. As Justin had previously mentioned, the chemical in the ayahuasca that catalyzed the journey was naturally occurring in the human body. In order to feel the desired effects, one must drink an inhibitor to shut down the body's natural defense mechanisms to the chemical, an inhibitor that Kenneth had already ingested. The cup that Justin was pouring was the actual ayahuasca.

Five...

Justin handed him the second cup. He drank it. Unbelievably, it was worst than the first.

Four...

He was seated between Justin and Ishaan, and waited as Justin poured the next cup that he was to pass to Ishaan. His skin began to tingle, perhaps in anticipation, perhaps in reaction to the horrid taste of the drink.

Three...

Bugs were crawling on his skin. Everywhere.

Two...

He passed the cup to Ishaan. His breath was quickening. He couldn't sit up anymore.

One...

He crashed lifelessly into a horizontal position and closed his eyes.

Ignition.

Like a plague of cockroaches, it was narrowing in on him from all sides. Miles away yet right beneath his skin. The blackness was sporadically interrupted by beams of green light. His breath was panicky. His hands moved from his sides to atop his belly to atop his thighs back to his sides back to his belly back to his sides. Nothing felt right. This was bad. He could already tell. It was like that feeling you get when you are jarred from a nightmare and your body comes leaping out of REM paralysis, but right at the pinnacle where you are between sleep and waking, that split second where the tension comes rushing in like a tidal wave, just before the body jolts. It was that moment stretched across hours, barreling at light speed and somehow constantly accelerating.

Justin turned on the music. A Hindu woman was chanting a dirge and accompanied by instruments that were either nonexistent or the likes of which Kenneth had never previously known. He felt it coursing through him, thick and sludgy, sprouting thousands of legs and crawling through his veins, its thickness ripping him apart.

Something in his head was wrestling him for the controls. He could feel the wheel of the ship spinning with the waves. He could feel his hands unable to slow the rotation. He could feel an outside entity reaching for the wheel, nudging him out of the way, but he couldn't do it. He couldn't surrender all that he was to this dark and ambiguous figure, this cloaked assailant shadowed by the recesses of his mind.

A green crucifix beamed out brightly but distant, shining through the blackness ahead like a fading nebula.

He could hear Ishaan vomiting, and he instantly did the same. Justin congratulated him as he emptied the contents of his already barren stomach into the white bowl beside him. Something about good job, get it out, that's all the negative energy inside you.

It didn't stop. He purged and purged again. It was the only thing in the physical realm that he could see. Justin spoke to him from above, like he was sitting on a bar stool up above while Kenneth was lying on the ground, but more realistically, he was probably hovering somewhere around the ceiling.

The music was like a puff of smoke, beginning in a tiny ember, then veering off in the thousand directions that were his auditory hallucinations, vast and indecipherable, a haunting cacophony. Behind it was the static of a hard rain. Among the noises that spun around his head were machines grinding, oboes blaring, children screaming, and poor Ishaan puking his guts out in the corner, just as Kenneth was.

The shadow was now wrestling Kenneth for the controls of the ship. His mind was hollowing out as if acid was poured into his brain, reducing all of his thoughts and memories to liquid, as some parasitic entity slithered in to work him like a puppet. In response, Kenneth's muscles all tightened with bone-shattering force. He twitched in violent subtleties.

Then came the visual hallucinations. Pictures moving too fast to discern, but sharp and abrasive, tearing through his hollowed out skull like a vicious swarm of red hornets. He felt like he was crouched beneath an onslaught of raining arrows, turning his shield to deflect them, but they came from every direction, even straight up from underneath. He moved around in convulsions and wondered why no one was intervening, but his body was paralyzed and motionless in the physical realm.

Tiny meteorites the size of golf balls rained down and tore through his flesh with minimal resistance.

Bleeding gums.

A stranger's face.

Complex machines.

Paul.

Each was a rock tearing through his flesh and turning him into a giant sieve.

The nausea was thick and abrasive. Whether it was the sludge of the ayahuasca or the demons that haunted him, it thickened his blood to a muddy acid, coursing through him like magma, burning, ripping, then erupting in frequent upheavals.

"I... can't..."

Justin was sitting up watching over the ordeal from between sleeping bags, galaxies away from where Kenneth was lying. He smoked on the rolled tobacco and blew smoke on every sleeping bag containing a body but no mind as each was journeying into realms unknown. The smoke escaped from both cheeks as he had removed the plugs for the night.

"I can't... handle... this."

Justin reached out and touched his forehead as if channeling the negative energy from Kenneth into his own body, just before vomiting into his own ceramic bowl. Nora put her hands under Kenneth's head and stabilized his neck. Justin puked again.

"Look at that," Nora said, her voice like a god rushing into Kenneth's rearview as he sped by. "So much negative energy. Look at the bile. It's thick with demons."

Justin began singing in Hindi as Nora adjusted all of Kenneth's limbs as he must have borne the body position of someone who had just jumped off a building.

"Can you hear me?" Her voice was sweet and assuring, but so many light years away that Kenneth couldn't even reach for them. "I'm going to turn you on your side so you don't choke on your vomit, okay?"

Kenneth couldn't respond. Not with a grunt. Not with a blink. His body had already been abandoned.

A thousand faces were staring at him. Not one was familiar. Razor blades were cutting through his face.

Justin and Kenneth both puked simultaneously.

"Get it out for him, Justin," Nora pleaded. "He needs help. Puke for him some more." He did as he was told, but none of this was heard by Kenneth. Although it was said to be the negativity leaving the body, nothing was getting better for Kenneth.

As if Kenneth's body heard Nora, he then proceeded to shit himself.

This brought Kenneth a little closer to the physical realm as he heard Justin pleading with him to stand, to help him get to the toilet. Kenneth swore he spoke and told him that he couldn't, but Justin only saw a pale, dead face, eyelashes lightly fluttering as the friend he knew was far, far away.

Justin hoisted him into a standing position and bear-hugged him, dragging him into the bathroom while Nora pulled his pants down. The two of them guided his body to the toilet and sat him down. His body, lifeless and top-heavy, crashed to the ground after catching a corner of the hot dog grill, piercing Kenneth's back, a pain that didn't reach him, that was miniscule to the torture he was enduring.

The miles of intestine that stretched between his esophagus and his rectum were full of this so-called negative energy and emptied themselves into the bucket like a serpent in a twisted Garden of Eden scenario, so much that Kenneth thought he was eviscerating.

In every second, a hundred faces of strangers flashed before his eyes. And then, a familiar one.

That little girl. She had dropped from the rowboat and sat at the bottom of the Ganges River long enough to be completely picked apart by scavenging marine life, but now she looked directly into Kenneth's eyes. He suddenly understood all of the faces staring at him. They were the recently deceased, the souls that would accompany him in crossing the Great Divide. They all looked enraged and ready to attack.

And then came the deity.

She wasn't Mother Ayahuasca. She was something much more. The only relation between the drink and her was the relationship that a door had with a beautiful woman standing on the other side.

He shuddered in her presence, knowing that she was near enough to feel his breath, but her position still unknown. The blackness was all-consuming. The beams of light were fewer and revealed nothing. But she was there. She was watching. She was judging.

Kenneth felt weak and exposed, more naked than he had ever felt, like he was ripped open to reveal every darkness that existed within him, every secret left untold, every lie, every sin, every dark desire swallowed down inside him. They all escaped like a swarm of bats erupting into the night sky.

She showed comfort. She showed mercy.

The pain, for the first time since ingesting the poison, was gently subsiding, yet all the knives were still in place, the blade of the guillotine rising to its pinnacle.

She wanted to show him how to die. She wanted to show him that he could cross through miles of Hell to feel the light of her presence, but he would have to do just that. The torture was only beginning. Everything up to that point was akin to a needle prick, and he was about to be drawn and quartered.

I will show you everything.

I will peel your skin from your body. I will dissolve your muscles in acid. I will burn your insides to ashes. And then the pain will be gone.

I will show you everything.

I will show you beauty.

Take me back.

He cried. He was weak. He was an infant. He wasn't strong like Justin. He wasn't smart like Narayan. He wasn't new like Paul. There was nothing unique about him. He was dead. He was erased.

Take me back.

The auditory hallucinations that spiraled around him slowed to a halt, like truck tires on a highway or a machine after being shut down, beginning with a high-pitched humming and winding slowly down into a grumble. His vision of the world, the everything that she had lain out for him, sucked away as if through a vacuum, and the physical realm seeped back in.

And so he returned to the broken and ugly world with vomit on his tongue and shit smeared across his ass. He opened his eyes and saw the pink glow of dawn. He vomited. The pain was gone, aside from the sharp pain in the center of his abdomen, just below his sternum, right where his pancreas was shutting down.

The cold morning breeze brought with it a hangover of epic proportions. His legs were just learning to walk again. He didn't pack a toothbrush, and he had vomit encrusted to the backs of his teeth. His muscles were sore from twitching. His face was swollen from crying. He took shelter under the blanket of his sleeping bag, hiding from his own shame. To escape any questions about his journey, he taught himself to walk again with the pleasant task of digging a hole out in the bushes to bury the waste from the toilet bucket. He felt like he was going to collapse.

The others carried the supplies down the stairs while Kenneth disrobed around back and washed off his backside with a garden hose. He dug another smaller hole and buried his underwear.

As they loaded up the car, disappointment rumbling in Kenneth's gut, like a family packing up after driving across the country to find that Disneyland had closed down, Ishaan spouted off in enthusiastic sentence fragments filled with grammatical errors about his intense journey, about the life lessons learned, about the changes he would make, about the glorious new perspective he had gained. Kenneth wanted to vomit on him.

Kenneth, Nora, and Justin got into the car and bid farewell to the new Ishaan. He waved at them through the windshield as they backed out, his face overcome with profound joy, like he was watching his kids being driven off to their first day of school.

The car belonged to Narayan, and borrowing it was a tough sell. First he had to convince Narayan that he had an Indian friend who could drive on the unforgiving and chaotic streets of New Delhi, then Kenneth had to organize the pickup at a time when Narayan would be out of the house so that he wouldn't see that Kenneth's 'Indian' friend was Justin. Narayan was gone for the weekend on his other vehicle, a white scooter.

Justin proved to be an excellent driver. Being a good driver in the states had no bearing on abilities in India. To conquer the streets of Delhi, one had to be an experienced stunt driver. Justin's calmness behind the wheel, the antithesis of the hysteria in every window, was a testament to the highly adaptable world traveler that he was.

Justin asked Kenneth about his experience, if there was anything to be gained, if maybe the pain was presenting some moral deeply entombed in torture and diarrhea. Kenneth dismissed this quickly, not wanting to tell of the maggots, the millipedes that crawled through the letters "F A I L U R E" as he descended back to the physical realm after asking the deity to release him.

After the silence burned through him, he sat in the back seat and tried to discern among the *millions* of images seen throughout the night, all of them meaningless and mostly forgotten. He clawed through his brain for some gift that she left behind, any alternative denouement to his life than the epiphanic prophecy that he failed in everything he had ever done and the parting gift of a pair of shit-stained underwear.

He brought up the green-lit cross that brought him through the doorway into his tortuous journey. Nora looked dumbfounded, but she was probably just exhausted from wiping a grown man's ass all night.

"You know," Justin responded, "there are many different meanings behind the cross. People have seen symbols that they had never seen before while journeying and later learned of their significance. The meaning of the symbols completely coincided with everything they experienced during the journey. And I know that the cross had many other meanings *before* Christianity. You should look into it."

Religion was such a logical answer, and that was why they were so quick to dismiss it. They existed on the fringes. They feared the mainstream, and any answer that required no arduous path to get to it wasn't worth entertaining, even if it meant missing the bigger picture.

Kenneth was equally disappointed and relieved by this explanation.

As the pollution thickened and the density of the buildings multiplied, as the city began to sprout up around their car, Kenneth felt like he was abandoning hope. He kept searching for some greater answer, some unseen epiphany that would make everything okay, but seeing the dense smog wrapped around the tan clumps of city that lay ahead, he knew that he was crossing the boundary back to reality, that the fantastical and unknown solutions were now in the rearview. There was no turning around.

They dropped off Nora at her hostel just inside the city. She exited the car with a solemn gaze in Kenneth's direction, but offered no verbal farewell. She passed the derelict owner conversing with this neighbor and entered the glass doorway into the ramshackle building and exited his life forever. He felt like an angel had just departed from his life. Although he only knew her for a brief evening while in the grips of a psychedelic nightmare, he somehow felt unsafe, like some force field had opened up and left him naked and vulnerable now that she was gone.

Justin took a highway that circumvented the city to get to the north side as driving in the streets of Delhi was dangerous enough for a native. Justin smoked one of the remaining tobacco cigarettes. He wasn't a smoker outside of the ceremony, but his gears were turning and grinding and blowing out puffs of steam, his teeth once again grinding visibly through the periscopes in his cheeks.

"I'm sorry, Ken," he said, his voice direct yet saturnine.

"Don't be... I mean... It's not your fault."

"Nah, man. I'm sorry." He turned away from the road and looked deeply into Kenneth. "I wanted this to be huge for you. I wanted you to walk away feeling better about your life than you ever had. But it did the inverse – *I* did the inverse."

They both wanted to say more, to hug, to bring the night to some beautiful conclusion, but there was none to be had. Justin opened his mouth to speak once more, but as he did three airplanes rocketed by overhead with supersonic force, the G's screaming off the fins of the aircrafts sounding like they were tearing apart the sky.

Just like a boxer faking a strike with his left just before a right jab, the roaring engines drew their attention to the skies that offered no visible explanation to the sound, then created the real spectacle in the direction that Kenneth and Justin were previously staring in the form of three mushroom clouds of fire and smoke, spewing up into the sky, followed by three booms that shook the windows and compressed their lungs like plastic bags getting ready to pop, leaving both of them gasping for their next breath.

PART III

1

THE YEAR THAT LITTLE PAUL got caught saying his first curse word was the same year that he got his first computer. The two incidents were entirely unrelated, yet elicited a similar sensation. They were both new and dark, seemingly boundless in their possibilities. They both landmarked a new territory, a step up on the ladder that pinnacled at manhood. They paved roads into thorny woods filled with howling unknowns. And although they both could possibly be used for good purposes, they were so much more commonly used for the more intriguing bad ones.

It was his mother's idea, and his father fought it tooth and nail, but as always, he conceded to Mom's almighty reign of the household. She won the debate by means of argumentative blitzkrieg, throwing lines of reasoning like hand grenades at her speechless husband. *All the other kids have them. It'll help him study. It'll help him socialize with other children. It'll act as a babysitter.* Kenneth's arguments were Neolithic by comparison.

Meredith walked her son through the basic operations of the laptop computer, then left him to explore. The computer in his room was like a doorway to a limitless realm where everything was accessible, nothing was impossible. During the first week, Paul's average nine hours of sleep per night had been reduced to four. He marveled at the infiniteness of the virtual world. The longer he was lost inside, the smaller his room, his house, his street, and his town seemed. Breakfasts were bland. Bath time was meaningless. Every second away was spent in yearning.

Meredith's 'study' argument was quickly proven null as Paul wasn't completing his assignments on time. While before he had to ask permission to use one of his parents' computers to complete his assignment and do so under scrutiny, he now had the freedom to do his work in his own sanctuary and at his own leisure. But the addictive lure of the internet dragged him away from responsibility no matter how hard his parents tugged on the other end.

It wasn't long before Paul discovered pornography, and with it, he discovered masturbation. Parental controls were so easily circumvented, even by an adolescent new to the virtual world. More and more sharply pointed doors opened and revealed newer and darker territories with every pornographic movie enjoyed. The female form was so enigmatic, yet so simple. Where men had this hanging appendage with so much versatility in rigidity, size, shape, color, and texture, the woman had *nothing*, just a flat surface. Beneath that, a mysterious line of flesh, an entrance point. How could something so simple, something concave and mostly unseen, something so small and lacking be so *beguiling?* And the act of fornication, it was so intrusive and ugly. It was as filthy as viewing a surgical operation. It was as abrasive and violent as an assault, and yet it was the most alluring image he had ever seen.

More and more sites were visited. Assignments were procrastinated. Doors were locked. Socks were dirtied.

About the time that even the various acts of sex that flashed across his monitor were bordering mundane for little Paul, he came across a category of pornography that incited a curious feeling of intrigue: cartoon pornography.

At first it was simple curiosity, a novelty that had to be investigated. The video was a popular animated series about a farmer and his wife and the animals that resided on the farm, one that he used to watch on Saturday mornings. Only in this episode, the plot went straight to… what you would imagine. And something about this allured Paul. Those characters that he had grown up with were now engaged in such an adult situation, the worlds of his past and present colliding in an act of cartoon intercourse. The sanctity and wholesomeness that came with characters drawn on the screen rather than just filmed was now compromised, and that break from the anticipated, that drastic left turn from morally decent to wickedly depraved had Paul working his joystick furiously.

One thing that was different from animated pornography and live pornography was that cartoons had the ability to change scenes quickly and tended to do so as either the people who viewed those sort of videos were looking more for rapid humor, or they were just notoriously premature ejaculators. As Paul broke out into a sweat watching the farmer's wife bounce up and down atop her husband, the scene quickly shifted to a cow standing on its hind legs with four, humanlike breasts down where its udders should have existed, engaged in unspeakable acts with a plump, pink pig. It was then that Kenneth walked into the room unannounced, witnessing his son, sweat beaded on his upper lip, pants shackling his ankles together, a long white sock perched up from his lap before hanging lifelessly like a windsock on a calm day. In front of him was an act of cartoon interspecies fellatio. It seemed that even the cow and pig stopped for a moment as the four of them retained a silent, paralyzed stare, shocked and unable to move to the next moment, whether that moment be scolding, denying, screaming, lying, or just walking away. Kenneth's eyes finally made the long, darting scan of the room before turning his head outdoors, mumbling something about dinner being ready as he closed the door on his foot that struggled to keep up with the rest of his body.

After tidying himself up, a mortified Paul descended the staircase like he was walking to the electric chair. He entered the kitchen, pale and uncomfortable, as his mother was just sitting down at the table. Kenneth was at the counter pouring himself a drink, his back to Paul, his hand on the crown of his head, scratching frenetically. Meredith's expressions were always quite transparent, and her blithe smile proved that his father told her nothing of the atrocities witnessed upstairs. She asked questions about his day and his growing pile of schoolwork. He gave low-decibel, one- and two-word answers. His father sat down at the table.

An undeniable tension existed. Paul kept waiting for the blade to drop. No punishment could be worse than this, aside from the three of them having an open discussion about the matter. Kenneth's mouth opened to speak, and it seemed that he had granted him amnesty.

"How's the schoolwork coming?" he asked.

Paul was caught off-guard, going through the answers he had prepared for dinner table accusations and sex talks, and now had to sift through them for a rebuttal to a question of schoolwork.

"It's... It's alright, I guess."

"Well," Kenneth continued. "You need to keep up and stop playing so many of those video games." His tone didn't fluctuate, but both of them knew the second he said 'those video games' exactly what he meant. Paul finally gained the confidence to make eye contact with his father. Kenneth smiled. It was a confused, distraught smile, a struggle to appear unworried, but he pulled it off. The event was never mentioned.

It wasn't until Riya spoke of her father and the odd and sometimes abusive ways that he treated her that this moment came back to life in Paul's memory. She said that mothers were adaptable, were guided by their hearts and with the unconditional love of a mother, they could shake off any hurt, embrace any deformity, and keep running full speed no matter the terrain of the road. Fathers, on the other hand, were constantly trying to figure out their children. Any discrepancy between the men that they were and the people that their children became was a Rubik's cube, a riddle that toyed with them with every glance at their offspring. They wanted to love and to teach and to mold, but they never imagined that the child they produced wouldn't be identical to themselves. Fathers dealt with this differently. Some tried to understand, and some just tried to cope. Those who coped might run away, they might abuse, they might ignore their children. It's an ugly fact of life and a strange way that our DNA fits imperfectly in our society, but it's just one of many hardships that we must face, and just as our fathers, endure.

Paul thought about this and remembered that look on his father's face at the dinner table so many years ago. Now, as an adult, Paul could look back and discern so many things to which he was oblivious at the time. Kenneth was perplexed, perhaps even disgusted at his own son's actions, but he did all that he could to mask that discontent to shield his son from the shame.

Paul thought about the father he never really knew, the father who existed in the shadow of his mother, and now that she was gone, the two of them seemed to stand face-to-face for the first time and just didn't know how to act. The father who was now dying. It seemed that they had missed so much that was right there in front of them, but they just didn't know how to tell one another. If they had just opened their mouths and let it all spill out, they would've found some common ground. Just like Paul and Riya, existing in cultures that disdained one another, forcing themselves in one another's proximity and learning to love one another, so would have been Paul and Kenneth if they had just found a means to do so.

Paul thought about this as he watched Riya's father, instead of charging toward Paul's home, withdrawing into his own. He watched as the curtains shuddered. He listened as doors slammed and screams yelped across the distance between the two houses. The only curtainless window revealed Riya, her head shaking to and fro, those wide eyes of hers drawn downward at the sides, just before being viciously slapped across the face, her body dropping inanimately beneath the windowsill and out of view.

Fear electrified Paul. His thoughts raced through ideas of fathers and daughters, unknown cultures, empty distractions. He thought about Riya's explanation of fathers not understanding their children and acting out in different ways. Basically, Paul was searching frantically for justification to stay hidden inside his house, any reason that could trump the motive of cowardice.

In nearly inaudible shrieks, fading in the wind and distance, her voice rang out in quick squeals with every blow delivered, but her strength kept her from any elongated bellow of pain or cry for help, and with every blow, Paul despised her father, Paul feared for his love, but could do nothing to intervene. He thought about everything that went on behind those walls to which he had no knowledge. Anywhere in the country, he was the outsider, but even a native had to have the strongest of inclinations to enter another's house to challenge the patriarch of the household. Everything beyond those walls was off-limits, or at least this was the explanation that Paul gave to combat his spinelessness.

He wasn't so much afraid of the physical pain of being beaten, but the shame of it. He didn't want to be emasculated in front of Riya, in front of anyone for that matter. He chose not to think that merely entering the house to come to her aid would give him godlike status in her eyes, no matter the beating that would follow. And besides the pain, Paul was the enemy from the first day of his arrival in the country, and the newfound information issued by Rajeev would certainly push the beating at least to the outer boundaries of *murder*, if not completely over and past them.

Riya's father emerged from the house. A hundred times more frightening than the enraged expression he bore when entering the house, his face now seemed blank. Devoid of emotion, he was robotic in his movements and motives. His chest and shoulders moved up and down with his heaving breaths. A long, wooden rod hung down by his side, the diameter of a thumb, thin enough for rapid movement and thick enough to deliver serious pain and injury. He was walking straight toward an unseen Paul, still hiding on the floor, peeking through the lower corner of the open window.

Paul's initial instinct was to hide. He ran frantically around his house, choosing a spot that would keep him safe from the violently charged assailant sauntering robotically toward him. He looked in the pantry, the closet, under the bed, but the house wasn't very large and didn't offer the variety of options that most American houses did. He came to the realization that hiding was a stupid idea as Riya's father would rip the entire house apart to find him, so he decided to run.

He crept around the house, avoiding the windows. He exited the front door as fast as silence would allow him. Before setting off in a full sprint, he peered around the corner of the house and saw Riya, desperate but not crying, one eye swollen from the assault to which she had just been the victim, running toward her father and shouting one word over and over again. *Nahin! Nahin!* In the hours and days after this event, Paul would question the meaning of that one word. He would hear it repeat in his dreams. More than likely, it meant 'no' or 'stop.' 'Please,' maybe. But as words were presented in foreign languages as phrases and vice-versa, perhaps that short utterance could have meant something larger, like 'fuck you,' 'what is wrong with you?' or 'kill him.' And in those moments of retrospect, of the past haunting him with an attack of that word repeated over and over like a merciless swarm of bees, Paul would seek a more pleasant meaning to attach to the words, but he found that the most pleasurable meaning was also the most damaging, and forever he would remember the love of his life chasing down her enraged father, shouting, "I love him!"

With a movement so swift and hidden behind the mass that his body displaced, Riya's father head-butted her as she approached and dropped her once more to the ground. Paul ran.

He ran faster than he ever had. He ran into the streets of New Delhi, an atmosphere that once elicited the greatest of fears and discomforts within him, and now was his only safe haven. He ran to outrun his attacker, but more prominently, he was trying to outrun his shame. Behind him was his one true love and her livid and armed father. In front of him was a swarming chaos that didn't concern him. He ran faster and faster, ignoring the bile churning in his stomach, his breath that just couldn't seem to match the speed to which his legs were moving. Love and pain in the rearview, nothingness ahead, he once again chose to remain stagnant. He fled.

Something inside him was ripping apart. Although the pain had begun in his gut, the effect of unprecedented physical exertion, it was now in his head, tearing his skull in two. He couldn't hear anything as the rumbling within took over all of his senses like an earthquake in his brain. It was deafening. Just as he realized that the cacophony was not coming from the inside, an unseen force pushed from behind, and with one movement, hurled him forty feet forward. Flying through the air, his arms waved as if he could just grow wings to deny himself the pain of hitting the ground. His stomach fluttered just as it did in all of those dreams where he would wake just before impact. But he did not wake up. He hit the gravel road, the outside of his right forearm and his forehead striking first with a position that somehow left his bones miraculously intact. One half of his vision was the vertical horizon of the gravel road that his face lied upon. The other was glowing with the light of a thousand fires. The ringing in his ears drowned out the screaming around him. Another body dropped to the ground ahead of him momentarily after his own impact, only this body was much smaller, missing various parts, just an asymmetrical lump of brown flesh and red blood. His vision faded to black as that one word from Riya echoed repeatedly beneath the screaming tinnitus.

2

THE BLASTS SEEMED TO RID Justin and Kenneth of their thought processes. As Justin sped back into the city limits, all that either of them could say were random curse words like they both had Tourette's syndrome. Kenneth's "fucks" and "shits" were growing in frequency, curses like the pings of a heart monitor on a patient who had just done an eight-ball of cocaine, as they got closer and closer to the blast sites, and at the same time, closer and closer to his home. Just as parents do when their teenagers first get their drivers' licenses, they hear sirens and fear that they are ambulances screaming toward their hurt children, but they always know that the thought is asinine, that the sound is unrelated to them. Kenneth neglected to believe that out of the entire gargantuan city, an air strike would target his neighborhood, and knew that Paul was alright. But with every turn, every block gained, he was proven wrong.

When they got within a few blocks, they had to abandon the car, which was fine as Kenneth was already hanging out the door and ready to begin sprinting. He had to find his son.

The streets of Delhi were always bustling, but the activity took a different face. People were running – in both directions – instead of walking. The banter of a thousand people was now issued in screams. Every voice was filled with agony, with mourning, with alerting purpose, with terror. Windows were shattered. Faces were covered in soot and dirt.

Kenneth and Justin passed by their first body. Both glanced at it and glanced back, pretending not to notice as they had a greater priority at the time, but neither could deny that the image would stay with them until they reached their own fates.

Buildings that had always looked on the verge of collapse had now been properly obliterated. More bodies were strewn across the street. Some were surrounded by mourners and observers, making it difficult for Kenneth to catch a glimpse. He began praying in his head, the god on the other end of those prayers some molding between Jesus Christ, the elephant goddess that he had seen painted on the walls in Varanasi, and the goddess from his ayahuasca journey, and every time he saw a body with the dark skin of a native rather than the pale skin of his son, he thanked God.

He reached the site where his house used to exist. He had to look around at the destruction for minutes to ensure that this was, indeed, his home. Every landmark had been destroyed. It was nothing but rubble, chunks of buildings twisting his ankles and slicing at his shins as he climbed. The higher the debris got, the more he wondered if there were bodies buried beneath his feet. He wondered if somewhere down there was his son.

He began clawing at the rubble beneath him, hysterically, hopelessly. He lifted blocks of concrete with all of his might, pointed rebar protruding out like the broken off bones of severed limbs, scraping against his skin and covering him in rust and blood. He moved a block and hurled it off the edge of the mountainous debris pile. And again. And again. Tears were flowing. Desperation and despair were setting in. He wiped the snot from his nose with the back of his hand, a motion that distracted him from moving debris from where his living room used to sit, a motion that directed his attention to a spot of ground where no debris existed, but another body did.

This body, luckily, was standing upright, walking with a slight limp, looking dazed and perplexed, eyes wide at the hell surrounding him, and as those wide eyes connected with Kenneth's, his limp seemed to disappear as the two sprinted toward one another and embraced for the first time in more than a decade.

J USTIN HAD PUT ON A dark gray hoodie he had stored in the car. The three of them instinctually knew that making their distinguished appearances hidden would be to their advantage. Paul, having never seen Justin before, shuddered at his mutilated face, then looked incredulously at his father. Their friendship seemed so unlikely and mismatched, but in light of everything else happening around them, it was a conundrum easily passed over.

They had made it back to the car, but driving out was a bit of a challenge. Justin looked like he enjoyed the danger, like he was fully assuming the role of getaway driver in his own action movie. His villainous face cloaked in his gray hoodie made it seem that he wasn't quite the hero.

Kenneth was thankful to have his son with him, alive, although something was obviously consuming him. At first it was an expected reaction, the same look of confusion and disbelief at the horrors outside their windows that existed on everyone's face. Then Paul's cogs started turning, grinding on some foreign object wedged in his gears. His brow furrowed as if he was trying to do calculus in his head. A darkness grew within him, a cloud so deep and black that it encompassed the atmosphere of the car, so cold and infectious that Justin didn't even need to check the rearview to know the state that Paul was in. A deep breath hollowed him out, and his breaths began to come in whimpers.

"You okay?" Kenneth asked. No reply.

Whimpering became bellowing. Paul brought his knees to his chest and began rocking back and forth. Justin's face was somewhere between concern and agitation. Kenneth was terrified.

"What happened? Are you hurt?"

Paul shook his head back and forth answering 'no,' but his groans were getting louder and sounded like an animal, like a cow squealing out into the air for any help as a band of coyotes tore apart the flesh. It was a sound that Kenneth had never heard a human make, something deep and seared in pain, the tone jumping from high-pitched squeals to demonic groans.

"PAUL! WHAT THE FUCK IS GOING ON?!"

Kenneth hopped into the back seat with his son and wrapped his arms around him, less of a hug and more of a restraint. This seemed to calm Paul slightly as the bellowing lowered a few decibels.

Paul had gotten into the car thinking about his career and wondering why in the hell no one had evacuated him, let alone notified him. Something was most definitely awry. He felt abandoned and used, but just couldn't piece together the puzzle of his betrayal.

A sound brought him out of this line of thinking. It came on softly like the drip of a faucet late at night, waking you softly from your sleep, so subtle that you don't even know it truly exists until you open the door to the bathroom. It grew louder and louder until it drowned everything else out, and suddenly Paul remembered.

Nahin!

Riya. She was temporarily erased from his memory, then brought back with the force of a tidal wave. She had seen his true self despite all of the distorted mirrors they had placed between them. She had shown him a love that he never knew existed. She had fought for him. In return, he had waged a war on her country, had posted her face as the enemy to the entire world, had watched idly as she endured an assault on his behalf and, ultimately, killed her. He couldn't bring her back. He couldn't recreate her with synthetic scents and kissing his own skin, just as he couldn't bring his mother back despite all of the complimentary comments she still posted on his webpage. Almost stronger than his love and mourning for Riya was his hatred of himself.

And so he bellowed.

He tried to calm himself with the thought that she could have survived, just as he did. *How far had he run before the explosion? How far were they from their house?* Nothing outside was recognizable. But if she was really alive, what did that mean? What fate would she have in store for her? That would mean that Paul had not only delivered this upon her, but now left without even looking for her. She would arise from the rubble, homeless, most likely orphaned, and unknowingly made the enemy of her own country. Nearly everyone in the nation had probably seen her face in his advertisement by now. She would be completely alone and more than likely injured. And once she herself saw the advertisement, how would she react? Could she ever look past something like that, as she had looked past his subjectively strange hobbies? No, surely not. He had abandoned her three times now, it seemed.

Kenneth calmed him down, his touch reminding him that there were others in his presence, and although this show of loathing and remorse needed to get out, it would be done better in solitude, possibly ending in a deserved suicide.

Kenneth's phone rang. He felt bad answering it as he tended to his son's needs, but it seemed that the entire country was in a similar state of need. The number was unknown, and Kenneth optimistically believed it was Bobby on the other end offering them a plan of evacuation.

"You need to see this," Narayan spoke from the other end. Before hanging up, he added a daunting forewarning, "Don't make any calls." Narayan was at the jobsite that Kenneth was at two weeks prior. Kenneth directed Justin.

Roads were blocked by traffic, by soldiers, by chaos. Justin weaved through the pandemonium and adjusted routes with the swiftness and calm demeanor of a secret agent. Paul's cries had reduced to irregular breathing and occasional light whimpers. It was now his blank stare and lack of response that worried Kenneth. At first he tried to coax answers out of his son. When that approach proved futile, he conceded to the gravity of the events that surrounded them and allowed his son time to react in whatever manner suited him.

"Nahin," Paul whined, still unsure of the word's meaning, but broken down by its repetition in his head.

"Huh?"

"Riya."

Paul's eyes were still locked on some point in the distance, some imaginary spot that remained untouched by the violence that surrounded them. Kenneth had completely forgotten. His son had finally experienced what was probably actual love in the real world, and she was more than likely dead. How much could his baby boy possibly endure? First Meredith, now Riya, and his father would be quick to follow. As the adrenaline wore off, the pain in Kenneth's gut and back came back with mounting new heights. It took all of his strength to keep from doubling over and moaning in agony, but he had to remain strong in light of all that they were undergoing. Slight winces in his eyelids were all that he let on.

Another blast echoed in the distance, unfelt and unseen, but its mighty implications were felt with the same magnitude had it landed on their heads.

"What the fuck is going on?!" Justin shouted, still navigating the mayhem. "Have you checked your phone, Ken? Mine's been out of service since this morning."

Kenneth didn't have the finger dexterity and technical savvy that Justin and Paul had, making it an arduous task that stretched all of two minutes. Oddly enough, the screen that greeted him was another advertisement, urging him to vote against budget restrictions that would reallocate state and local government funding offered by the federal government, a law that, if passed, would centralize government funds and therefore give other jurisdictions the ability to vote on how much each state and county should receive based on need. Kenneth didn't quite grasp the concept and didn't care to. He was never a frequent voter.

The next screen read in huge, flashing text, "AMERICA GOES TO WAR WITH INDIA." Beneath the headline it read as follows:

After efforts by U.S. officials seeking to extradite suspected Hindu extremists residing in the Haryana state of India were hindered by Indian president Mayank Kapoor, the U.S.A. has launched a series of airstrikes throughout northern India intended to dismantle terrorist groups residing in the area. The Indian government has denied any possible connections between the targeted groups and the terrorist activities that have killed more than a collective six thousand American citizens over the past four years. In response to the attacks, President Kapoor has made no comment if he will retaliate with force, but has vowed to restrict trade to the U.S. and negotiate new trade agreements with China.

The most debated issue with these initial strikes has been the manner in which they were voted into action. The initial attempted extradition of the suspected terrorist groups was voted on after several weeks of the issue being broadcast into the public eye, receiving a 99.4% voter turnout, 91.2% of which voted for the actions taken by the U.S. government. Advertisements bringing the issue to the public first appeared more than a month before it came to election. The declaration of war, however, was taken to the polls with a speeding urgency. A mere two hours after the first wave of advertisements making the potential war public information and presenting views that both supported and challenged the idea of war between the two nations, the ballots closed, only twenty-two minutes after they opened. Not only did the U.S. government claim that declaration of war had to be done in a timely fashion to make way for military strategy, but stated that 68.1% of the American public still voted despite the short notice, and 89.9% of those who voted elected to go to war with India, meaning that over 61% of eligible voters supported the war. Despite the outcry of voters who did not get the information in time to cast a ballot, the numbers deny any possibility that the decision could have been overturned.

None of this came as a shock to any of them. It only supported what they were all thinking. Growing up in the states offered a sense of entitlement and superiority, a beautiful fact ingrained in the American way of life: we were number one. But once expatriated, the views of outsiders shattered that image and made one question all he had been taught. While all three still maintained fleeting senses of patriotism, the car was slowly filled with shame and confusion, like the actions of the man behind the curtain had stained them all.

From an aerial perspective, the site looked like an eyeball. The pupil in the center was black, but with a shimmering silver reflection. The iris, like most, was one solid color defined by the combination of many. At first glance, it appeared brown, but upon closer inspection, it was an array of blacks, tans, silvers, and reds commixing together. The sclera was an unhealthy shade of tan yellow, fading to a lighter shade toward the outside, like the sickly eyes of Kenneth.

At ground level, these colors weren't quite discernable, but the causes of them were. The tan and yellow on the outside was dirt and rock, stones made into sand by the force of the blast. The iris was constructed of many elements: the destructed steel structure of the rig, the scattered supplies that it housed, and the bodies, mostly. Metal and rock, bone and blood, a shoe here, a beam there. It was a jumbled mess of death and destruction, and in the center, a black hole. Darkened by shadows, it cratered into the earth deeper than they could see. The center of the hole was drilled out by their co-workers, by them. A finely targeted missile struck dead center, widening the hole drastically at the surface, more narrowly as it sank deeper into the earth, creating an elongated, upside-down cone, and at the surface where the diameter was at its greatest, the hole was not black, but an earthy silver, the smoky color of neodymium.

Narayan's scooter was parked outside the destruction. Kenneth, Paul, and Justin had to climb across the debris and death toward the crater where Narayan was standing, staring down into the bottomless silver pit. The images of the mutilated bodies that they had to circumnavigate were chillingly seared into all of their memories. Each wondered separately how much more death they would be subjected to and if they could actually be desensitized to such horror.

Paul came across a familiar face, although it was attached to a legless and charred body. It was the fat man, the one whom he used in his first advertisement for war, the one whom he thought he had gotten fired. Relocated, obviously. Paul stared down at that hideous face, now lifeless and bloodied. The last time he saw it, it was caged in his computer screen giving Paul the feeling of victory. Now, he looked at the man and realized that he was right all along. Paul *was* the enemy. He was there to take their jobs, then their lives. The man was now dead, his futile actions proved righteous, yet they still only sealed his fate as the altercation only fueled the American people to support Paul in his selfish and narrow-minded endeavors that would end all life in this country.

Although the revelation that Narayan was alive was as joyous as everything else was devastating, they greeted each other wordlessly. The four of them stood side by side, lost in the black emptiness in front of them.

"Neodymium?" Kenneth questioned. Narayan nodded gravely. "You were right."

"I really wish that I wasn't." His voice was shaky with tears. Paul and Justin were understandably confused, but equally transfixed on the vast darkness before them, a sparkling hell that sucked endlessly down into the earth.

"Have you spoken to anyone from Echo?"

"Briefly," he replied pessimistically, "but it doesn't look good. Getting flights out right now is next to impossible. They're trying to contact the American Embassy, but even they are too busy to help. I, personally, think it would be easier to get flights out on our own. We'll probably have to fly to Bangladesh or Nepal first. I can purchase tickets as a native much easier than you or our company. I think that should be our next move, right after tossing our phones into this crater."

"Alright, I've gotta ask," Justin interjected. "What the fuck is going on? Neodymium? Echo? What the hell are you guys doin' here?"

"We work for a drilling company," Narayan answered. "We were supposed to be looking for oil, but instead have been drilling for this." His hands spread out in front of him, angled downward, palms up. "Neodymium. It's used mostly in computers, and it is very expensive these days. Your government has framed the Indian people for terrorist activities so they could essentially steal this right from the ground. That's what this war is about. It's about theft."

Justin's teeth were grinding through the periscopes again. He took a solid step in Narayan's direction.

"First of all, don't call them "*my*" government. They're over there. I'm over here. My connection to all this is as weak as yours. I didn't come here spewin' that propaganda horse shit, so don't throw it at me."

"I'm sorry, I didn't—"

"And so what you're saying," he interrupted, Justin's way of accepting an apology, "is that you all were the gambit by the U.S. to incite a war? Holy fuck, man, this is heavy."

"Well, I wouldn't say *gambit*," said Kenneth. "More like reconnaissance team – unknowingly, of course."

"And why do we have to throw our phones in this giant asshole in the earth?"

"Because," answered Narayan, "they may be trying to get rid of us, to cover up any ill motive. It would probably look good for us to have died on this strike."

"Me, too? I ain't even heard of your company."

"It couldn't hurt. There is no telling what they know, and they have no way of telling what *you* know."

The three of them tossed their phones into the eternal darkness below. They dropped beyond their vision without ever issuing the sound of impact, like they could have dropped all the way to the center of the earth, floating in limbo.

"And yours?" All three of them looked at Paul.

But his phone was still sitting on his desk when he fled from his home just before the strikes began. It was then that he realized why their neighborhood, of anywhere in the country, was targeted. Above all Echo employees, Paul was the highest on the list of people whom the American government needed to silence. As of now, this war was waged against him.

"What the hell is that?" Justin asked, his index finger pointed above them to the top of what appeared to be a plateau, but no, it was merely the fact that they were inside a crater. Small black dots lined the horizon and moved across and inward.

"I think we need to get moving – fast!" shouted Narayan. The four of them hurdled the wreckage and carnage back toward the car. Narayan pushed his scooter over to make it look like part of the debris. Justin hopped into the driver's seat. Narayan sent an incredulous look to Kenneth, who returned the glare with one that said he needed to allow it to happen. Justin started the car and pulled the hood from off the top of his head as it impeded his vision when reversing. The dots on the horizon were growing larger. They sped away, hopefully before being noticed. Paul glared out the back windshield and saw the black dots grow into a military convoy. The smaller of the vehicles were tanks and Humvees, the larger ones were excavators and dump trucks, ready to haul away the loot. Paul watched and remembered his first advertisement for the road construction. He remembered his father questioning why all of the roads back in Texas were under construction, yet all of the trucks were empty. Paul watched the line of construction vehicles and wondered how much each cost. He wondered if his first project that granted three and a half million dollars to local road construction bought one of the machines. He wondered how essential he was to this campaign of genocide. He wondered how guilty he really was.

4

IT'S STRANGE HOW WHEN THE inner monologue of an individual begins ranting, when the thoughts pile up faster than the brain can comprehend, the mouth goes silent. These are the times when people need one another the most, when emotions overpower the mind's ability to cope, yet they are the times when people isolate themselves.

The car was heavy with silence, yet all four of them were screaming on the inside. As the terrifying activity of the city made way for the muted chaos of stationary highway traffic, their collective anxiousness pulsated and seeped out the cracks in their windows. Paul had finally calmed himself, and even Justin, who was growing increasingly agitated by Paul's outbursts, suddenly missed the distraction. It was Paul who threw the first stone through the glass house of their silence.

"So, Dad. You're dying, right?"

The sinking implications were made drastically more devastating with the unmatched tones. Paul had alluded to his father's impending death with the same inflection of asking if it was going to rain that day. Kenneth was taken off-guard.

"Um... Yeah. How did you know?"

"P.T.A.T.T."

Justin stared straight ahead. Kenneth and Narayan both looked at him perplexedly.

"Put three and three together." No one bothered correcting him, save for Justin scoffing under his breath as he lit his last cigarette.

The following silence that lingered was like an ocean. All four of them lost in that sea, each on his own lifeboat, but instead of paddling toward one another and linking vessels, each fought against the elements on his own. Kenneth yearned to say something, anything, but nothing came to mind. It was bad enough that he had waited this long, and now finally his secret came to light, but not of his own doing. Now whatever profound father-son moment that should come after such a discovery would bear an audience, something that muted any possible verbal reaction from Kenneth. He wanted to reach across the seat and hug his son, but for some reason, it felt so *unnatural*. How poorly had he done in raising a son that not even their eternal parting could elicit physical contact? Kenneth no longer blamed the times. This was his fault. He remembered the word FAILURE as it was presented to him the night before. He had failed. It was his primary job in life, to raise a son, and he had forsaken his duty.

"Where are we going?" asked Narayan, graciously ending the silence. Justin had exited the highway and made a detour into the outer limit of town.

"There's a market right here," he puffed through a cloud of smoke. "We'll probably need to pick up some phones. You know, the prepaid, off-the-grid type. If we get separated, we'll need to be able to contact each other, right?"

Narayan nodded with one short dip of the chin. Justin hadn't made the best impression on him, but then again, it was an odd time to be introduced to someone. Everyone was in crisis mode.

The market existed just off the highway. Kenneth was still impressed by Justin's knowledge of the city and his ability to survive. Most of the stores were shut down, a metal garage door pulled down, barricading the only entrance. The streets seemed less frantic than before as the chaotic activity of the people's first knowledge of the transpiring events had led to retreating indoors. Even those without families stayed inside, boxing themselves in the psychological barriers from potential airstrikes that would offer the same amount of protection as a sheet of notebook paper.

One store remained open. The man behind the counter was ancient. It was always difficult discerning the age of foreigners, but if Kenneth had to guess, the man was well into his eighties, if not nineties or triple-digits. He seemed unfazed by all that was happening to his country. His face contained a sense of numbness, like he had seen all of this before. Perhaps his family had all been taken by similar events, and he was the only one left behind, awaiting the same fate so he could rejoin his loved ones or be doomed to start again. Maybe was just too old to understand what was going on.

The four of them perused the store individually. Kenneth, Justin, and Narayan were quick to purchase, first asking the necessary questions – prepaid? Chargers? Network? – then forking over the money. Paul wanted to shop for styles and colors, but was degradingly hurried by Kenneth and Justin. Kenneth paid for all five phones – Paul said he *had to* have two – for an outrageous price by Indian standards given the current status of the nation, yet still quite modest in American terms. Paul straggled behind as the other three hurried out the store with their purchases. Something had caught his eye.

It rested beneath the glass counter. It was curved smoothly. The colors of ivory and beige enveloped the piece in no apparent order, the two shades entirely separate from one another, never influencing the tone of the other. At one end it was inharmoniously rounded, perforated like a sponge, with a diameter of about one and a half centimeters. At the other end, about three inches away, it narrowed to a fine and lethal point. Just beneath it lay a name card, barely taller than the strip of paper inside a fortune cookie, that read in Hindi and English: Golden Eagle Talon.

It had a striking resemblance to the horn that used to perch up on the shelf in his old room, like it was a miniature representation. Both pieces were as beautiful as they were deadly. They were both torn from living animals, the phallic and dangerous appendages that sprung to mind at the mention of either species. Paul had to have it.

"How much?" He spoke slowly and over-enunciated while pointing down at the artifact, a habit that seemed courteous, but in fact was a pet peeve of most natives.

The old man held up an index finger, then brought his four fingers in a circle to meet his thumb, then touched them together three times like a shadow animal speaking on the wall behind him. Paul threw the thousand rupees onto the counter and ripped the artifact from the man's hand the second he brought it out from under the display counter. Justin was already yelling from the car, agitated that he would have to wait for a shopper in a time of war.

When they reached the airport, the entire surrounding area looked like a riot. Everyone who was not taking refuge in their homes was there, and all of them were frightened and furious. Some were trying to push their way through the crowd to the inside, succeeding only in agitating the masses. Others were around the side of the building, hurling rocks at the third story windows. Fights had already broken out.

"Look at this shit, man," said Justin. "Even when you show 'em the face of the enemy, they all just attack each other." Narayan glared across the console at him with a stern look, but before he could interject, Justin concluded with, "All people, I mean. Not just Indians."

After programming the other three's phone numbers into his new phone, Narayan exited the car and plunged into the mayhem, stating that he would 'see what he could find out.' None of them had more than a speck of hope, but let him fulfill his duty as they didn't have any alternative solution.

As they waited, Justin poked at his new phone angrily with both thumbs. Paul did the same, but without the ferocity and with more of the dexterity. Kenneth ransacked his brain for anything to say to his son, anything to make things better. He thought about all of the great lines in movies when disaster struck, how the Hollywood fathers always knew how to console with a few simple words. With a short anecdote or even a heartfelt look, they could make everything alright. Whether they lived or died, Dad just brought all of their tribulations and heartaches to a warm light that negated any previous tensions and explained his undying love. The climax and denouement were deemed unnecessary.

Kenneth had nothing. Were it Narayan or Justin to whom he needed to make a deathbed speech, he could have gone on for hours. He just didn't have that connection with Paul, and that, he knew, was highly indicative of his failure as a parent.

"I hope you're not logging on to your accounts back there," warned Justin from the driver's seat. Kenneth pretended that the interjection came just as he was about to deliver his speech to his son, but he was still unprepared.

"Of course not," Paul replied without looking up from his phone. "I made new accounts under fake names."

Kenneth couldn't fathom what possibly could require logging on to any form of social media in a time like this. Contacting loved ones, sure, but shouldn't that be done with a phone call rather than an impersonal message? These were the thoughts that forced the distance between Kenneth and Paul, the silencing agent that sealed his lips even while his soul was being hurled into the darkness, screaming toward death.

Narayan hopped back into the passenger seat and slammed the door shut behind him, his breaths heaving as if he had just lost a wrestling match.

"All flights have been grounded." He allowed a moment for the weight of the information to sink in, but the three were already awaiting bad news, and Justin and Paul had more than likely already found the information on their phones. Justin still hadn't looked up from his phone. "It seems that a plane crashed a few hours ago. They're unsure of whether it was shot down or brought down from within. Of course, America is claiming that it was another terrorist activity thwarting efforts of Americans residing in India to return home. India is claiming that it was shot down by the Americans. Regardless, flying out is impossible. Perhaps we drive across the border. The highways will be slow and the lines at the borders will be long. We could take a train…"

"You know, Narayan," Paul said accusatorily, "you could fix a lot of this shit if you'd just give up the rhino horn."

Narayan twisted around in his seat lividly. "What?!"

"The rhino horn. If you'd give it up, you could cure my dad and probably still have enough left over to just *buy* us an airplane and get us the fuck out of your country."

"The rhino horn?! Don't you think if I had any ability to save your father, I would? You keep emphasizing these things that don't matter. You sound like a little baby! Waaah! The rhino horn! Waaah! My pretty shirt! Maybe you should be speaking to your father and enjoying his presence while you have it. You should be comforting him in his time of need instead of worrying about a stupid rhino horn! Maybe you should—"

"Hang on a sec," interrupted Justin. "I need to get something from the back seat."

Justin opened the door directly behind his own and yanked an unsuspecting Paul from the vehicle, threw him forcefully to the ground, and landed a powerful right jab to his forehead, the back of his head bouncing off the pavement and leaving him slightly concussed.

"WHAT THE FUCK?!" Kenneth screamed incredulously.

"Take a look for yourself, Ken." Justin tossed his phone onto Kenneth's lap. He picked it up, but kept his eyes on Justin for a few moments to ensure that the beating had concluded. Fearfully and shamefully, he looked down at the screen and saw the pretty Indian girl who lived across the way from them. The girl whom his son was dating. The girl who died in the blast.

The commercial played through as Kenneth watched in disbelief. He had seen these election advertisements before, but never featuring anyone whom he knew personally. It was a strange sensation, almost like being starstruck, but as the message revealed itself with every utterance, Kenneth understood exactly what his son had done. Before he could question how much of the footage was real and how much was edited by Paul, another advertisement began.

He saw the obese man he had pranked that first day at work. His livid outburst was just as he remembered it, only from a slightly different perspective, and in this footage, he was wielding a gun. Just as the previous advertisement, the video ended with insane propaganda narrated in an ominous voice.

Three or four videos played through, seemingly unconnected, but all concerning issues facing his local government back in Corpus Christi, Texas. Every time he glanced away from the phone and started to hand it back, Justin would hold up an outward-faced palm and encourage him to keep watching. By the fifth video, he saw what he was waiting for.

The video began in his own car. Kenneth was driving, Paul was in the passenger seat. The heartfelt chat that he had been trying desperately to initiate over the past five minutes, the past five months, was playing back at him through edited video and audio footage, sporadically interrupted by another narrator. Kenneth, watching everything that he should have said, was crying. On the screen in his hands, he was grabbing his son's shoulder, something that he remembered as an awkward and forced moment, followed by him telling his son, "I love you," something that never happened. The tears were now dripping onto the phone. As the second tear splashed in a small droplet on the center of the screen, the car exploded, and Kenneth flinched reflexively, an embarrassing whimper escaping his windpipe like an effeminate hiccup.

The video ended, and Kenneth looked up, his face newly gaunt from the cancer, yet puffy from the crying. His cheeks were jaundiced, yet blushed. His bottom lip was quivering. The phone in his hand was vibrating, but no one was calling. His hands were shaking, as was most of his body, almost similarly to his seizure-like twitches from the night before under the influence of ayahuasca. Paul was crawling back to a standing position, his hands climbing their way back up on the door handle and seat, his face looking confused, yet slowly drawing back into reality, the expressions of the three other men – Narayan's one of disdain, Justin's one of wrath, and Kenneth's one of despair and depression – telling him that the jig was up, his secret was out, and they were all doomed.

5

THE SILENCE THAT HAD PREVIOUSLY filled the car had now taken a much more violent tone. Justin had mentioned the prospect of going off on his own, possibly rafting the Ganges River all the way into Bangladesh. He had heard of other adventurers making the journey, and it seemed like a great time to do the same. Kenneth rallied against it, stating that they should stick together. He tacked on the responsibility of Justin getting the word out of the true nature of this war and the innocence of the Indian people, should something happen to the three remaining employees of Echo residing in India.

"Don't get me wrong," he responded, "I mean, I prefer the role of 'Citizen of the World' to 'Savior of the World,' but I'll rise to the call of duty if it's inescapable. But I think you're severely overestimating the American public. *Neodymium* just isn't as sexy as *Curry Terrorism*. It won't take."

Narayan further pushed the responsibility issue, but Kenneth didn't have the willpower to supplement his argument. Not only was he already doomed, but ensuring his family and friends' survival seemed endlessly more pertinent than global issues. Maybe he was being selfish.

Paul hadn't looked up from his phone since the altercation. Perhaps it was shame. For once, Kenneth didn't blame him. He, too, would be lost in anything that could take him away from the inside of that car if he could. The pain in his gut was becoming unbearable, and no longer could he mask his reactions. His head was receding down to his knees. His groans were becoming audible. Everyone in the car did all they could to ignore it. There was no consolation, there was no aid. There was no turning back.

As Kenneth's body rocked back and forth to alleviate the pain, he stared at his son. He was no longer searching for a deathbed speech, but an agreeable way to address his son's crimes. Scolding, screaming, and fighting were arbitrary actions as the whole ship was already going down, but the exposure of Paul's cataclysmic misdeed led to no grand closure. This wasn't just a slipup. Paul had been covertly sinning against all of them for their entire stay in the country, longer even, but what could Kenneth possibly say? What action could make his fleeting life any more valuable? Nothing came to mind, so he resorted to glaring at his son through a painful grimace. His thoughts were so easily read by all, especially Paul.

"I know, Dad," he responded to his father's glower. "I fucked up, alright? I thought I was doing good. I thought I was doing the right thing."

Everyone in the car heard his interjection, and they all understood. Paul was young and lived in a virtual world that was nothing but superficial highs and endless propaganda. They understood his mistake, yet no one said anything in response. The silence that followed was far more abrasive than any harsh word or violent outburst. Paul sank back into himself and pushed a black piece of thread through a pre-drilled hole at the base of the talon. He tied a knot and looped it around his neck. The index finger and thumb of his right hand caressed the smoothly fierce appendage, just like the chess pieces with Riya, just like the rhino horn, but despite the beauty and lethality of the talon, it offered little in the way of condolence or self-esteem.

Justin suggested they hide out at Ishaan's farmhouse for a while. "Get off the grid for a bit," was how he put it. Narayan questioned the whereabouts of this hideaway. Paul did not.

So they went back to where they had come from – half of them, at least – where mere hours previous, Kenneth was visiting gods and crossing abysses, returning shamefully to what turned out to be an even greater hell than the one of his psychedelic trip. Ishaan was still on the porch, just as they had left him, the same, enlightened and incorrigible smile plastered across his face.

As they exited the car, Kenneth pulled Justin aside before approaching the house. He leaned in and whispered, "I've never understood him, myself, but please protect him. Please don't tell anyone." Justin answered with an affirming nod.

Ishaan hugged each of them as they entered, like all four of them were his long-lost siblings. Justin kissed him on the temple. With Kenneth, Ishaan embraced him for an exceptionally long time, even in comparison to the others, asking how he was feeling, if he had made any sense of last night. This did not go unnoticed by Paul, but he also hadn't the slightest clue to what he was alluding. It gave the entire location a cryptic undertone, like the night before they were performing some experimental, back-alley type cancer treatment in the storage cellar. Perhaps they all had been snorting lines of rhino horn. Truthfully, it wouldn't have surprised Paul one bit. With Ishaan's state of permanent elation and Justin's twisted physical appearance, something of that sort would actually make perfect sense.

The house looked relatively new and unused, yet also ignored in the way of upkeep. White tile floors were made beige by a layer of dirt. Two ceiling fans spun lopsidedly, the blades drooping down at the tips like dying flowers. Carpeting was something that Paul had not seen since his arrival in the country, yet finely threaded gray carpet lined the stairway up to the second floor – a multi-floor domicile something else that seemed strictly western. In the kitchen, the black granite countertops appeared faded through the dust. Every cabinet was stocked full of new dishes and cookware, most still with the tags on them. It was as if Ishaan had won the lottery, built a mansion in the middle of nowhere, then abandoned it.

The group huddled around the island in the kitchen.

"Should I call Bobby?" Kenneth asked, initiating a meeting of strategy.

"I don't think so," replied Narayan.

"Who's Bobby?" asked Justin.

"Our employer," answered Narayan. "I've spoken to my contacts with Echo already, and they can't do anything for us."

"But Bobby has always been so good to us. If he knew we were alive, I feel like he would be the one to try the hardest to pull some strings."

"But the fact that he thinks we are dead may very well be the thing that is keeping us alive. When I spoke to Echo, I was calling from the phone of a dead man. It was after the first blast, but before the site we were at was destroyed. I left the phone there, so if there were any trace back to me, it could be presumed that I died at our drilling site that we just left."

"And don't you think this Bobby dude will realize that somethin's severely fucked up?" asked Justin.

"What do you mean?"

"When the U.S. is supposed to be targeting terrorists and they bomb all of his drill sites and kill all of his employees, he'll have to know that shit ain't right."

"Not necessarily," replied Narayan. "Only ten people have been contracted from Echo. The rest are native workers. And although the equipment was manufactured by Echo's subsidiaries, it was bought by the Indian corporation overseeing the drilling. Even if Echo wanted to try to come back and search for missing employees or missing equipment, by the time they could get into the country, it wouldn't be strange to find that it was all gone, whether by the airstrikes or by looting afterward."

"And how the hell would looting explain the loss of *employees?*"

"I guess it was a euphemism. Let's just say that enemies of the nation *do* tend to go missing."

"I'm sorry." Ishaan's voice was soft even at high volume. It was no longer a tone of timorousness, but one of tranquility. "But I do not wish to talk of these things. I will be outside."

Paul followed Ishaan. The rest looked on, confused, wanting to convey the importance of the next step, and every step after, for that matter, but then excused his dismissal, understanding that it didn't matter to Ishaan. Nothing did, apparently, and therefore, Ishaan didn't matter to the plan. As for Paul, his absence was greatly appreciated. As he walked out onto the patio, a thick undertone of derision left with him.

Paul sat at one of two wicker chairs that faced away from the house, Ishaan on the other. Paul observed him with intrigue – his unwavering smile, his shimmering eyes, his gentle demeanor, and his complete lack of concern for the white enemies that he was now harboring all suggested that he was of monk status. Despite his interest in the subject, it wasn't research that Paul was after. It was documentation.

"So, you know my dad?" Paul asked, the camera of his phone peeking out of his breast pocket.

Ishaan nodded serenely. Paul didn't know how to interview or prod for the answers that he sought, so instead he questioned for more personal endeavors.

"Did something happen here yesterday?"

Another tranquil nod. This was going to be difficult.

"You know my dad is dying, right?"

Nod.

"I feel like something is going on with him, but I just don't know what. I'm worried. Can you tell me something, anything? Because you just might know more about my father than I do."

He glared into Paul.

"She showed us the truth. But she is... confusing, sometimes. She didn't show him like she showed me. His was... much more difficult."

Paul was ostensibly befuddled. Rather than questioning as to whom 'she' was, he felt that attempting to level with such bizarre lines of thought would prove to be much more beneficial.

"What did she show you?"

Ishaan cleared his throat. He leaned forward in his chair. His eyes widened. All were slow and deliberate actions made to emphasize the gravity of everything he had to say. "Everyone is the same. We all want. We all need. We all love and hate and laugh and cry. We feel hunger the same. We feel joy the same. But we fight. We hate. We hurt. We all want happiness, and we all want to end our suffering." It sounded like Riya, only with worse English. Paul wanted to cry. Ishaan continued, "And when we hurt others to get happy or to stop suffering, we die. We hurt others, and so we hurt. We destroy happiness, and we, ourselves, become sad. Even if someone has hurt me very much, I must not want to hurt. I will only hurt myself. The more we hate, the more we hurt, the more we die. It is stupid, but we still do these things. She showed me happiness. She showed me love. I no longer need hate. I don't want to hurt anymore."

His eyes glazed over, his smile widened, and he glared back up into the sky, into nothingness, completely content.

Paul remembered Riya. With so much going on in his life, it became difficult to single out one feeling, but at that moment, it was all he could think about. He thought about all the ways that he had wronged her and all of the ways that she tried to steer him on a more righteous and substantial path. He remembered how much he wanted to die after he came to from the blast. He still did. She had shown him all the ways that his life was a trivial existence. All of his desires and achievements, she whittled down to nothing. All that was true and good in the world, she gave him. And he murdered her. He felt that there was nothing to go back to, so he might as well die. But not yet. He needed to do one thing right by her, then just maybe he could be lucky enough to join her in the afterlife. Maybe his father would be there, too. At least by Riya's belief system, Paul could only be born again and wouldn't have to burn in Hell. Dying didn't seem so bad.

With Ishaan still lost somewhere in the sky, Paul edited the footage he had just taken, only discarding the first minute or so where Ishaan spoke in pronouns, telling of 'her' and how 'she' made it more difficult for Kenneth. Paul set up an internet channel called *War of Lies* and tagged it with keywords like 'India,' 'terrorism,' and 'bullshit.' After doing the initial work and uploading the first video, the site took about a minute to boot up, during which time another advertisement was shown, only this time – for the first time – it displayed an advertisement promoting an issue that had already gone through the voting process, an issue already in action.

It began with a body. Brown skin cocooned in a white cloth emerged at the top in the form of a face, old and wrinkled, lifeless yet pain-stricken, mouth agape, eyes squeezed tight. The sheets were then pulled shut to hide the face just before the body was set aflame. The camera panned out, and another body came into view, and another. All three were spewing flames into the evening sky, surrounded by dirt and garbage. Before those wading through the water and sifting through the ashes could be seen, the video switched scenes to a little girl, a dead little girl who lay directly in front of Paul. In a few short seconds, the video captured her being loaded onto a rowboat, then dumped into the river, the driver of the boat not shedding a tear. This was all Paul's footage. It was never submitted. It was never edited. But now, over various clips of bodies being dumped into the water and men delivering torches to wrapped bodies, a narrator read the words, "If this is how they treat their own, how do you think they will treat us?" The scene shifted suddenly to a series of buildings being detonated, railway station bombings, suicide bombers, all taken over the past few years. "Let's keep America safe." No voice nor caption told the viewer for what to vote, because it was already finished. There was no purpose other than to make the American people comfortable with the genocide they had just set into action. It was like they knew Paul's plan before he executed it. Their preemptive actions had negated his own.

The advertisement came to an end, revealing a screen that read SETUP COMPLETE. It could have just as well said, YOUR MOVE, PAUL. He felt so weak and powerless, yet at the same time empowered by the less and less he had to lose.

He set up a live video feed to his channel and hit record.

He walked around the side of the house and aimed his phone back toward his own face.

"I'm… I'm in India right now. The first wave of strikes has devastated much of the country, or at least, the part of the country I'm in. Bodies are everywhere. It's… I can't describe it. It's terrible. And worst of all, I'm responsible."

He began making his way into the house.

"I've been in charge of making promotional videos to advertise the war, but I didn't realize what I was doing. These are good people here. We're taking refuge in an Indian man's house right now. And I've come to realize that this war may have been started under false pretenses. We've lost everything, and we're trying to find a way out of… Look, here's another Indian man who's been helping us." Narayan's face – confused, terrified, and enraged – entered the shot. "He could just up and leave, but instead he chooses to help us get to safety. And the man that—"

The camera was slapped out of his hands by Justin, the image presented on the channel now of the ceiling, spinning, slower, slower, then stopped.

"What the fuck do you think you're doin', man?!"

Paul picked the phone back up and aimed it back at himself.

"As you can see, the only asshole of the bunch is the other American. Quite suiting, huh?"

This time Justin grabbed the phone and slammed it into the tile floor. The tile cracked. The phone disintegrated.

"Are you really this fuckin' stupid, or are you *trying* to kill us?!" shouted Justin. "You do realize what this means, right? We're next. This house is now seconds away from being fuckin' obliterated, minutes if we're lucky."

"It's all under a false alias," Paul retorted.

"*A false alias? That's* gonna help us? If you're really that dumb, then you need to stop making executive decisions."

"I'm trying to help," Paul pleaded pathetically.

"I think we've had enough of *your* fuckin' help for one lifetime."

"Hey!" Kenneth shouted, still doubled over, one hand clutching his gut. "That's enough!" He wanted to speak more, but it was all he could muster, physically and verbally.

"Well, let's fuckin' pack up, then," said Justin in a snarky tone. "You guys get to the car. I'll get Ishaan and tell him that he's homeless."

Narayan hopped into the passenger seat, assuming the role of navigator and submitting to Justin's driving skills. Before Paul could open the back door, Kenneth caught him by the shoulder.

"Paul, listen," he gasped in painful breaths. "I know you're trying to help. I know you made a mistake. But just stay with us. You know, *with* us, not on the internet. Be with me. Here."

And that was it. That was his profound deathbed monologue delivered to his son, yet it somehow felt like a speech given to an ex-girlfriend, begging her to come back, oblivious to the fact that she was already fucking somebody else. Paul looked completely unmoved, like he might not have even been paying attention, but he nodded quickly and jumped into the car.

In the time they waited for Justin, they began to think that he had fulfilled his plan to set off on his own, walking out into the great unknown, east being his only direction. Narayan was beating the heel of his hand into the door handle at an accelerated rate. The rising tempo filled the car with his nervousness. Kenneth was clutching his stomach, groaning out every breath. Paul just looked lost, like a child searching for his parents after the initial fear and anxiety wears off and he just accepts his fate with a fleeting endeavor to find his way back home.

"Narayan," said Paul. "I'm sorry. For… For everything."

Narayan peered back at Paul, then went right back to pounding at the door handle. Paul expected a reaction as such, but it didn't make it any less heartbreaking.

Justin finally dove into the driver's seat with a bloody nose. Ishaan was nowhere to be found.

"He ain't comin'."

"What do you mean?" asked Narayan.

"Couldn't make 'im. Believe me, I tried. Dude is lost somewhere, said he don't wanna run. I told 'im it's either run or die, and the crazy fucker is choosing death. I tried to drag the bastard by the damn ankles, but he kicked me right in the fuckin' nose. Ain't nothin' we can do."

With that, he screeched the tires, spinning the car one hundred eighty degrees, spewing dirt into the air. They drove with the haste of a racecar and the silent melancholy of a hearse. They found a highway and headed for the train station, at Narayan's request. When the traffic backed up, they drove through the dirt alongside the road. The only words any of them spoke were intermittent curses moaned by Kenneth as he rocked back and forth, now with *both* hands grabbing at his belly. Still, they all just tried to ignore it. They had confronted his death long ago, and they were all just out of words to say. There was only so many times one could say, "It's okay," or "Hang in there," yet when the empty phrases wore out their use, that was when it really hurt for all of them. Kenneth's moaning reached new heights, and their collective inability to soothe him felt sinfully awkward. They all loved one another, they all banded together, but truthfully, they all wanted to be somewhere else, with any*one* else. They were inescapable thoughts, thoughts they all wished they could suppress or otherwise mute so bad that when the blast that was sure to be Ishaan's farmhouse boomed and echoed behind them, they were almost grateful.

6

ENNETH'S FACE WAS SMASHED TOGETHER like an accordion. He slumped over, his right cheek resting upon the door handle as his body had given up fighting the cancer. His jaw hung down lifelessly – such a perfect adverb to describe his entire state of being. His face had paled. His eyes were glazed, and his sockets were sunken. Paul would watch intently for movement. It seemed that minutes would go by between his breaths. Paul remembered those bodies strewn about the banks of the Ganges. Most of their faces bore the exact same expression as they would if they were sleeping, but something was most definitely missing. Whether it be a soul, a spirit, a beating heart - its absence was seen just as easily as a toe tag. Those who have watched a loved one take his final breath know, even after weeks of resting in a vegetative state, surviving only by the surrounding machines, the moment the soul would depart couldn't be more discernable if a buzzer sounded. The mouth gapes open. The eyes glaze over. But more than subtle movements and the easily described aspects, a blankness washes over. They can wonder for days if their loved one is still in there, if he is still contained by his quickly expiring shell, if he can sense their presence. They give up hope. They believe he is already gone. They mourn, and then they wait for it to become official. But the moment the body signs its last resignation, they realize that they grieved too soon. He was in there. If they're calm enough, still enough, they can almost watch him exit, maybe through the breath, maybe evaporating through the head, as subtly as when they look to the distance on a hot day and their vision blurs in a mirage-like steam, they can see him disembark to another realm.

As Kenneth's sickness choked the air inside the car, Paul noticed his skin going pale, his eyes staring off in the distance, and his face going blank, and for a brief moment, he honestly thought he saw his father's soul drifting toward the crack in the window. Kenneth would cough, saliva cascading down to the floorboard, and the entire car would take a collective breath, then all four would hold the air in their lungs until Kenneth allowed them to breathe again.

While Paul was still struggling to grasp the concept of existing without parents, he suddenly felt the severe consequences not of losing a father, but of losing his last ally. Justin and Narayan may have understood his confused motives for the pro-war propaganda that he created, but the explosion that still echoed behind them, as far as they were concerned, was *murder*. Paul knew this, just as he knew his father's breaths were winding down to the last, and when that moment came, nothing stood between himself and the onslaught of enemies that he produced over the past few months.

The car still sped alongside the freeway, leaving a cloud of dirt in its wake, along with a trail of cars following the hazardous example. Justin was constantly dodging light posts, trees, and holes in the ground, obstacles that were surely harder to avoid in the smokescreen he left behind. The speed seemed so futile, like an ambulance running a red light on its way to the morgue. Kenneth was more than unnecessary. In fact, he was somewhat of a dead weight. Narayan could surely make it on his own. Justin had always existed as a loner and would probably survive better in this fashion, even in the apocalyptic times they were living in. And with Kenneth came Paul, the catalyzing agent of all of their misfortune, the Grim Reaper to the entire country. Still, every step Kenneth took toward the great abyss filled them all with an undeniable sense of hopelessness.

But Kenneth wasn't dead yet. Although his stare appeared blank and thoughtless, he was glaring at his son's tattoos that peeked out from beneath the neck of his shirt. *3612016*. The day that Meredith brought their son home with that hideous barcode permanently scraped into his skin was the same day that Kenneth gave up. He gave up trying to connect with his family. They say that people drift apart, and his son had boarded his wife's life raft. He was alone and the current was taking him in the opposite direction. He knew this. He no longer tried to paddle toward them. Everything that they were was everything that he disdained. He couldn't deny it.

Meredith had always been on an adjacent track to Kenneth that was constantly veering away. Her life existed primarily in social media, and Kenneth didn't even have a Facebook page. He had always reached across the widening gap between them to make a connection, but no longer. And yet all this time, a critical detail went unnoticed: Meredith had no ink of her own. In fact, she and Kenneth spent ample amounts of time sitting at restaurant booths ridiculing the tattoos of those seated around them, whispering and giggling like children. Perhaps Meredith and Paul weren't as alike as Kenneth always made them out to be, but she just put forth a greater effort to coincide with the person he chose to be rather than veering him toward the person that she *wanted* him to become. There were so many ways that Kenneth had failed, and it seemed that their revelations came in a parabolic curve in frequency, peaking at his death, whispering inaudibly his entire life, then firing at him like a machine gun when the time came when he was no longer able to alleviate any of the pain that he had caused. His tongue was dry and cracking inside his mouth as all of his saliva leaked right down to the floor. His lips smacked together. He tried to speak, but it just wasn't working anymore.

Plots of farmland, uneven paths, and barbed wire fences forced Justin to merge the car back into the traffic on the road, bringing them to a standstill. They let out a collective groan. Getting to Bangladesh could take weeks at such a congested pace.

"Do we have to go to the train station?" asked Justin. "Every other asshole's gonna be there. There's gotta be a more open road between here and the border."

"Yes, but it would be wise for us to travel parallel to the train tracks," answered Narayan. "Gas will be difficult to come by. Should we run out – or encounter any other automotive problem – we can try to board the train to Kolkata."

The longer they stayed stationary, the thicker the desperation that filled the air.

"What if we bought more phones?" Paul asked desperately. "We could load up and create a new profile for each. Then we could post everything we know and all that we see before tossing the phone out the window, then move on to the next and drive the car in a different direction to keep them off our tail. I know you all hate me right now, but one thing I'm good at is gaining a following online. I could give us the podium to make our voices heard. It could work."

"It couldn't," grumbled Justin.

"It could, but maybe you're just too scared to do it."

Justin took a deep breath and did his best to reply calmly.

"I'll fight the good fight. But I'll do it on my own terms."

The heel of Narayan's hand was still pounding on the door handle. The others probably would have mentioned it, but the sound was infinitely better than Kenneth's wheezing breaths and hacking coughs. Kenneth and Paul had gotten so used to Narayan's presence as the leader, Narayan himself, as well, but he was speechless. He was the passenger. He had no narration nor comforting words. He was just along for the ride, and that was good enough, because they all knew that he didn't need to be.

Justin, growing perturbed and impatient, plowed through a weak section of guardrail, careened the car down the embankment, and sped through the farmland. He never was one to sit still.

He watched the needle on the speedometer hover around seventy kilometers per hour, a quick pace considering they were driving off-road through crops of ripe tomato plants. Again, the speed combined with the hopelessness that filled the car and made them all just want to give up. Justin prodded at his phone in his lap with the hand that was not perched over the steering wheel. His eyes would glance briefly down at his screen before returning to the dangerous road ahead. He glanced in the rearview. He could see the miles between the father and son in the back seat and could sense the aching to reach one another across that vast canyon. It always seemed that the strongest connections were only realized just before severance. With one final tap at the screen, he picked up his phone and tossed it out the window. In the cloud of dirt behind them, a white screen on a phone discarded along an Indian highway revealed a message sent to Justin's father.

Don't come looking for me. I'm already dead.

No one in the car bothered to comment on the action. Perhaps they didn't notice. With Narayan tapping the tempo of his terror, Paul lost in his shame, and Kenneth dying, no one bothered giving too much attention to the others' actions.

Justin was almost beginning to enjoy the setting. Soil and tomato juice were spewing out the backside of the car. Behind the cloud of dirt in the rearview was an entourage of speeding cars like a pack of hyenas, following Justin's example and chasing them down. He kept his eyes on the mirror and almost believed his fantasy in which the dozen cars that followed were the only enemies they needed to escape from. He became so fixated on outrunning the pack and plowing through a fresh crop, he almost didn't notice the road cutting across the land in front of him, loaded with cars. A hydroplane through the farmland put them in the direction of traffic as they vigorously pushed their way in, no other drivers courteous in the way of allowing a newbie to merge in front of them.

To combat the rising level of discouragement in the car, Justin reached in the floorboard behind his seat and retrieved his backpack. He shuffled through its contents before producing a digital music device and plugged it into the dashboard on the car.

The sounds emanated through the interior of the car, slow and contagious like an infection. Sitars quietly accompanied one another like the flicking of tightly wound springs, raindrops on spider webs made of steel. High-pitched like bells yet played at such a low volume and without any discernable melody, they issued more of a feeling than individual notes. Tabla began beating softly, slowly, nudging everyone awake. The combination of the noises was still so gentle that they felt like a lover's eyelashes fluttering against the skin. Then her voice rang out. It was smooth and resonating. It sang with such depth and raw emotion, like she was singing from beyond her vocal chords, from the pit of her stomach, her soul. An open vowel sound cried with the pain of a thousand deaths and the supplementary joy of a thousand rebirths, all without bringing the syllable to a close. It jumped and shifted tones wildly, skipping across octaves, then settling on one note as it bellowed from her soul and into theirs, transcending language. As it skipped over notes like a stone over still water, so did the emotion conveyed. She went from the deepest of sorrows to the most uplifting of joys. Somewhere between a dirge and a hymn, a call for serenity and a call to arms, she brought them all to life. Slowly, they all woke up just a little bit – even Kenneth – and allowed an unspeakable thought into their heads: they just might make it.

The traffic crawled forward. They inched toward their fate. They couldn't tell if they felt like gladiators waiting for the Colosseum doors to open or Holocaust-era Jews waiting to be gassed. The asphalt beneath their tires nearly smoking from the heat, the road burning and alive with impending destiny, it was just a question of hope. Something among them was binding them together. Just like the ayahuasca ceremony where they journeyed in separate realms galaxies apart, yet breathed as one organism, even vomited for one another in their times of need, they were now bound together by hope. It fluctuated, and they all knew that it was a dangerous drug - a little could cure, but too much could kill. Just as the Jews and the Roman slaves, they wondered if hope was a weapon or a distraction, if it was the adrenaline needed to face their assailants or their fantasy they journeyed to while succumbing to their fate. Only time would tell.

Their speed picked up incrementally as cars ahead veered off the road, most turning around and heading back from whence they came. As they mounted a small hill that revealed the valley ahead, the image that turned the vehicles to other directions sat in the distance like an enormous omen.

A massive commercial airplane – a Boeing 777, to be precise – had crashed directly onto the stretch of highway before them. At first glance, it wasn't recognized as an aircraft. It had dyed the land black with fires that had burnt out, the black spot on the landscape surrounded by small glowing fires that had yet to burn out. Only on the outermost parts of the wreckage could one distinguish the severed appendages of the aircraft. The tail turned in the wrong direction. The tips of the wings, one larger than the other. The massive nose looking almost completely intact, like the pilots might still be in the cockpit attempting to address their passengers through their headsets. The scene looked like the decaying corpse of a giant, the abdomen hollowed out by ants and scavenging animals. The ants came in the form of cars, and just like ants, they moved in straight and seemingly orderly lines in every direction – some traveling directly to and from the carcass, others veering off in tangent lines, still others attempting to circumvent the massive obstruction – yet despite their coordinated and precise movements, all the moving food lines looked like one gigantic swarm of chaos.

The four of them stared silently at the colossal obstruction of death and destruction ahead. Kenneth even sat almost completely upright and gazed at the monstrosity. He looked at the wreckage in the same way he stared at the Taj Mahal. It was so titanic in its physical presence as well as its implications, but neither offered much suggestion as to what those implications might have been. They both symbolized widely coordinated efforts, unspeakable pain, and a thousand other monumental secrets that would keep people guessing for centuries to come. Take away the suffering and loss, and the sight of the crash was quite impressive. Almost beautiful.

"What do you think?" Justin asked Narayan. It seemed that he was catering to Narayan's fleeting need to be in a position of leadership, but more than anything, he was just out of ideas.

"The train tracks should be to the north. If you can cut across the highway to the left, just head in that direction. Eventually we will find something." Although no one spoke of it, they all heard the word 'something' and interpreted it as an intentional landmine placed by Narayan, an insinuation that the 'something' that they find might be a train, and it might be another catastrophic pile of death blocking their next path.

Forcing their way through the traffic was like running through a stampede that ran in all different directions. It seemed that every window revealed another vehicle approaching them like a speeding rhinoceros, head cocked down, horn ready to impale. It was the first time that Justin didn't appear comfortable behind the wheel. His head whipped around in every direction, spinning the wheel vigorously like a sea captain caught in a violent squall. Eventually he made his way to open field and picked up speed, attempting to gain ground between themselves and the rest of the pack, away from the huge, metal, two- and four-door cannonballs that were rocketing in from all angles.

Emerging from the hopelessness like a flower from a pile of cow dung, Paul sensed the faint presence of camaraderie. Utter despair worked marvelously as a sort of counselor. Had the potential danger lightened a bit, they all more than likely would have been shouting their ideas on where to go, how to get there, and what to do, but as options dwindled and destruction multiplied, they all went silent and trusted Justin and Narayan, trusted one another, as any action was as good as any other. Paul's previous feelings of mistrust and dislike toward Narayan gently lifted. His preconceptions of a man with giant peepholes in the sides of his face faded away. They were now just four human beings struggling to survive, depending on one another. He really, *really* hoped that the feeling wasn't exclusively his own.

The city ahead – a town by the name of Bulandshahr, unbeknownst to them, even Narayan – began as a distant skyline interrupting the vast empty landscape, then quickly surrounded them. By the time they reached the first city street, driving became an impossibility. Before the airstrikes began, pedestrians and vehicular traffic co-existed in the streets and moved in and around one another with the grace and consciousness of a school of fish around a shark, some clinging to its underbelly and some frantic to avoid it. But in that first street where the crowds poured out into the streets from every alley, it seemed that no one was conscious of anyone but themselves and treated all others with a fearful hostility.

Justin parked the car and looked at Narayan.

"What do you think?" he asked. "Abandon ship?"

Narayan nodded gravely with one dip of the chin.

Kenneth had been summing up all of his strength over the past hour, knowing that this time would come, the time when he would have to use his dying body to bring him to his destination, his destiny, rather than the automobile that had been carrying him, and he refused to be the flat tire holding up the group. He emerged from the car, still clutching his stomach, but his face no longer a grimace of pain, but tight with determination.

A dark-skinned man with a mustache and a face wrinkled and worn by years of manual labor and struggle was exiting his home just beside their parked car. A burlap sack the size of a beanbag chair containing all of his belongings that he refused to abandon balanced on his head. One hand stabilized the load, the other clutched the tiny fingers of his daughter just old enough to walk.

Justin tossed the keys to Narayan. Narayan handed the keys to the stranger. With the look of a beaten and starving dog, the man accepted. His eyes were weary and untrusting, yet overcome with desperation. He took the keys the way the starving dog would take a treat – nervous, fearing the backlash, but more importantly, needing to survive. He offered a sullen, "Namastay," then loaded his belongings in the back seat, his daughter in the front.

Plunging into the crowds that all migrated toward the train station, it felt like battle. They were truly at war, pushing their way through the crowds with vigilant aggression, strangers throwing elbows to forge enough space so their children weren't trampled. They felt like spies as they constantly had to hide their pale complexions because they were, in fact, the enemy. But if they had the same view as the vultures circling above, they would see that it wasn't a battle, because the word 'battle' assumed two opposing sides fighting one another. If they would have seen the vastness of the crowds that surrounded them, the desperation that drove them to their selfish aggression, the bodies piled on the outside of the trains so densely that the metal of the train was entirely hidden on the top as well as all sides, even on the front where clinging passengers ignored the constant threat of falling under the wheels to a gruesome death – a threat that became a reality for many – the screaming mothers clutching infants, the children boarding cars crammed full of bags and strangers as their parents wailed their goodbyes through the windows in hope that their children could reach safety even when they couldn't, the peaceful men driven to assaulting drivers and commandeering vehicles to protect their families, they would have seen that this was not a war at all. This was more like a beating. An extermination.

Witnessing the desperation burning behind the faces of even the strongest men, they all envied the cows that wandered aimlessly through the mayhem, still adorned with flower garlands and vibrant speckles of paint, unconcerned with the doom that hovered behind the clouds.

Paul set his phone to record and placed it in the all-seeing nook of his breast pocket. He justified this action by the knowledge that any skilled hacker or computer savvy anti-war activist could access his page and post their own videos. Paul tried his best not to allow his father's nor Narayan's faces into the shot. He would discard the phone after boarding the train, and they would escape to safety.

Nothing, not the explosion that claimed their house and neighbors, not the wreckage of the plane that claimed more than four hundred lives, not the realization that they were being targeted, none of it could have prepared them for seeing the trains. It was such a simple and seemingly benign image, yet it so clearly illustrated the despair that had washed through the country with the sudden and unforeseen impact of a tsunami.

Bodies covered the entire surface of every car. No metal was visible aside from the turning wheels that cut their way through the fallen bodies. People were stacked between the cars like mortar, those on the bottom bellowing as the weight atop them multiplied, crushing them, sending them under the train. Children screamed as they were hoisted overhead and passed atop the crowd, lifted to the tops of the cars. They clutched at the bodies of strangers to keep them from falling, yet some of them jumped foolishly, refusing to consign to such a quick admission to fate, such a rapid and all-consuming turn in their lives. Some landed in the dirt and raced back into the crowds to find their families. Some went under the wheels.

As all human contact was to be addressed with vigilance, when Kenneth felt a hand grab at the back of his neck, he flinched back reflexively and braced his muscles for a potential struggle. But the hand on his neck belonged to Justin, and with it, he pulled Kenneth's head toward his own and kissed him gently on the temple right at the hairline. They connected eyes, and Justin slunk back into the crowd, then turned and walked away down a perpendicular alley. Kenneth watched in disbelief as Justin retreated. He stared at the back of Justin's head as he closed the hood of his sweatshirt over his head, then pulled earphones over the top of the hood and secured them, a layer of cotton fabric between the earpieces and his ears. Passing strangers obstructed Kenneth's view. He struggled to watch as his friend departed. Justin turned his head and made one last glance in Kenneth's direction, his eyes searing into Kenneth, no smile nor pursing lips offering any suggestion as to the feeling he was trying to convey. His eyes were as sharp as needles and equally indecipherable. Was it a look of compassion or blame? Was it meant to say 'Godspeed' or 'God damn you'? It was a question that would haunt Kenneth for the rest of his life.

Justin started singing loudly, blithely, seemingly unfazed by the terror around him, in horrible French. "Bonjour, amoureux, bonjour!" He turned his head back in the direction he was walking, showing Kenneth the back of his hood, and disappeared forever.

The rest of the group didn't notice Justin's departure, but as they trudged their way forward, Kenneth noticed both of their heads turning this way and that, searching for the lost member of their party, then looking at Kenneth, and with a simple frown and look of confirmation, they understood. They kept moving.

Narayan instructed them to move away from the station and back west along the tracks. There, they might be able to catch a train before it made it to the station and could stake out their spot atop one of the cars. Kenneth limped as the pain spread to every cell in his body, but lingered no more than a few paces behind his son.

For once, fortune seemed to be on their side as another long, metallic serpent was slithering across the desert toward them, covered in the white scales of robed bodies. After running for the better part of five minutes, they had reached a spot along the tracks where the crowd had finally thinned out. Waiting for the train that had seemed so close was an anxiety they weren't prepared for. The building tension of reaching this point in their journey didn't warrant a comfortable moment to pause. They awaited the train coming in from the west, and the doom of the crowd following their example from the east. If the rest of the crowd made their way as far west as they were posted, it would make climbing aboard the approaching train virtually impossible. Moving farther westward would mean the train would not yet have slowed enough for them to embark. Waiting felt sinful.

Luckily, the crowd seemed too distracted to make the same assumptions that Narayan had made, and the train became larger and larger as it gained proximity without an onslaught of desperate people attempting to board running in their direction.

In a miraculous feat of strength and without notice, Narayan crouched down and hoisted Kenneth onto his shoulders. As the train gained ground, Narayan started trotting eastward in an attempt to match the speed of the approaching locomotive. Paul trailed closely behind.

The white skin of the train presented emotionless faces as it neared. Kenneth's condition was abundantly apparent as all of the passengers clinging to the steel reached sympathetic hands out to receive the suffering man perched atop Narayan's shoulders, slumping over just beneath the chest. Kenneth felt like he was floating as he was transported by ten sets of hands to the roof of the train. Paul's ascension to the rooftop wasn't quite as graceful as he didn't bear a debilitating condition to gain sympathetic assistance, and he had to claw his way up, tugging at clothes and shoulders, feet scraping against agitated bodies as he made his way to the top. Eyes from all around glared at him in anger, then dismissed him. All except for one pair.

Narayan found a sturdy branch the width of his arm that stood up to his shoulders, resting in the dirt beside the track. He picked it up mid-trot and used it to push his way up the side of the train, not quite a pole vault, but still quite impressive. He joined his friends, oblivious to the man in the white turban clinging to the side of the car behind them, shouting accusations in Hindi in Paul's direction. They were huddled together as it seemed just as crowded atop the train as it was in the streets. Narayan's attention was on the speed of the train, wondering if it would stop at the next station or if it was merely slowing down to avoid any more casualties. He prayed that it was the latter.

The screams of the brakes slowing the metal wheels of the train were diluted by the screams of all around. Narayan's fists tightened. Every degree of speed they lost, the more he willed the train to keep moving. But misfortune prevailed, and the train came to a halt.

The turbaned man on the car behind them was rallying the crowd on the ground and pointing in Paul's direction. They had grown so accustomed to the incessant shouting all around them that the sounds of shrieking anguish and bellowing desperation became the static noise that was the background to all of their thoughts. But in a moment, a wave of anger flowed through the crowd, and although it was heard as shouts among shouts, the wavering tone was quite obvious. They saw heads all turning between the car behind them and the car they were standing on – more precisely, at *them*. They noticed the turbaned man and identified him as the catalyst to this shift in emotion, but couldn't make sense of the commotion. And then, like a holy artifact extended to the heavens, a tablet was hoisted above the crowd by two hands with no face, and even at the distance they were from the screen, Kenneth and Paul could see themselves staring back from the front seat of Kenneth's old truck in Paul's very first advertisement.

Just as the cold weightlessness of the reality of the situation hollowed them out from the inside, Narayan began pushing them to the side of the train. They both thought he was trying to push them off, whether it be to get them to safety or to act as the savior of his country by eliminating the antagonists. They saw the lonesome and stationary train car on the adjacent set of tracks. It was out of commission and appeared to have been that way for a long time. The gap between their car and it was the length of a human body, a disheartening distance to leap, especially for a man in Kenneth's condition, but Narayan's forceful nudges didn't offer the option of backing out. Miraculously, Kenneth made the jump, as did his son and his Indian friend. As his feet hit the rusted steel of the stationary car, Narayan swiveled around on his heels and wielded the tree branch that he used to board the last train. The mob on the train they had just disembarked was one of ambivalence. Some looked ready to make the leap that the Americans had just made, but knew they would be met by Narayan's flailing wooden club. Others were the face of disarmament. They turned away from Kenneth and Paul and faced their own people with wide eyes and downward-facing palms pleading to pacify the crowd. Without them, Kenneth, Paul, and Narayan would have already been pulled apart and dispersed in gruesome cutlets to the ravenous masses.

Paul looked at his father with wide, terrified eyes. He spoke with the speed of an auctioneer in frantic sentence fragments, a petrified confession offered in a frenetic stream of consciousness.

"I'm sorry! I know I fucked up! I fucked up! I ruined everything! I love you! Please, please forgive me!"

Kenneth was calm and meditative. His eyes glazed over, almost as the body does as the soul disembarks, but more serenely. His back straightened. He was no longer doubled over in pain. His wincing cheeks sagged back down in a state of relaxation.

"I think I know where it is! I know now! I know where the horn is! We can run! We can get home! It can cure you! We can be safe! Please, Dad! Please! I'm so sorry!"

"Don't worry, son," Kenneth replied calmly, his tranquil voice barely heard over the howling mob.

"How can you say that?!"

"Because I've been through this before."

Narayan was still swinging his club from side to side, fending off assailants. Although unseen, Paul heard Narayan's voice, animalistic in his rage and vehemence.

"Nahin!"

The word reverberated through his skull. Both times he heard the word, it was a plea for peace, but now it sounded more like a culling song, a lullabye sung to a dying soldier.

A rock was thrown. The first rock that would end their way of life. The rock that would irreparably alter the course of human existence. It missed.

Tears of joy streamed down Kenneth's face. He tasted the salt as they traveled downward and took refuge in the crevice between his lips. He had feared the face that death would bear for so many months, and after thirty-seven years of waiting in trepidation for death to show up to his door, its face was amiable, ethereal, beautiful – chaotically so, but beautiful, nonetheless. He was so relieved, and for the first time, so proud of the person who stood before him. He had wasted decades of scrutinizing and picking apart the distasteful outer layers, and now Paul was exposed in his rawest form before him. And it was her. It was the deity from Kenneth's journey. She was Paul. Kenneth had always wanted a girl. When all other fathers wanted boys, Kenneth always knew that he would bond better with a daughter.

Somewhere beneath the enraged shouting of the collective mob, he could hear a scraping sound, like feet shuffling in the dirt, fingernails scraping up stones like a thousand death rattles.

"I love you so much, Dad! I'm so fucking sorry! I'm so fucking sorry, Dad! Can you hear me? I'm sorry!" A newfound and flooring respect danced in his squealing voice. His eyes gazed up at his father's. Since the pain of his cancer set in, the curve in Kenneth's back put their eyes level with one another's, but now he stood tall, and Paul had forgotten the commanding presence of his father's stature. He looked up at him like he was God. "Please, Dad! Forgive me! Forgive me!"

A rock struck Kenneth in the left shoulder, but his face was unwavering and didn't offer so much as a flinch of the eyelids, as if the pelting stones went unfelt. His cheeks were wet with tears. His teeth now peeked out through his parting lips in a smile of supreme satisfaction. He reached his hand out and grabbed Paul's shoulder just as he had done in the car back in Texas, just after receiving his cancer diagnosis.

Paul's rambling confessions petered out like he had just felt the effects of a tranquilizer intended for a much larger animal.

"I'm... sorry."

They could almost hear the gushing wind as the wave of rocks soared overhead. Despite the impending doom, the imminently violent and catastrophic backlash, the precedents set, the sound was quite beautiful.

"I love you, son," Kenneth said contently. "I love you."

EPILOGUE

IS NAME IS QUANG, BUT he calls himself Ken. He works as a computer technician for a corporation specializing in electronics. He mostly does house calls and installations of new software. He doesn't speak much to the customers. At night he sits in a small studio apartment and practices his pronunciation. Although he is not Indian, although the facial features of Vietnamese and those of Indian men are worlds apart, although there is no connection between his people and the people at war with America, he must hide his heritage. Xenophobia in its heightened form has swept the nation. No one has the ability nor cause to discern among nationalities. Foreigner equals villain. Ken can almost say the word 'readily' without rolling the 'r' and flatten the ending vowel sound in a pronunciation that could pass for American. He is currently installing a new 2034.0HSX computer and Suit in a pretty blonde girl's house. The new series of Suit (that must be matched with an entire CPU upgrade) is said to be able to inseminate during sex. A bottle of a thick, syrup-like fluid good for three uses comes with the startup kit, but it can be purchased in mass quantities via the online store. They call it 'blank semen.' There is a separate container and distributor for the fluid in the female version of the genital compartment. The male's version of the upgrade is just a collector, but it is quite phenomenal in its abilities. It can decode the DNA in the sperm and the female end can encode that series into the fluid, which is then injected vaginally at the exact time that the man orgasms. Touchless insemination. The 2034.0HSX version of the Suit, along with the necessary CPU upgrade, costs around $14,000. The same company is developing new programming they call Remote Father Software. There are endless new programs for recreating anything from horseplay to life lessons that can be experienced by both the father and the child from across the globe.

Ken tries to give the girl a brief introduction to the new software. She doesn't pay any attention to him. He finishes the job, and she pays on her phone. She never looks at him. She doesn't say a word.

After he completes the job and exits her house, she continues posting her e-journal to her FlashConnect page.

The Darkest Day, and the Brightness that Followed

I couldn't believe it, watching the man I love on screen being assaulted by maniacs just before getting blown to shit after the town of Bulandshahr was leveled. And all from his perspective. I could see what he saw and feel what he felt. I CMEO [cried my eyes out] for days. Nothing seemed real.

Those fuckers will pay for what they did to me. They will pay for fucking with America. WYB [watch your back(s)]!

But after Paul died, my FC [FlashConnect] page blew the fuck up. In the first day, I got messages from 396 people offering their condolences. By the end of the first week, it was 10,485. I had never felt so loved.

Since then, I've had a SBA [super badass] following. People all over the world have been reading about me and Paul and all that we've been through, so

I've been giving everyone more to read. We've had a great run, baby! I'll keep it going for the both of us!

Thank you to everyone who has been with me through all of this. Despite the tragedy, it has been almost a blessing to me, gaining so many great friends.

So this is Chrissy telling everyone to keep your head up, help one another, and support our troops who are over there kicking those Curry Terrorists' asses!

-C

Throughout her blog about her and Paul, before and after India, she never mentioned how she used to vandalize his house in hope to scare him into commitment. It wasn't her fault. Paul was spineless, and he needed to be coerced into her loving arms. He was always so terrified of everything new, so she knew that the only way to get him to commit was if she surrounded him with new and horrific events, solidifying her as his safe haven. If only he had done as she wished, he'd still be alive today, but then again, she wouldn't be famous. Or rich.

During one of her e-journal posts, she mentioned something about the talon that Paul had around his neck in his final transmission looking like this rhino horn that he had and was so in love with. A few of her followers messaged her about the beliefs of the abilities of rhino horns throughout Asia and the price that they were selling for. Aarav454rocks27 bought the horn from her for $890,000. She viewed it as a posthumous gift from her late boyfriend.

Aside from the horn, she always makes a point to be completely honest with her fans. She is very sincere in her appreciation. Even when she was with Paul, before he left for India, she had always had this small hollow spot deep inside. Late at night, when it sucks at her like a hunger pang, she thinks about all of those people who tell her day in and day out how much they love her and respect her, and she feels almost fulfilled in a way that is so familiar yet so foreign, like a nostalgia for something she has never experienced. Something bringing her back to childhood. The hole still exists, but has been numbed by the fame that overshadows it. Chrissy comforts herself in the knowledge that the pain will go away when she has a baby sleeping beside her.

Printed in the United States
By Bookmasters